THE FALLOUT

NAMELESS - BOOK TWO

NIKKI ROBB

THE FALLOUT

NAMELESS - BOOK TWO

NIKKI ROBB

ISBN: Paperback: 978-1-964036-06-9
ISBN: Hardcover: 978-1-964036-07-6

This novel is a work of fiction, any similarities to real people and events are entirely coincidental.

Cover design by Nicole Tuttle
Interior design by Rachel McEwan
Printed and distributed by Kindle Direct Publishing

First Printing Edition

CONTENT WARNINGS

This novel includes and alludes to things that may be concerning such as murder, vampires, blood drinking, graphic sex, sexual assault, rape, cancer, descriptions of torture, death of a parent and family member, victim-blaming, panic attacks, brief thoughts of self-harm, PTSD, discrimination, hate crimes, a brief reference to the LA Times Bombing, parental neglect, and harassment.

Please consider these before continuing.

ACKNOWLEDGMENTS

This novel would not exist if it weren't for some incredible people in my life, and I simply must thank them for everything they've done for me. To my husband, for always reading my books and being my number one fan. To my mom, for showing me that I could actually be a writer and for being my momager. To Mariah, for encouraging my creative side and for always being a sounding board. To my dad, for reminding me how to use commas correctly (just because I still don't understand doesn't mean you didn't try your best, so thank you).

Once again, if you're in my family and you somehow didn't get the memo to NOT read this book, I urge you to listen to me now. Please. Seriously. This book is dirty and smutty, and there are things in this novel that I don't want you to know that I know about. So please, if you love me, put this book down and stop reading it immediately. Thank you! Love you!

To all my incredible ARC Readers for their continued support and encouragement. Your kind words and love of my stories are what keeps me going.

And finally, to you, dear reader. Thank you for falling in love with these monsters the way I have. Welcome back to Shockgrove.

To anyone who thinks they have to limit how much love they're allowed to accept.

Open your heart and let it all in. You deserve it.

SAMARA

PROLOGUE

There is nothing quite as beautiful as a vampire joining ceremony. Although, I may be a little biased. Moonlight flooded the small clearing, casting a soft glow across the faces of the people I loved most in this world. Standing off to my side was Laz, their face was lit with the brightest smile I'd ever seen grace their features. To my left was Orpheus, his usually cold exterior softened in this moment of love and light. He wore a suit, as always, but he had swapped his usual dark tie for a bright red one to mark the occasion. Across the way, Silas stood with his hands clasped in front of him, an eager excitement coursing noticeably through him. He wore what he wore every day, dark jeans and a tight t-shirt, but he had the good sense to swap his jean jacket for a grey sport coat at least.

And then, standing before me, hands in mine, was the most beautiful creature to ever exist. My love. My chosen. My Alora.

Her golden hair was pulled up into a delicate tangle of curls and braids at the top of her head with stray pieces falling to frame her stunning face. She had that perfect olive complexion, a testament to her human parents' Sicilian ancestry. Her eyes were the color of the ocean, and their gaze felt just as deep. Her delicate frame was draped in a blood-red gown, as mine was. Her dress had a corset bodice that hugged her soft curves perfectly. Mine hung off my shoulders, showing off my dark brown skin that was illuminated by the light from the midnight moon, and flowed loosely down to the grass beneath our bare feet.

There was a soft ethereal nature to her as if she were some sort of mythic beauty. My own personal Helen of Troy. Her plump lips called to me the same way they had every day since I met her. Ever since the day she and Silas joined our coven, her intoxicating scent and mesmerizing gaze had laid claim to me.

She wasn't my mate, but what I felt for her was so powerful that I truly couldn't fathom any bond being stronger than the one I shared with her. That is why I asked her to commit to me, mate bond be damned. I didn't need some cosmic intervention to tell me that I belonged to this woman, and she to me.

The stars in the sky served as a million little reminders of the days I'd already spent worshiping this beauty before me, and a promise of the days I was swearing to devote to her from here on out.

"Alora," Orpheus began, but neither of our gazes traveled to him. We were too enraptured with each other. She had that effect. "Do you swear your commitment to choose Samara, tonight, and every night beyond?"

"I swear." Her voice was steadfast despite the happy sobs that were slipping past her delicious lips.

"You may now offer your promise."

Alora cleared her throat, pushing the flooding emotions down, and squeezed my hands in hers. "Samara, my love." She inhaled sharply, holding back the wave of cresting emotions. " I have spent so much of my life, both this one and the one that came before, feeling like a nomad. Wondering if I'd ever find a place to settle, a place to belong. And I did." She glanced at our friends, our family. " Here with The Wanderers, I found a home. But I didn't know the true meaning of the word until you offered me your love." Tears streamed down her face, painting her gorgeous features with crystalline streaks. "I make this promise to you before the stars and before our coven. A promise I will spend the rest of my unending existence upholding. You will be happy. You will be content. You will be loved." She was staring directly into my eyes, into my soul. "This is my vow to you."

I reached up to wipe my own tears away, smiling so wide that my cheeks were beginning to burn. I welcomed the pain though. It was a good pain.

"Samara," Orpheus continued. "Do you swear your commitment to choose Alora, tonight, and eve-"

"I swear," I interjected, eliciting laughter from all in attendance, but the melodic shimmering laugh of Alora was the only one that mattered to me.

"You may now offer your promise," Orpheus offered with a chuckle. He didn't often smile, but I saw the hints of one gracing his lips.

"Alora, I have known you were my chosen from the moment I laid eyes on you. There is nothing I wouldn't do to protect you, to honor you, to adore you. Our connection is something only a few are lucky enough to experience and I am bewildered and honored that you would ever consider allowing me to share this love with you."

She was crying now, tears of pure happiness, her face blurred in my vision as my own tears spilled.

"I will never love another the way I love you."

Orpheus held up a goblet between the two of us, the silver design was delicate and intricate, climbing vines and steadfast trees. "Fortify your bond. Make your choice."

Alora and I raised our wrists to each other's mouths, letting our fangs sink into the flesh there and drawing the venomous blood to the surface. Once the flow was steady enough, we allowed the essence of our individual lives to drip from our veins into the goblet, mixing together in a swirling whirlpool of life and promise.

She drank first, taking the cup eagerly in her hands, and sipped the proof of our commitment hungrily. When she pulled the cup from her lips, they were stained with a red tint, I couldn't wait to taste them. But first, I reached for the cup in her outstretched hand and took a sip of my own. It was a burst of sweet flavor, assaulting my senses with a slight jolt of euphoria. I smiled, handing the now empty vessel back to Orpheus.

Then I claimed her lips with mine, sealing the promise between us.

I meant what I said. I would never love another the way I loved her. Not as long as I lived.

ATHENA

ONE

You never know how you're going to respond to life-threatening situations until you're in one. Are you a fighter? Someone who pushes back against the threat and refuses to be a victim? Do you default to flight? Run away at the sign of trouble and never slow until your feet have carried you to safety.

In the past, I've been known to freeze. To completely shut down and while my body remained and endured the trauma, I was somewhere else. Deep inside the recesses of my brain where nobody could touch me.

"Mate".

Their long claws were thick and vicious-looking, sharpened to a point in a matter of seconds. Their eyes were red, the whites disappearing entirely, giving way to the veiny crimson hue, and their once rounded ears had tapered off to a fine point. But that wasn't the most terrifying part. Nor was the way their mouth hung open in a snarl to reveal razor-sharp teeth and two elongated fangs. No, what scared me the most was how they were watching me. Like I was their prey.

So, realizing I had found myself in this life-and-death situation, staring into the ravenous faces of four vicious-looking creatures, I didn't freeze.

I ran.

Leaving behind the blood-covered rose, I sprinted to the back entrance of the store, a scream stuck in my throat. I didn't waste any time, throwing the door open and delving into the eerie night. The setting sun cast an orange-red glow on the town, and a soft layer of fog was rolling in from the ocean. Everything looked warmer like I was looking at my hometown through a sepia filter. It wasn't lost on me how quiet it was on the pier. Not a soul in sight. Normally, I enjoyed the peaceful calm that came from the small-town atmosphere. But at this moment, as I sprinted down the boardwalk, with my heart racing beyond what I thought it was capable of, I was begging for a savior.

I didn't dare look behind me to see if they had followed.

I wasn't naive enough to think I could outrun them - whatever it is they are, but I could make it to civilization. I could make it to safety. To anyone.

The sound of my feet pounding the wooden pier below echoed in my skull. Despite the quiet Shockgrove evening, the sounds in my head were loud, violent, and terrifying.

I felt them then, their presence. It was all-consuming, intoxicating, and dangerous. I had once craved that feeling from them, but now it felt like a chain around my heart. Goosebumps erupted across my skin and the hairs on the back of my neck stood at attention. A mangled cry escaped my lips. I felt so hopeless, but still I pressed on.

They were going to catch me. I was going to die. But I was never going to stop running.

Leaving the pier, I hung a right and sprinted toward the lighthouse subconsciously, letting my feet take me through the fence and toward the tall white and blue structure. Slowly, I realized I had no plan. I was headed toward the cliff, a dead end. Just as I was deciding if I'd rather take my chances with the rocky coastline below or the creatures in pursuit, I saw a figure standing near the base of the lighthouse.

Hope blossomed in my chest.

"Help!" I screamed out, making a beeline for the figure. Whoever they were. They turned to face me and I got a quick glimpse of their dark hair under a baseball cap.

Relief flooded me, the man from the store. He stepped forward to meet me and I didn't bother stopping my trajectory, I slammed into his firm body and held on for dear life, violent cries falling from my lips.

"Whoa, um, are you ok?" The man, Archer, I think he said, put his strong hands on my shoulders and gently peeled me from his torso. Then and only then did I look back.

Their presence wasn't as strong anymore, maybe they had given up the chase. But either way, I scanned the area behind me with fervor. My chest rose and fell as I struggled to regulate my breathing, still ragged from the fear and the fastest mile of my life.

"Chased… they're…" I stopped. My words fell silent. They're what? What were they? I'd never seen anything like it before. Were they monsters? Yes, they had to be. That much was clear. But somewhere beneath the fear, beneath the obvious, I remembered the way Silas made me laugh, the way Samara comforted me, how Laz worshiped me, and Orpheus grounded me. How could I reconcile those creatures I saw, with pointed teeth and bloodthirsty gazes with my wanderers? The ones I was starting to… truly care for?

"Breathe, ok?" Archer spoke, drawing my eyes back to him and away from the empty town behind me. I followed his command and let my breathing return to a relatively normal pace, but my heart still sped within my chest. "Tell me what's wrong," he pleaded, his eyes also scanned the area as if he was looking for the threat. There was a slight tick to his jaw, and one of his hands came to rest on something on his hip. I didn't bother looking at what it was.

For a brief moment, panic seized my heart as a horrific thought came to me. What if I led the threat to him, what if Archer gets killed because of me?

"I…" What the hell was I supposed to say? 'I think the people I was sleeping with are inhuman monsters and then they started chasing me?' Not the most believable claim. While I took a few more calming breaths, and my sanity returned with each passing second, I thought carefully of my next move. "I saw something, like a big creature of some kind." That much was true. "I ran. It chased me."

Archer's eyebrows furrowed, but not in disbelief, more like he was trying to decipher my words.

"What kind of creature," he asked, the muscles in his arm tensing as his hand closed tighter around whatever it was he was holding at his side.

I panted, taking a steady step away from Archer and the intensity of his questioning glare. He seemed genuinely worried for me, which was a sweet notion, but he was a stranger and I was a raving lunatic who nearly tackled him.

"They were…" I stopped, his eyebrow rose in question. "I'm sorry, I wish I could describe it. I just… I didn't stop to take mental pictures, you know. I just ran." That was a lie of course. I'm not sure I could ever close my eyes again without seeing the image of their warped and terrifying forms burned on my eyelids. He nodded, seeming to accept that answer, then lifted the hem of his shirt to cover whatever he had hiding in the waistband of his pants. A gun maybe?

Why did that thought make me even more uncomfortable? I took a step back, assessing this new potentially threatening situation for the first time.

"You're safe, there's nothing here now," Archer confirmed in an authoritative voice. He seemed calm and collected, but on edge like he was preparing for the creature I spoke of to show its face.

"I'm sorry, you must think I'm crazy," I offered, pathetically. Archer looked down at me, his eyes harboring a hint of fear.

"I don't think you're crazy at all." He held my gaze and all I could think of was how nice it was to have someone believe me. That was not always the case. In fact, in this town, it was quite the opposite all those years ago when I told them what my stepfather had done to me. Instead of comforting words of encouragement, instead of support, I received accusatory looks and disbelief. But Archer wasn't giving me one of those looks I knew so well, the kind that had a sort of pity to them. No, this look was genuine and I knew, without a doubt, that he believed me. "It's Athena, right?"

I nodded, pressing a hand to my chest and feeling the beating there as it gradually slowed to a more appropriate resting rate.

"How many did you see? Was it just the one?" He asked, and I looked up at him again, hoping my wide-eyed reaction didn't give me away.

This man believed me, he believed I saw what I saw. He seemed actually interested in helping me. I could tell him the whole truth. Tell him what I saw, and what they looked like. I could give him names.

I could do that.

But I didn't.

I shook my head. "Just one," I lied. He nodded again, mentally filing away my answer.

"You're hurt," he said, pointing to my palm. Glancing down at the wound, I noticed it had stopped bleeding, but my run had splattered the red substance all across my arm and onto my shirt.

"Did you hurt yourself before or after you saw the creature?" he asked, eagerly. I glared at him in question. This stranger is asking the type of questions someone might ask if they knew something. Could he?

"Before," I claimed, gauging his reaction. His breath hitched in his throat and he nodded to himself continuously for a few seconds. He slid his backpack off his shoulders and placed it on the ground. Kneeling, he grabbed a small box from the pack. I tried not to glance inside as he unzipped, but curiosity got the better of me. I caught a glimpse of several paint-covered rags and the blue cap of what looked like a can of spray paint.

Maybe he was a graffiti painter who tagged buildings illegally, and that was why he was so cagey when I asked if he was an artist. He closed the bag quickly before I saw anything else and produced a small first-aid kit.

He handed me a wet wipe and I thanked him, getting to work on cleaning my skin of the blood. Then he handed me some antibacterial ointment and I carefully smoothed the cooling substance into my palm, ignoring the sting and focusing on forcing the memory of the roses from my mind.

How had the sweet, kind, protective individuals who brought me those roses become the stuff of nightmares? There was this blanket of fear cloaking me from seeing past those red orbs to the eyes I'd become so fascinated with within the last week. Their hands had claimed my flesh, their mouths had been on my center. They kissed my neck. A shiver wracked through me at that thought. Those fangs, they've been so close to me. They could have killed me.

But they didn't.

That doesn't matter. They're still monsters.

Right?

After cleaning the wound, he offered me a bandage and helped me wrap it around my hand and secure it on my palm.

Archer and I stood facing each other, and a strange energy was coursing between us, something like camaraderie. I liked it. After a few moments of silence, I realized I had no idea what to do next. They know where I live and where I work. I left the store unlocked. I can't go home. I can't be alone.

My breathing was shallow again all of a sudden and Archer caught the shift in my demeanor.

"Hey, it's ok," he cooed.

"I just realized I have to go back to the store and that's where… Um, that's where I saw it."

"I'll go with you," he offered, earnestly. I sighed, a weight lifting off my chest.

"Are you sure?" He nodded before I'd even finished the sentence.

"I won't let anything happen to you, I promise." It was a sweet gesture, one that made me feel safe and protected. And I think the fact that I could tell he was hiding his own fear made him seem even more trustworthy.

I nodded a few times, taking long languid breaths before turning to face the direction of the pier.

"You're ok, Athena. I promise." He knelt down, returning the kit to his backpack. He dug for a brief moment into the pack to grab what looked like a canister of pepper spray and then he stood, slinging the bag over his shoulder.

He caught me looking at it and shrugged. "Can't be too careful, right?" I found myself wondering if pepper spray would work on those creatures. Probably not, but it was better than nothing, right?

Together, we left the clearing at the base of the lighthouse and I tried not to let the memory of Silas' lips on mine the last time I was here distract me from the very real danger he posed to me.

Because he is dangerous. They all are.

I can't forget that.

Archer and I slipped through the fence and out onto the quiet Shockgrove streets. The sun was setting rapidly, and I couldn't ignore the dread that was enveloping me at the thought of being outside at night, with whatever they were on the loose.

The walk to the store was slow. My paranoia caused me to constantly look over each shoulder. On the plus side, Archer seemed to be reacting similarly to the threat, his eyes scanned the space methodically, almost militant. I then noticed the toned arms and the broad shoulders that held his tactical backpack. Not to mention whatever weapon he had in his waistband.

I wanted to ask him if he was a soldier, but I couldn't bring myself to make a sound. I felt so exposed out here in the open, walking amongst the quiet storefronts, venturing onto the pier. Toward the monsters.

The closer we got, the harder it was to breathe. Archer placed a comforting and encouraging hand on my shoulder and led me to the front door of my store. The fairy lights were on, the open sign hung in the window, and the stacks of books inside stood steadfast and unchanged. It looked as if nothing was different, but that wasn't true, was it?

There was nobody inside. At least not that I could see. I paused with my hand on the cool metal handle before pressing inside. The chiming of the bell frightened me and I jumped slightly as it rang out. Archer was close behind me, and again he squeezed my shoulder, encouraging me forward into the store.

The memory of what I saw here only minutes ago felt so visceral, and yet so blurry at the same time. Like a dream.

A nightmare.

Everything was unchanged, except for me. I was changed.

The single pink rose I had left behind on my way out was gone, but the bouquet atop the counter remained in its vase. I hated the way my confused heart leaped at the sight of them.

Was it fear that made my heart beat faster, or something else entirely?

"Lock this door," he said pointing to the front door. I did. flipping the sign and securing the metal gate in its place. "I'm going to sweep the place, don't go far." Archer moved forward, disappearing into the stacks of books. Just as he rounded the corner I swear I saw him reach for whatever he had tucked in his waistband. I moved to the cash drawer quickly. Thankful for the first time all off-season for the slow day that made the final count incredibly simple. I secured the cash into the safe in the office and by the time I returned to the cash register, Archer was back. Whatever weapon he had grabbed was hidden again, but he still had that canister of spray in his hand. A faint smell of garlic pervaded the air.

"There's nothing here. We're safe, but it's getting dark and we should head out. Do you have someplace safe to stay tonight?"

I nodded. Davia would let me stay over without a doubt.

"Good, I'll walk you there."

I pulled my phone from my pocket and shot off a text.

ATHENA: Can I sleep at yours tonight?

DAVIA: You never have to ask that. But why?

ATHENA: I just don't wanna be alone.

DAVIA: None of your new fuck buddies wanna volunteer to keep you company?

ATHENA: I think I need my best friend tonight.

DAVIA: Then get your ass over here. I'll cue up Love Island.

I smiled for the first time since before seeing the real faces of the people I was falling for. It felt foreign on my face, but I enjoyed the hopeful bloom in my chest nonetheless.

After shutting the lights off and locking the back door behind us, the two of us headed back down the pier toward town. The red-orange light was fading with each step giving way to the soft glow of the stars and moonlight. With each inch that the sun sunk, my fear ramped up just as much. There was an almost inhuman quality to the stillness in town. Like the ghost town from all those horror films. I tried to keep my overactive mind from filling in the blanks of the story that was unfolding with images of death, blood and fear.

Was I the unsuspecting human who was seduced by the creatures only to be their victim? I shivered at the way that thought made me feel. I'd told them about my own issues with being a victim. They know I've had my own run-in with monsters in my past. Why now, were they here doing this to me, again?

I never wanted to be a victim again. I never wanted to feel helpless, like I had that night.

I led Archer through the streets toward Davia's house. Archer remained vigilant and I couldn't express how much it meant to me to have someone so clearly devoted to keeping me safe.

I just hoped this one didn't turn out to be a monster too.

Even I have to admit my track record isn't the most promising.

When we turned down Davia's driveway, the sun had completely disappeared behind the horizon and I felt a chill crawl down my spine.

"Thank you, Archer. You have no idea what you've done for me tonight." He nodded, a soft smile gracing his lips

"I'm just glad you're safe." He sounded like he meant it. "Listen, if you see anything else I want you to text me, ok?" He was reaching into his backpack, grabbing a pen and a scrap of paint-stained paper. He scribbled a number and handed it to me. He must have seen the apprehension in my gaze as I looked at his outstretched hand because he quickly added, "I'm not hitting on you in a moment of vulnerability if that's what you're worried about. I just want to make sure you're ok." There wasn't a hint of manipulation in his gaze or tone, so I was inclined to believe him. I grabbed the number and nodded.

"It, um, well it means a lot that you believed me," I whispered the confession into the quiet night air. Archer sighed, not in pity, but something else colored his expression.

"I've seen my fair share of monsters," he said with a small melancholic chuckle. I watched his dark eyebrows scrunch together as he took a contemplative moment to gather his thoughts.

"Me too," I admitted, but it wasn't the transformed, blood-thirsty faces of the wanderers that I thought of, it was *his*.

His charming smile, the deep dimple, the perfectly coiffed blonde hair. He was one of those all-American homegrown hero types. The kind that had such a perfectly crafted and iron-clad public persona that nobody could even imagine their perfect golden boy was a villain behind closed doors. Mom fell for his charms, hell, we all did.

"Have a goodnight, Athena." Archer began back down the driveway, his eyes returned to their scan of the surrounding area.

"Be careful, Archer." He looked over his shoulder briefly and smiled.

"Always am." As he continued down the street, I watched him go, and found myself increasingly nervous for his safety. Maybe I should have told him the full truth so he could be prepared. Walking alone at night with *them* on the loose could potentially be life-threatening for him. But something about him told me he could handle his own.

Once my most recent savior was out of eyesight, I felt the eerie chill return, as if there were eyes watching me. I quickly slipped into Davia's home and locked the deadbolt. Leaning my forehead against the wooden frame, I sighed, releasing tension I didn't even realize had been gathering in my tight shoulders. An almost suspicious feeling gripped my heart. Why have I been so willing to place my trust in strangers who save me? Maybe I should have been more careful with Archer. I certainly should have been with the others.

A sinking feeling erupted in my chest at the thought of sharing my body with them…whatever they are. Although, beneath the fear and disgust there was another, heated emotion. Something that felt wrong, and dangerous, but exciting.

"Athena, that you babe?" Davia's voice called from the living room. Composing myself, I turned on a heel and walked in to greet my best friend.

A night with Davia was exactly what I needed. Despite the growing fear in the pit of my stomach and my jumpiness at every little sound, she had me laughing and relaxing within an hour. She didn't ask questions or comment on my obvious nervousness, which continued to be one of my favorite things about her. Eventually, I started to feel a little more back to normal, except for that soft nagging voice in my mind.

Just as I was beginning to feel like I was back on solid ground, my phone buzzed with an incoming call. Before even looking at the name on the screen, I knew who it was. Dread filled my heart and my palms were sweating as I lifted the phone to check the source of the call.

SILAS

I watched the name on the phone flash as the vibrations numbed my hand. I was still lost somewhere between fear and anger. They had lied to me. Had deceived me. Had hidden who they were.

I let the call go to voicemail, but I only had a moment of reprieve before the phone was ringing again.

I watched the call continue again, Davia's voice as she explained what was happening on the screen was a distant echo. Another minute passed and he called again. This time, instead of letting the phone ring, I pressed the power button, sending him to voicemail after a single ring, hoping that sent him the message.

A moment later, a text arrived.

SILAS: Athena, please let us explain.

I swallowed the lump in my throat and took a few steadying breaths as another number joined the barrage.

LAZ: Darlin', where are you? We should talk.

SILAS: Bookworm, please. It's me.

My heart tightened, I drew my knees up to my chest and hugged them, reading and rereading their words. A tear slid down my cheek.

SILAS: I need to talk to you.

LAZ: It isn't what it looked like.

The anger that was already pooling in my chest was burning brighter with each text.

SILAS: Baby girl, text me back.

Trying to command me? Fury grabbed the wheel and I found myself excusing myself to go to the restroom. By the time I was leaning over the sink with my hands on the vanity, I had several more text messages.

SILAS: We would never hurt you.

SILAS: I'm sorry we scared you.

LAZ: I swear you're safe with us.

SILAS: We need you.

I saw the bubble, informing me they were texting again, but before he got the chance to send it, I blocked their numbers. There was a quiet relief in that silence.

It was a hollow victory.

On one hand, I needed this space. On the other, something told me that whatever they are, they're not going to be deterred by a simple block button. But tonight? Tonight, it was enough for me.

I returned to the living room and when Davia talked about the hot couple on the tv screen and their dramatic relationship troubles, I listened.

SILAS

TWO

The world was black and white before. I only thought I had experienced the joy of color, but the moment the scent of her blood reached my nose everything exploded into vibrant rich hues and I quickly realized I had never experienced what it meant to 'live' in my long life. The light felt brighter, and the smells were stronger. Hell, even the air on my skin felt softer, like a careful embrace. It was more. Everything felt…more. But it wasn't *everything* I was feeling, seeing, smelling… It was her. Her scent was thick, it invaded every single one of my senses, holding me in a vice grip. Wintergreen. Fresh, vibrant, and cozy. Sensual. Her blood called to me like a siren song, I'd welcome the depths of the ocean if it meant I could have a taste of the blood that ran in her veins, and the woman who owns my soul.

My vision zeroed in on her. There was no past, no future. There was only this moment. Heedlessly, I watched her. Her flushed skin, her perfect red hair. I needed her. My cock strained against my pants and my fangs ached with the need to sink into her perfect skin and drink the sinful elixir.

I knew then for a fact, a confirmation of what my soul already knew, this human was my mate. The one for whom I was created. The other half of my existence. I was incomplete without her, a shell of who I was destined to be. I belonged to her, mind, body, and soul. I would go to the ends of the Earth to protect her, to find her. To worship her. There was nothing in the world that could keep me from her.

So why the fuck was she running away from me?

She darted from the bookstore and I was so caught off guard that I couldn't move for a moment, a frustrated groan escaping my lips. My logic was locked in a cage of mindlessness. There was no rhyme, no reason, only her. My fingers gripped the stem of the now blood-covered rose. Her scent was addictive, beckoning me to have a taste. But no, the first taste I have of her will be directly from the source, not lapping drops from the thorn in my hand. I sprinted in the direction she retreated, only vaguely aware of my companions who were quick to follow along. Her long red hair bounced with each stride as she ran down the pier, away from me.

That simply wouldn't do.

I could catch her in a few seconds. I could have her blood on my tongue in a moment, driving my cock into her heat. She could be mine.

Just as I prepared to dart forward and catch up to her, I felt a powerful palm against my chest.

A growl wretched itself from my throat at whoever it was who dared to keep me from my Athena. My eyes settled on the figure before me.

"All of you, stop! Right now!" Her voice was strong, familiar enough to give me pause, but in the fog of the mate bond, I wasn't able to place it entirely. My eyes glanced after my mate again.

"Fucking stop! You're terrifying her!"

I cocked my head, how could my mate be afraid of me? I was her mate. I was made for her. It didn't make sense.

"Snap the fuck out of it, right now!"

I felt the hand on my chest push back harder and the sensation was almost grounding. The red vignette of my vision slowly receded with every step she took away from me.

I pressed forward against the hold on my chest because suddenly my mate was too far from me and I couldn't understand why.

"Silas, please!" The voice, Samara, I think, pleaded. "Laz, shake it off. Fuck. Orpheus. Help me."

I knew those names. They meant a lot to me, I think. Not as much as Athena. Hers was the only name that truly meant anything and ever would again. I needed her blood. Immediately. With every fiber of my existence. If I didn't, I would cease to be.

"Damnit," Orpheus exclaimed. I didn't turn to look at him though. My eyes were still trained on my mate as she ran. "God Damnit!" He yelled again.

"Shake it off, Orpheus, and fucking help me. If they go after her like this, they'll kill her."

At merely the thought of Athena in pain, I felt the world snap back into focus, the red film the world had taken on dissipated, and the fog of mindless want and need started to recede. My fangs retracted, and my fingernails returned to their normal length and suddenly, I had regained a hold on my actions. And the reality of what I had been prepared to do hit me.

"Shit," I exhaled a long breath, feeling the effects of the forced shift.

Samara sighed with relief, letting her hand drop from my chest. I glanced around at my companions, each of them breathless and tired. Their eye color had reverted to normal, but they were sunken, hollow. I'd never seen Orpheus look so…out of place.

"Thank you, Samara," Laz said, placing a hand on her shoulder. She nodded, focusing on her breathing. Again, I found myself utterly amazed by her willpower.

I glanced down the pier, noticing Athena had disappeared around the corner. Fuck.

We shifted in front of her.

And we all…

Double fuck.

I was hit with an intense wave of hunger as the aroma of her blood called to me from the pink rose in my hand. I felt my already delicate will being tested. The barrier between myself and my monster was so thin it was nearly nonexistent.

Before I could fall even further back into the mindset of lost control, the rose was ripped from my hands. I growled as Orpheus tossed it over the ledge into the ocean below.

"You were losing it," Orpheus claimed, although, from his ragged breathing and strained voice, I knew I wasn't the only one.

"We need to get home now. We all need blood," Samara winced as if merely speaking the words was painful. A deep grumble sounded in my chest at the idea of drinking blood that wasn't Athena's, but I knew she was right. If we had followed through, the four of us? We would have killed her.

Samara kept us from doing that.

It was tense, and we had to hold our breath as we sprinted away so as not to scent her as we made our way back to our rental. Every step in the direction opposite of Athena was painful, it was like there was this hook in my soul begging to drag me back to her, but I knew I needed to get this hunger under control before we spoke to her again. After what she saw, we had a lot of explaining to do. We needed a clear and collected head to do that. Who knows how strong her pull will be the next time we see her? We need to be prepared.

There were only a few flasks left from Orpheus and Samara's trip to the city. We each grabbed one and gulped down every unsatisfactory drop, but it tasted wrong somehow. It filled my stomach and satisfied my hunger, for now, but my nearly-dead heart was begging for something else. Something I couldn't offer.

We had denied the nature of the mate bond, and somewhere in my mind, I knew we would face serious repercussions for that. The fact that I had just drank an entire flask of blood and could already feel the slight pang of hunger in my stomach was one issue.

The way I was so desperate for my mate that I felt the shift constantly dancing just beneath my skin was another.

"Fuck, this cannot be happening," Orpheus mumbled, his hands running through his hair as he paced the living room. Laz was rubbing their face in their palms anxiously.

"Except it is," Samara interjected, sinking onto the couch, her composure returning. I made my way across the room to her, sliding down onto my knees in front of where she sat.

"Thank you for stopping us," I whispered. Orpheus and Laz both paused, turning their gazes to watch our exchange.

Samara sighed, a tired smile playing on her lips. "You're welcome."

"How did you regain control?" Orpheus asked, coming to a stop near the edge of the couch. Laz leaned against the wall across the room, listening intently.

"It was blinding. The want," she started. I nodded, understanding completely. "We chased after her, but when we got outside, in the fresh air, I felt like I could breathe a little. Then reality hit me. Breaking through the frenzy."

My breath hitched at the memory of how mindless I had become, how willing I was to chase Athena and sink my teeth into her without any regard. I shuttered.

"There was a voice screaming at me, telling me that if we went through with it, we would kill her."

Laz, Orpehus, and I all growled at that sentiment.

"I think I was able to break free because I was reminded of how it felt to lose the love of my life. The memory of the pain and the desperate need to avoid ever feeling it again was what brought me back."

Silence filled the room as the four of us exchanged knowing glances. This new development not only changed our present but our future. There was no plan anymore. There was no more running away. We all knew it.

I allowed a moment of reflection before I spoke again. "Multiple mates," I barely murmured, but they all heard me.

It wasn't impossible, but unlikely. Especially for who we were. We weren't from any royal line, and while we were powerful individuals we weren't the most powerful of our kind by any stretch of the definition. Not when there are some vamps who have the ability to literally alter time and space. There was no logical explanation for why Athena Landry, a human from the middle of nowhere, was now at the center of our coven. The keystone to our delicate structure.

"I need to do some research," Orpheus exclaimed, angrily. I could see the delicate hold he had on his control and how close he was to losing himself again.

"I'll help you," I offered, standing up and making my way to him.

"I don't know much, but I know we can't deny the bond for long without experiencing ramifications." He grabbed the knot of his tie and pulled it down, removing it over his head. His collar was crumpled, and I took in the sight of him. Orpheus had never been this off-kilter before. I'd say we were dealing with the ramifications already.

"We can accept the bond tomorrow. After we feed again just to be safe," Laz piped in eagerly.

I nodded.

"You're all forgetting something."

Our heads turned toward Samara who had stood from the couch. She placed a hand on her chest and breathed slowly.

"She saw us shift, she's afraid of us. She won't let us anywhere near her."

A whimper escaped my mouth at the thought of Athena being afraid of me. Doesn't she understand I am her protector?

I reached for my phone then, seeing Laz do the same out of the corner of my eye. I called her. It rang for what felt like hours until it went to voicemail.

"Hi! You've reached Athena."

I felt my heartbeat in a single powerful thump at the sound of her voice. How had I ever not had that voice in my life?

"I'm sorry I couldn't answer the phone, but go ahead and leave a message!"

I hung up before the tone. When I said what I needed to say to her, I needed to know she was listening. I called again. Each ring felt like she was slipping away from me.

And again. When the third call was sent to voicemail directly, I felt a desperate fear grip my soul. I texted her, ignoring the questions slinging my way from Orpheus and Samara.

SILAS: Athena, please let us explain.

She had to give us that. She knew us. She knew who we were. She had rested her head on my chest, she had cried with me, she had screamed my name. She knew. She had to.

SILAS: Bookworm, please. It's me.

I was slipping into a frenzy, different from the one from before. This one was the flailing dance of a man who felt his whole heart being ripped away from him. I was only slightly aware Laz was also glued to their phone. Were they getting an answer?

SILAS: I need to talk to you.

Orpheus grunted in anger, and I heard the crashing of something against a wall and pieces of glass clattering to the floor. I was only vaguely aware of Samara comforting him.

SILAS: Baby girl, text me back.

I was running out of excuses to not run to her house right now and beg her to listen to me, but even through the fear of losing her, I knew she needed time to process what she saw and come to us on her own terms.

SILAS: We would never hurt you.

I hated that I had to even remind her of that. She should already know I'd never do anything that brought harm to her. She was everything to me. She will always be everything to me.

SILAS: I'm sorry we scared you.

Please answer me.

SILAS: We need you.

Each unanswered text was a scar on my heart. I glanced up at Samara who was doing her best to calm a raging Orpehus. Laz looked nearly as dejected as I felt, so I could imagine they had the same amount of luck getting through to her as I did.

I let my thumbs fly across the keyboard and typed another response.

SILAS: It's ok if you're afraid. I'm sorry we never told you what we were. Give us the chance and we will explain everything, we will answer every question, and we will grovel as long as you need us to. But don't shut us out, bookworm. Please. Let us back in.

When my phone buzzed with a message I gasped, my entire body flooded with endorphins. Everyone was to me in a flash, gathering around trying to peek a look at the screen.

"What did she say?" Laz.

"Is she ok?" Samara.

"Where is she?" Orpheus.

I flipped to the message and felt the venomous blood drain from my face, the pit in my stomach deepening.

Message Undelivered. The number you are trying to reach is temporarily out of service.

Just like that, my already dead heart broke into a million pieces.

ATHENA

THREE

I didn't go home for two days.

I stayed with Davia, who only asked a few questions to ensure I was safe. I wasn't sure how to answer her, but I assured her I was ok. Whatever that meant. Grandma worked The Maine Plotline on her own, which made me feel horrible, but the idea of returning there nearly had me spiraling into a panic. I wasn't ready to face them again.

Not the monsters from that night, or the saviors from the bar. I couldn't face either version of them.

I tried to do research, but I had no idea what to search for. I didn't exactly understand what I saw, so I had no idea what words to even use to describe it. Turns out though there was a whole message board site dedicated to the sightings of monsters these people described as something eerily similar to what I had seen.

I read a lot. And no, not just smutty romance books. I read non-fiction, and contemporary, even books for knowledge, not pleasure. I feel like I have a rather wide range of understanding with which I use to view the world. That is why it is so disconcerting to be forced to rework the way I looked at my existence, to shift how I saw everything. If monsters exist, then what else is out there?

On the morning of the third day, I was exhausted from the night before when I spent countless hours scrolling through the message board. Scrolling past pictures of missing people whom others were convinced were taken by the creatures of the night. Some swore they saw werewolves out in the woods at night, complete with blurry pictures to 'prove' it. Others were adamant they had experienced alien interference. Ghosts, Gollums, Witches… reading the erratic wordy claims of these individuals a week ago would have made me laugh, but now all I could think of is how I would sound if I were to describe what I had seen. I typed it once. Fully prepared to anonymously post it to the board in hopes someone could give me answers, but it was so unbelievable I ended up deleting the entire thing and tossing my phone across the room for a solid hour before the potential answers the message board housed called to me again.

There was a knock on the front door and I heard Davia venturing to answer it. I tidied up her guest room, bracing myself to leave the house today when she called for me.

"Athena, someone's here to see you, babe."

Everything stilled. The blood in my veins, the beating of my heart. I felt each individual pump as if it were the drum pounding, beckoning me to my execution. Had they finally gotten tired of me hiding? Were they going to kill me for what I saw?

Fear froze me in my spot for a few moments until an unsettling thought entered my mind. What if they hurt Davia? Suddenly, I was jogging out of the guest room and making my way to the front door, expecting to confront the very demons that had entered my heart and my bed before revealing their true face.

But it wasn't them that was waiting for me just beyond the threshold. My relief lasted only a second before the two individuals standing on the porch flashed their badges to me. A sinking feeling rushed through me and suddenly I felt my very foundation shift.

"Athena Landry?" The woman closest to me said, her light brown hair pulled back in a bun, accentuating her angular features. I nodded, unable to use my mouth. "My name is Detective Barnes, and this is my partner Detective Argent." She nodded to the stout man to her left. He had dusty blonde hair that was combed back. They both wore dark black slacks and dress shirts. I swallowed the lump in my throat and nodded my acknowledgment.

"We have some questions we'd like to ask you, mind if we come in?"

I glanced over to Davia, who looked calm and collected despite the law enforcement officers standing a few feet from her. She nodded, ushering them inside. I stepped to the side, letting the two brush past me. Claustrophobia blanketed me the moment they were in my space like their mere presence was suffocating.

Davia sent a reassuring glance in my direction before shutting the door and following the detectives into the living area. The two of them took seats on the large beige couch.

"Can I get you anything to drink?" Davia asked, ever the gracious host. The two politely declined and Davia took a seat on the loveseat and gestured for me to join her. I hadn't realized my feet were cemented to their spot near the door. I took a settling breath then made my way to the loveseat, sinking onto the cushion next to my best friend. Her steadying presence was comforting despite the pairs of accusatory eyes that were now analyzing my every move.

"Miss Landry, do you know this man?" Detective Barnes asked, drawing a picture out of a folder at her side and sliding it across the coffee table toward me. Louis' smug smiling face looked up at me from the portrait and I hated the way even a picture of him made me feel weak.

"I've met him once, yes," I answered. I felt Davia's hand squeeze my thigh and I let her reassurance calm me.

"He was reported missing by his friend Mr. Greg Holden. When was the last time you saw Mr. Dells?"

Dells. Louis Dells. A weird sense of comfort floats over me, knowing the name of my villain. There's power in names. Rumplestiltskin could tell you that.

"Last Friday night, at the Craving Crab."

The stout man took some notes on a small flip notebook as Detective Barnes kept eye contact with me.

"Did you two leave the bar together?"

I tried not to let the memory of stumbling out the front door and into the dark alley enter my mind. I could tell them the truth right now. Tell them what really happened to me. Maybe they'd be sympathetic. Maybe they'd believe me.

But they didn't the last time.

My hands were sweating, and the skin around my fingers had been nearly completely peeled off, a nervous habit that had only been exacerbated by this entire ordeal. Mom sat outside the interrogation room, her simmering anger was a constant presence today, never directed at me, but I couldn't help but feel like I had played a crucial part in the events that led to her current state of mind. The older gentleman sat across the metallic table from me, his grey mustache was long and hanging over his upper lip as he took a sip of his coffee.

"That's how it happened," I finished, timidly. It was the first time I was taking my experience to the authorities. It took nearly a month to gather the courage to tell Davia, and a few weeks after that for her to convince me to tell Mom. It was a night he had to work late. I remember standing on the edge of the kitchen, watching her as she danced freely to the music playing from the baby blue record player while she cooked. I loathed the idea of ruining her lightheartedness. Ruining her relationship. Her life. But I had to do it. I had to tell her. It wasn't my job to protect her from the truth, it was my job to protect her from the monster living and lying in our house.

After a long night of tears, reassurances, and promises. We got a room at the motel, and she asked me to write it all down. Every word, every moment. I hated it. Of course, I hated reliving the worst night of my life, but it was watching her face as she read the words that hurt me the most. Seeing her face fall, no matter how hard she tried to stay neutral for me when she read the things he said, the things he did. The way he stole my innocence out from underneath her nose. No matter how many times I told her it was not her fault,

I could tell she believed it less and less each time I uttered the words.

She woke me up the next morning with breakfast from the continental buffet in the lobby and then told me she wanted to take me to the police station. I argued, of course, fear coursing through me, but she convinced me it was the right thing to do. She told me he should not be allowed to get away with what he did to me. She spoke with such fire and such passion that I believed her. I believed her when she said that others would want to protect me too.

It wasn't her fault she was wrong.

"Your father is a good man," the detective replied. My skin crawled.

"Stepfather," I corrected, meekly, with only a fraction of the ire I felt.

"I know how some kids get jealous when their parents remarry." He leaned back in his chair, nonchalantly and relaxed, like I hadn't just rehashed the entirety of my horrific assault for him moments ago.

"I'm not…I wasn't jealous." I stuttered through the words. Why was I defending my story? Why was he questioning me?

"Listen, I know him and there's no way he did what you're claiming. You teenagers need to learn not to make these false accusations just cause you're upset. You could ruin his life with talk like this." He took another languid sip of his coffee and my jaw fell open.

"You think I'm lying?" I asked although I didn't need to. It was all over his face.

"I think you're acting out because your Mom hasn't been paying you enough attention. See it all the time. Most try underage drinking and smoking before they go flinging baseless accusations around."

I felt my whole body tense, anger, fear, fury.

"I'm not lying. He did this. He actually... He drugged me."

The detective leaned forward on the table.

"And conveniently you waited over a month to come and report it? When we couldn't do a blood test to confirm your story." The way he said 'story' made it sound like I had told him a bedtime tale. Something insignificant. Not the biggest, most traumatic event I've ever had to endure.

"You're not going to do anything?" I asked, tears falling steadily down my face.

"Of course, I'm gonna do something." Relief. "I'm going to tell your daddy what you're lying about so he can discipline you." Fear. Unrelenting, uncontrollable, fear. Sobs ripped from my throat. "The police are here to help you when there are real problems, girl. You need to learn not to waste our time with lies."

The next hour was a blur. Mom was screaming at the detective, being restrained and then he came. At first, he looked terrified, like maybe he'd been caught and this was his end. I relished that look on his face. The guilt painted on every expression he made. But quickly enough he discovered just how wrong he was to be afraid. His perfect mask was firmly in place and he had the audacity to apologize to the detective that his wife and daughter took up his time with this. The graying detective shook his hand, muttering something about going golfing when he gets a handle on the two of us. I felt sick to my stomach and bile rose in my throat.

Mom refused to go home with him there. He rolled his eyes, denying every single thing I had admitted. But she did not back down. She believed me with every breath in her body and not once did doubt creep its way in.

Every once in a while, I felt him cast a disapproving glare in my direction as if I was the one in the wrong. As if I had broken some sort of silent twisted promise by revealing his true nature.

Fucking lot of good that did.

Mom and I moved in with Grandma when the divorce process began. It got messy, only in the sense that the entire town knew about it. The rumors ranged all over the board, but always painted Mom and me as ungrateful liars, the promiscuous whores. In every version, he was the one who was wronged. In every version, he was the victim.

The stares and whispers continued for years, every time I went to school I'd feel their stares on the side of my face, and hear their words in the hall. People would come into The Maine Plotline, only to get a good look at us, like the circus freaks we were. It didn't help that he still retained his portion of the business from the divorce. For years, I'd see him, work with him, and feel his eyes on me as I grew up. He finally moved out once the divorce was final and let us move back into my childhood home, but it felt tainted somehow. Mom did her best to keep us separated, but without the support of the law, there was little she could do besides get into screaming matches with him when he showed his face. Do you know how horrible it is to see your tormentor every single day and know that nobody who could do a damn thing about it cared enough to try?

When Grandma found a discrepancy in the books it felt like the universe was finally throwing us a proverbial bone. The trial was quick, painless even. The amount of clear evidence we had found in the financials of the store was enough to put him away for a long time.

The worst part?

Even when the town found out about his illegal activities, he was still the golden boy. The town still came to his defense. No one admitted he may have been the one who lied all those years ago.

The villain was the victim until the very end, and the victim was forgotten.

"We walked outside together, but we went our separate ways in the parking lot," I said finally. I knew the truth, and while I hated the idea of another monster like him roaming the streets, I couldn't be 'the girl who cried rapist' in this town again.

"Did you see where he went?"

What was it Silas had said? I wracked my brain.

"I think he was headed to the gas station down on the corner of 5th and Lake."

More notes.

"Why are you not staying at your own home, Miss Landry?" We've been trying to find you for two days now," the stout one piped up.

"I had a fight with someone I was seeing and needed some time to recoup," I admitted, willing the images of the four wanderers to stay locked away.

"It's rather convenient," he started, "that you go into hiding after Mr. Holden visited you to tell you about Louis' disappearance."

"I did not go into hiding," I asserted.

"You didn't return home for two days, Miss Landry. The timing of that is-"

"I am here at my best friend's house. A friend that I publicly and frequently am seen with. There isn't a person in this town who couldn't make an educated guess as to my whereabouts. If I were trying to hide, I chose a pretty shitty spot." I was seething. I was tired of the police accusing the wrong fucking people.

"Please don't get hostile, Miss Landry," he offered, casually, making my blood boil again. His stupid face reminded me of that aloof bastard sitting across the metallic table from me in that fucking interrogation room.

"Louis and I said maybe twenty words to each other the entire night. I bought my own drinks because I knew the second he walked through the doors that I wanted nothing to do with him. When I left, we went our separate ways and I've never seen him again." I stood up, feeling years' worth of pent-up distrust and anger fueling me.

Detective Barnes stood to make eye contact with me. She smiled softly. "You are not a suspect, Miss Landry. We are not even sure he didn't run away of his own volition. We are simply trying to get all the information we can."

I nodded to her. She seemed to be the most level-headed of the two. I wondered what might have changed if I had taken my report all those years ago to a female. Would I have been heard? Would she have believed me? Would we both be buried by a man with more power?

"Do you have anyone who can corroborate your story?"

I swallowed, turning my head to Davia. She nodded, urging me on. Her face was stoic, but I could tell she was fuming beneath the surface.

"There were four people in the bar who were just passing through town. They saw us go our separate ways." She nodded, indicating to Detective Argent to take down that note. He stood and leveled his stare at me.

"Do you know how we might be able to contact them?" He asked.

I thought for a moment about lying, and protecting their identities, which was utterly confusing, but then a sickening thought occurred to me. What if they were lying? What if they didn't let Louis go?

Pulling my phone from my pocket, I offered up Silas' phone number without offering their names.

"Thought they were strangers just passing through?" Argent mused in an accusatory tone.

"They were until I started sleeping with them." I saw Detective Barnes' eyebrows shoot up at my confession. Davia stifled a laugh to my side. "You'll understand when you see them." I tacked on.

As Davia ushered the two detectives out the front door I found myself truly struggling to rectify that the people who saved me from Louis were the monsters I saw. But they were. I had seen it. I felt them chase me.

But if they were truly monsters, they could have caught me.

If they wanted me dead. They could have found me.

"We'll be in touch," Detective Barnes promised as she crossed the threshold. "Please give me a call if you think of anything else." She handed me a card.

"Don't leave town," Detective Argent added, unhelpfully. The two of them sauntered down the driveway to their black sedan parked on the curb and Davia and I watched them pull away before slowly retreating into the safety of the house.

"Are you ok?" Davia asked. She had intimate knowledge of my personal experience with law enforcement.

"I just hope they find him soon so I never have to hear his fucking name again." I offered with a little too much anger. I sighed, remembering I hadn't told Davia everything that happened that night.

"You know, just cause I'm headed out of town for this stupid summit, doesn't mean you can't stay." She meant it. And that made me feel safe.

"Thanks for letting me stay here, Davia, but I think it's time for me to rejoin society."

She smiled softly. "You're welcome to *hide* here anytime you need to." She laughed as she emphasized the word. I threw my arms around her shoulders and drew her into a tight embrace.

I made my way back to the guest room to pack up and get ready for a day at The Maine Plotline. My first day back since… Since them.

Was I ready to see them?

No.

Was I missing them?

Maybe.

I'd never felt this confused in my life.

I pulled my phone from my pocket and made my way to my jacket which was slung over the arm of the accent chair in the corner. I dug through the pockets until I found what I was looking for. A moment later, I was typing in the number that was scrawled across the slip of paper into my phone.

ATHENA: Archer. Hi. It's Athena.

It was a few moments before I saw his response come in.

ARCHER: I was wondering if I'd hear from you. How are you?

How was I?

Confused, angry, afraid, utterly lost. But he didn't need to know that.

ATHENA: Still trying to understand.

ARCHER: I get it.

ATHENA: I figured you might.

Which was a strange thought because I barely knew this guy.

ARCHER: You ever heard Float On?

ATHENA: Modest Mouse? I'm offended you think there's a chance I haven't.

ARCHER: Didn't wanna assume and embarrass you in case you had shitty musical taste.

I laughed. A full, belly-shaking kind of laugh. It felt good, albeit misplaced.

ATHENA: Of course, I've heard the song.

ARCHER: Listen to it again.

I don't know why, but I did. Pressing play, I tossed my phone onto the bedspread and fell backward onto the mattress, closed my eyes, and let the song envelop me.

Three minutes and thirty seconds later, I released the breath I had been holding. A cleansing one. I felt like I had been given the world's most mellow pep talk. Smiling, I reached for my phone.

ATHENA: Thank you.

ARCHER: Have you seen anything since that night?

ATHENA: I haven't left the house, truthfully.

ARCHER: Understandably.

ATHENA: You really don't think I'm crazy?

I waited with bated breath. Worry rushed over me. He had seemed truly understanding the night he walked me here. Never once making me feel like I wasn't worthy of being believed. Which was a really nice feeling.

ARCHER: Not in the slightest.

I didn't take the time to think about it that night, and how quickly he trusted me because at the time it meant the world to me. But I would be lying if I didn't admit that here in the light of a new day, it was a little strange he didn't question it once. He heard me speak of a monster and instead of questioning it, he gripped his weapon and walked me home.

Did he know more than he was letting on? Was he a paranoid nut-job, or did he have a deeper understanding of the world that I could only ever dream of?

ATHENA: I'm rejoining the land of the living today though.

ARCHER: Definitely a better place to be.

I chuckled lightly, but there was that slightly nagging feeling in my chest that told me there was a chance he wasn't joking.

ARCHER: Are you nervous?

ATHENA: Yes.

I sighed, finishing packing the final items from around the room into the bag that Davia let me borrow. I'd take the clothes she lent me home and wash them before returning them. Although, I loved the soft off-the-shoulder blue and white floral shirt she gave me to wear today. It reminded me of something Mom would have worn. Maybe Davia would let me keep this one.

ARCHER: Want me to walk you to work?

Did I? On one hand. I needed to go back to my real life and stop being so afraid. On the other hand, if I was going to be confronted by…*them*… it was entirely possible it would occur at the store where I last saw them.

ATHENA: I don't want to inconvenience you.

Which was the truth, but also I was silently hoping he'd do it anyway.

ARCHER: You still at the place I left you at?

ATHENA: Yeah.

ARCHER: Be there in 10.

I smiled at the phone, and slowly relief began to replace the cloud of fear that had been present for who knows how long. I took the next few minutes mentally preparing myself to exit the safety of this oasis for the first time in two sheltered days.

Venturing out to the living room, I saw Davia had dressed for work and was gathering her things into her large grey messenger bag. Her small black suitcase sat by the door. She had her blonde hair curled slightly, the top layer twisted up in a claw clip at the back of her hair. She wore a light pink dress with a grey overcoat which traveled down to her knees.

I used to think Davia was the most attractive person I'd ever seen in real life. And while she was undoubtedly, and annoyingly, stunning…I couldn't help but feel my mind flash to the faces - well the normal faces - of my wanderers.

No. Not mine.

I thought of Samara's flawless skin, and the way her eyes managed to make me feel like she actually *saw* me. All of me. I thought of Silas' powerful tattooed hands, the way they possessed my body in a way I'd never thought I'd want to feel again. But it was a worshiping connection, the type of domination that reminded me with each punishing touch that it was *I* who held the power. I thought of Laz's loving gaze, the way their soft hair fell so delicately across their forehead when they looked at me with what felt like an emotion I was not, and would never be, worthy of. I thought of Orpheus. Of his dark black eyes. Of his overwhelming scent. The way he so clearly understood how to calm me. As if he knew my soul more intimately than I could ever hope to.

I thought of them all. Their bodies, their souls. I had been drawn to them from the moment I saw them. Was that because of *who* they were? Or *what* they were?

Did it matter?

Maybe.

No.

I don't know.

"Are you ready?" Davia asked from over by the couch. I was shaken from my internal dilemma, the mental pictures of my wanderers slipping away.

"I have to be."

She nodded. She had been so wonderful these past few days, but I knew her nosy-by-nature personality was on the verge of exploding. "I got into a fight with them," I stated. Davia stopped to look at me. "I was falling too hard, too fast and I realized I didn't even know them. I needed to take a step back. To find myself again. Clear-headed."

She pursed her lips, seemingly absorbing this new development.

"Need me to kick their ass?"

I chuckled, before crossing to her and pulling her into a hug. She held onto me. "I could take most of them, I bet."

The humor dissipated and I pulled back, suddenly worried for her safety. Davia was one hundred percent the type of friend to confront them if she ever saw them about town, and while they hadn't come to hurt me, yet, that didn't mean anything when it came to her.

"Promise me you won't, ok?" I urged, infusing as much seriousness as I could into the warning. "Promise me."

Her face fell. "Are you scared of them, babe? Did they do something?" I saw the fire building in her eyes. Was I afraid? I was. Yes. But am I still? Working on it.

"No, nothing like that. I swear."

She sighed.

"I just…I don't think I'm ready to burn any bridges with them and that would be hard if you go over there pouring kerosene all over the place."

She smirked. "You say the word and the whole town goes up in flames. You know that."

I hugged her again. Letting my lips press a gentle kiss on her cheek. "I know. I won the best friend lottery."

She pulled back, gripping her bag and slinging the strap over her shoulder. "Don't you forget it."

Knock. Knock.

I jumped. How could I not? Now that I was aware, as vaguely as it was, of a world beyond what I could comprehend, I was jumping at everything.

Davia answered and I sighed as the door swung far enough to reveal Archer.

"Who the hell are you?" Davia asserted, and I jumped forward.

"Davia, this is Archer. He's…" I stopped. What the hell was he to me?

"I'm a new employee of The Maine Plotline. I'm training today and Athena is going to show me the ropes." The lie fell so expertly off his tongue.

"I didn't know you were hiring," Davia accused, an eyebrow cocked in my direction.

I hated the thought of lying to my best friend. Literally hated it.

"Grandma needs to take a step down." Truth. "Archer here is helping me out." Also true. Semantics didn't matter much, but it placated me slightly to know I didn't outright lie to her.

"Ok, so why are you here?" Davia popped a hip and rested her hand on her waist. She was without a doubt one of the most intimidating women in the world.

She could make people eat out of the palm of her hand and then thank her for the pleasure.

Archer was composed, but I noticed his eyes scan her, a coy smile playing on his lips. "Walking her to work. Wanna join?" When Archer smiled a small dimple appeared on his right cheek.

Davia's eyes narrowed and her tongue ran along her teeth as she surveyed him. "No," she replied plainly.

"Then, it was a pleasure." He tilted his head. "I'll wait outside, Athena." He took a few steps back, tossing another cheeky grin in Davia's direction before retreating hallways down the driveway. Davia watched him walk for a moment before closing the door and turning her attention to me.

"You have ANOTHER boyfriend? You're five for five with the hot strangers and while I'm incredibly happy for you, seriously so thankful that you're feeling healed enough to move on and take back your sensuality. Love you so much. I'm also so pissed because how dare you? Seriously. Leave some for the rest of us, Jesus." She pointed an accusatory finger in my direction.

"I am not dating this one, he really is just a friend who's helping me out," I replied with a laugh. She tossed her hands up and went to leave.

"Have fun living my dream!" She sauntered out the front door with her suitcase in tow, I was close on her heels, and she grimaced at Archer who was leaning against her car.

"Do you mind?" She bit. Archer shifted his weight off the car and smiled brightly at her.

"Not at all," he teased. She maintained her glare the entire time she slipped into the driver's seat, started the car, and backed down the drive. "I'll only be a few hours away babe, so call me if you need me to come back and castrate anyone." She called out the window, her eyes landing maliciously on Archer.

He laughed as we both watched her car disappear down the street. "Your friend hates me," Archer offered a few moments later, chuckling.

"She's just protective of me," I said, warmly. My best friend was the fiercest defender of my emotional safety. I loved her for that.

"You ready for this?" Archer asked, his gaze free of judgment. I appreciated that. Nodding, we began the trek to the pier. We made idle chatter, it felt comfortable between the two of us.

Arriving at the store felt like a dream and a nightmare rolled into one. I sighed deeply, resting my hand on the door before disengaging the lock and lifting the gate.

So many memories were made in this place in the last week. Reading that book out loud with Silas, feeling their heated gazes on me. The pink roses. Orpheus calmed me expertly, then pressed his lips to mine.

Their red eyes, pointed claws and sharpened fangs.

Too many memories.

"Give me a second, ok?" Archer offered before leaving me standing near the front of the store to go for another sweep of the space. Once again, like a militant soldier. I flipped the open sign in the window, switched on the fairy lights that danced along the display window, and decorated the ceiling. It felt good to be back at work, despite the fear that had me constantly checking the front door.

When I turned back to the counter, the dying pink roses stopped me in my tracks. Their petals had lost their vibrant color and instead were lightening to a soft brown. Their leaves, once rich green, were decaying. Their scent wasn't as strong. I found myself wishing I could simultaneously smell their strong aroma again, and never smell it again.

"Hello, there young man," a familiar kind voice called out. Archer's head poked into the office, his body going rigid. My grandma popped out of the room and smiled up at him. His eyes flicked to mine as if asking for confirmation of who this person was.

"Hi, Grandma," I offered, moving across the floor to embrace her. She held me back, planting a kiss on my hair. I looked over at Archer who relaxed slightly, and continued into the store.

"You're a sight for sore eyes," Grandma whispered into my ear as she held onto me.

"I'm sorry I've been M.I.A," I said as I pulled back.

She waved me off. "Don't worry about that one bit, you know I love working at the store."

I smiled, noticing how strong she seemed. She might not be able to do it every day like she used to, but she really did live and breathe for this place. "I know, but I've got it today. You go rest."

Her phone rang in her hand, she glanced at it briefly and I couldn't help myself but look at the screen.

My heart skipped a beat. "Is that who I think it is?" I challenged, as she sent his call to voicemail.

"Depends on who you think it is," she responded aloofly.

"Why the hell is my dad calling you?" I asked, probably a little too angrily, but I couldn't help it when it came to him.

"I know he's done wrong by you, Athena. And trust me, he's heard an earful from me about it. But he and your mom were together for a while before he took off. I knew him well once," she sounded pained by that.

"So he'll call you, but not me?" I didn't mean to sound so jealous.

"Now, I'm all for bashing the guy for his choices as much as he deserves, but he never called you because that was your mom's wish, not his."

I shook my head. "There's no way that's true."

"Listen, girl, I don't know what happened between them all those years ago, but what I do know is that he calls to check in on you every once in a while, so I tell him and then we leave the conversation at that." She waved me off. "I don't forgive him for his cowardice and for leaving, but I also know how hard it is to be separated from your daughter." A tear slid down her cheek, and my heart was constructed at the thought of my mother.

"Why didn't he call me after she died?" If my father cared so much about how I was doing, he should have the guts to ask me himself.

"He doesn't know," she replied, sheepishly.

"What?"

"He doesn't ask about her. He knows she didn't want anything to do with him, and he respects that. And I just… I guess it's nice to talk to someone who doesn't know. To talk to someone who thinks she's still living life to the fullest."

I sighed, grabbed ahold of her hand, and squeezed.

"How often do you talk?" I asked, not entirely sure I wanted the answer.

"Not very, I swear to you." She crossed her heart and held up a Girl Scout Salute. I smiled lightly, still feeling the twinge of anger budding behind the action.

"Who's your guest?" She teased and I rolled my eyes. "He's a cutie."

"Just a friend."

She smiled, crossing behind the counter and looking at the bouquet of decaying roses. "You never did tell me how that date went," she teased.

"It was perfect," I replied, honestly, with a hint of shame and sadness.

"You don't sound too happy about that," she accused. I moved to the counter and rested my elbows on the surface.

"I just think it was too good to be true, ya know?"

She squinted, a pensive look crossing her face. "Or was it too good for you to believe?"

"I've got the store today," I said, ignoring the way her gaze made me feel exposed. "Go home, and relax!"

She contemplated for a moment, and I thought briefly that she might continue to push the subject, but thankfully she finally agreed and headed toward the door.

"Just to be clear, I'm leaving because you have a handsome visitor and I don't wanna be a third-wheeler, not because I need a break." She winked and left before I had a chance to reiterate to her Archer was just a friend.

"Place is clear." Archer had come back from the back of the store and settled in near the counter. "If it makes you feel more comfortable, I can stick around. I was just going to be doing some research today and this is as good a place as any."

I smiled at him, without fully giving him my attention. My eyes were still drawn to the expiring roses.

"That would be great, Archer. Thank you," I offered, mindlessly walking toward the vase on the counter.

I felt the tiniest, most imperceptible draw to them grow with each step. Like a rope was wrapped around their stems and the other end secured onto my heart. The closer I got to those roses, the less fear harbored in my mind. With each step, the image of their monstrous faces was replaced with their soft eyes, gentle hands, and tormenting tongues. These roses and their withered existence ironically gave me a fresh perspective. A long time ago, people painted me the villain without letting me explain, without truly hearing me. Nobody cared what the truth was. I wasn't offered the option, but maybe my wanderers should be. If nothing else, they at least owed me their truth. And I owed them a listening ear.

So with newfound determination and resolution, I pulled my phone from my pocket and unblocked two very important numbers.

"So how long have you been working here?" Archer asked, finding a comfortable spot on one of the couches near the front. I slid my phone back into my pocket, suddenly feeling lighter, and made my way to the coffee machine. I made quick work of brewing us each a cup.

"My entire life basically," I answered, as the milk steamed. "This store has been in my family for a long time."

"It's a really cool place, when I'm in here I feel like I'm scrolling through a 'dark academia and woodland fae' Pinterest board."

When I turned, giving him an arched eyebrow he threw his hands up. "What? Can't a guy enjoy a little interior design?"

I fell into an easy laughter I hadn't experienced in a few days and instantly was once again thankful for his presence. "Sure you can," I assured him, pouring the hot liquid into blue ceramic mugs.

"All I'm saying is, you should be proud of this place." I turned to face him, mug in hand, and smiled.

"I am." I sat the coffee down in front of him, and then it hit me. "Oh, shit. I didn't even ask you what kind of coffee you like." I shook my head. "I'm sorry! I can make you something else!"

"Hey, no worries," he comforted. "What kind did ya make me?"

I glanced down at the cup on the table. "It's a white chocolate mocha."

"That's my favorite," Archer replied, earnestly. I tilted my head and eyed him incredulously. "No, I'm serious! I swear. It really is my favorite." He made a crossing his heart motion that looked so playful and easy. I couldn't help but notice that this was how it was starting to feel being around him. Playful and easy.

"It's my favorite too," I agreed and Archer took a slow sip of the coffee, releasing a satisfied groan of approval as the taste reached his tongue. I chuckled and sat down on the opposite side of the table from him, enjoying my coffee as well. We drank in comfortable silence for a few minutes.

"So, still not sticking around for the season?" I inquired, replaying his answer from the first night we met in my mind. He shook his head, swallowing his current sip of coffee.

"No, I'm not staying long," I couldn't help but feel a little saddened by that. Archer had quickly cemented himself as someone I enjoyed spending time with. Well, that and he willingly protected me the other night. That kind of chivalry makes an impression.

"That's a bummer. Who am I going to go to the summer series concerts on the pier with?" I teased.

Archer smiled, but then a small blush darkened on his face.

"I assume you could ask your friend… What was her name again? Danielle? Delilah?" Something in his coy phrasing and shy smile told me he knew exactly what her name was. I smirked and leaned back in my chair.

"Davia?" I said, amused. He nodded, over the top.

"Oh, that's right."

I watched him as he avoided eye contact, fiddling with the cup in front of him.

"You could always go to those shows with her unless she has someone else she normally goes with. Parents, boyfriend… You know. That kind of person."

"Are you fishing to find out if Davia is single?"

He had the gall to act appalled. "What? Jeez, no I'm just… you're… Ok. yeah, Yeah I was," he admitted, defeatedly. We devolved into laughter together, the melodic sound filling the space with a type of liveliness I had desperately been craving.

"She's single, and she's also a serial one-night-stander," I said, and Archer nodded his head, absorbing the new info. "Can't go to those concerts with her anyway," I resolved, downing the last of my coffee.

"Why not?" He asked.

"Davia doesn't know the difference between Kid Rock and Kidz Bop."

Archer visibly flinched. "Yikes."

I nodded solemnly. "So, where are you from? And why did you choose Shockgrove as your latest pit stop?" I asked, leaning my elbows on the table and resting my chin on my hands.

He looked like he was contemplating the answer, his brow furrowed.

"I grew up in the Midwest. I'm talking corn fields, cow-tipping, and 'drive your tractor to school' kind of rural." He seemed nearly ashamed of that fact. "Knew I wanted to get out of there, but it was kind of impossible."

"Why?" I asked.

"Because of the family business," he replied, sincerely.

"You didn't want to join?"

He shook his head. "No, but there wasn't much of a choice." He seemed upset, and I nodded. I understood the pressure of joining a family business, but the difference here was clear. I loved the work I did, and this was a passion I developed myself. It was a perfect fit. But if I hadn't loved this job, I still would have done it, out of obligation. And I would have been miserable.

"I'm sorry," I whispered.

He thanked me under his breath.

"Is it a painting business?" I asked, he looked up at me sharply, a confused expression on his face. I gestured to the blue paint stains on his hands that were receding, but still there. He anxiously clasped his hands together in front of him.

"Yeah, something like that." He seemed cagey and I decided it was best not to press the matter.

"What would you do if you got the benefit of a choice?"

He sighed deeply, a soft smile playing on his lips. "I've always wanted to be a musician."

"Do you play? Write? Sing?"

He nodded. "All of the above. I can play five instruments, but my favorite is guitar." The passion in his eyes was undeniable. I couldn't help but feel a prick of pain at the thought of him suppressing his dreams.

"That's really impressive," I gushed. "You'll have to play something for me sometime!" I eagerly offered. He leaned back in his chair.

"Maybe," he promised, with a slight smirk.

We spent the next few hours getting to know each other. A few customers came and went, buying mostly coffee and pastries, and one hardcover of Moby Dick. Throughout it all, the exchange between Archer and me was easy and freeing.

But the ease of this conversation and the vase of roses on the counter served as a reminder of the conversation I needed to have soon. And it was going to be anything but easy.

ARCHER

FOUR

I really couldn't believe my luck. When I arrived in this little town, I thought it was going to take me days to figure out where The Wanderers were hiding out, then days after that to plan my attack, and then probably a few days to gather the nerve to carry it out.

It was fate really that I had ventured out to the lighthouse that evening. I've been sent to enough coastal towns during my tagging assignments, but I never had time to just sort of soak it in. When I drove into town the decommissioned lighthouse felt like a beacon to me, despite its state. I was drawn to it, in a weird sort of quiet way. Like a whisper. When I got there, in the orange hue of the evening, with the fading light dancing against the waves as they crashed, I felt like a normal guy. Someone on vacation, just relaxing and taking in the view. Appreciating the natural beauty of what this world has to offer.

But I am not normal.

That truth slammed into me almost as hard as Athena had as she barrelled toward me. The look of terror and incredulity on her face was so familiar. I'd seen that look before. The way she was struggling to describe what she had seen, the fear hiding behind her mask.

A monster. She had seen a monster.

Now, unless Shockgrove had another monstrous visitor in town, I was positive that I found my trail.

Jackpot.

Walking her to her store was not entirely selfless of me. Not that I wanted her to walk alone with the creatures of the night still out and about, but if The Wanderers left a witness? Maybe having her near me was the bait I needed to capture them once and for all.

That was as good a plan as any. Stick close to their loose end in hopes they come back to tie it up. Then I'll be ready.

Fuck. When did I start thinking of human beings as bait and loose ends?

I always said I wasn't going to lose myself to this business, but here I was, not even a single kill in and already I'm hoping the vampires will come to terrorize this girl so I can capture them.

Who's the monster in this scenario again?

Them. Of course, it's them. Vampires. They prey on the innocent. They drain blood and leave their lifeless forms in a trail of death and destruction behind them. They kill without reason, take what they want, and damn the consequences.

They are the real villains.

The entire walk back to her store, I felt my heart in my throat, beating quickly and violently. My fingers were tense, holding tightly to the acidic spray. It would be enough to incapacitate them for a few hours. I just had to get close enough to do it.

The wooden stake that rested on my side felt like it was burning me alive as it brushed against my bare skin. I'd never used it on a living creature.

No, stop that, Archer. They're not living. Not anymore.

When we got to her store, I could feel it instantly. Hunters are trained to understand and recognize the smallest details about vampires. I could analyze anything in this room and decipher if they were here, but I didn't have to. The hair on the back of my neck stood at attention, goosebumps erupted across my entire body. The air was thick, like blood. They were here.

I found them.

"Lock this door," I offered to her, as I headed down the aisle to the back entrance I clocked the last time I was in the store. "I'm going to sweep the place, don't go far."

I knew she was doing as I asked, but I didn't bother to look back. I let my hand rest on my stake, and once I knew I was far enough from Athena, I pulled it from its place. Holding it in front of me. Ready.

The stake was a dark brown wood, meticulously filed to a sharp point. A metallic band encircled the girthiest part of the stake that read 'nisi nox'. The creed of Nameless. A promise our organization has made to the world of mortals, even though they'll never know.

Save the night.

That's what we're trained to do. To protect mortals from the vicious creatures who hide and hunt in the dark.

I let the air fill my lungs, willing my heart to slow as I take cautious steps forward. Stake in one hand, spray bottle in the other. Quickly, without stopping my motion, I spritz the mixture on either side of my neck. It was a little trick taught to us at the facility. If a vampire gets close enough to take a bite out of your neck, you're already dead…but this way you take them with you.

As I ventured through the stacks of books, the musty smell of paper in the air, I wondered briefly if I was hoping to find them, or hoping not to. I knew what my father had said. That I needed to make a statement. To prove my loyalty and allegiance to Nameless before they see me as a liability and erase me from existence. And a part of me really wanted to do that. Make my father proud. Make Nameless proud. Help rid the world of monsters. But another part of me, the part that has never done more in the field than paint a symbol on some walls, was panicking. I'm not cut out for this. I'm not a fighter. A Hunter.

But I have to be.

When I arrived at the ajar back door, I could sense them. I may not have trained against actual vampires, but I've seen them. I know what their presence feels like.

The first time I ever saw a vampire, I was nine years old.

"You're gonna be brave in there, right, son?"

I remember the way my father had bent down, his knee resting on the ground. His fingers came up to fiddle with the collar of my shirt. My palms felt clammy.

I swallowed the lump in my throat and nodded once.

"Good." His hands came to rest on my shoulders and his eyes searched my face. He only looked at me like this when he was serious. Which was a lot of the time, but I knew why today was special. He told me to be ready. To be brave. It was the day I was going to see my first vampire.

"I know you're probably scared," he started, but I shook my head. I was scared. Really scared, actually, but I knew better than to let him know that. "If you're going to be a Hunter when you're older, you need to learn how not to show fear. Vampires sense that and they will not hesitate to kill you."

I felt my heart beat faster and my chest heave with anxious breaths. I glanced at the large iron door that led to the vampires. Dad told me once that nightmares live behind this door. I used to lie awake at night, worrying about what was in there. Making up fantastical stories, and images in my mind. Today, I'd see if they were true.

"I won't be scared, Dad."

He shook his head, lifting a hand to stop me. "Don't call me that here, kid."

I shut my mouth, hanging my head in shame. "I'm sorry, sir."

He gave me a pat on the back and stood, his frame towering over me. He reached into his back pocket for something, producing it in front of me.

"Stay behind the red line, don't let them get into your head, kid."

I nodded to hide the way my body shook.

"I'll be watching." Then he slid the black mask onto my head, securing it over my face. I'd seen my father wear a mask much like this before. I remembered always wanting to wear it, wondering when it would be my chance. Now that it was here, I wasn't so sure I wanted it.

When he was satisfied with my preparations, he offered a quick nod and moved to the iron door. He slipped a key into the massive lock, the sound echoed in the empty hall... When he pushed it open, I felt the cold air brush against my warmed skin. There was so much fear. I felt like I was drowning in it... My blood pulsed with fervor as if it wanted to taunt the creatures beyond the door.

With one last swallow, I puffed my chest and stepped across the threshold into the long, dank hallway. My eyes slowly adjusted to the low light. There were only a few dull bulbs lining the space, casting an eerie shadow across the floor. The air escaped my lungs as the door was shut behind me, locking me inside. I forced long settling breaths, despite the growing panic. Knowing my father was watching my every move. Studying me. Judging me.

Large iron gates lined the walls and as I took tentative steps forward, I couldn't see into the darkness of the cages. I'd passed three sets of cells without seeing anything, but I wasn't relieved. It was only a matter of time. Only a matter of when.

I think I walked past seemingly empty cages for a whole minute before I heard the softest groan. My entire body froze, fear coursing through my veins like ice.

"Hello?" I called out meekly, toward the cell where the sound permeated from. In the darkness of the hallway, I couldn't see more than a foot or two into the depth of the cage. If there was a back wall I couldn't tell. My eyes glanced down at the red line on the ground, crudely painted. I planted my feet firmly behind it.

"Hello?" I asked again. I had almost given up, writing it off as my mind playing tricks on me when a soft, feminine voice spoke from the depths of the cell.

"Hi there." The voice was weak, but other than that, it sounded positively...human. My eyebrows rose in shock as a beautiful woman slowly appeared from within in the shadows. Her clothes were torn, and her face was dirty and sunken, but she was pretty.

Long blonde hair curled around her face, hanging down her back and over her shoulders. Her blue eyes were bright enough to reflect even the dim light. "What's your name?" She asked, tilting her head slightly, her blue eyes scanned my form. I swallowed the fear and confusion that were beginning to intermingle and cleared my throat.

"My.. um... I'm," I paused. I felt the cool fabric of the mask brush against my face, a reminder of my supposed anonymity. "I'm a Hunter," I replied with as much false bravado as I could muster, which earned me a soft chuckle from the woman behind bars.

"Do you want to know my name?" She asked, smiling down at me with a mischievous glint in her eyes. I nodded my head. "Evangeline. My name is Evangeline." It was a pretty name, fitting. She looked like an Evangeline. "How old are you?" She took a step closer to the iron gate, and I found myself glancing down at the line to ensure I hadn't crossed it.

"I'm not afraid of you," I offered. She smiled again, leaning her head against the bars.

"I don't want you to be." It was so matter-of-fact, so concise. I almost believed her. "I'm two hundred and seventeen years old," she whispered, a contemplative look on her face.

"You're a vampire," I echo her volume. Her eyes flicked to me.

"Yeah," she starts. "I am."

I studied her, she looked calm, sweet even. If I saw her on the street I might even feel comfortable saying hello.

"I'm not going to hurt you, Hunter," she expressed, sinking down onto the ground. She sat with her shoulder leaning against the bar, her profile turned to me.

"Do you know why they have me in here, little one?" She queried. I shook my head. "They think I'm a monster." She glanced up at me, her eyes met mine directly. She looked at me as if she could see right through the mask to the scared little kid beneath.

"You are," I asserted, shakily. She sighed, letting her head fall back and her eyes travel to the ceiling.

"You don't even know me," she scoffed. "Tell me, kid, what about me makes me a monster?"

I scanned her face, her weak form, and her soft eyes. She was right, she didn't look the part of a monster, but she was one. I knew that much. She was here for a reason, my dad wouldn't do this if he didn't have to. We were saving the world. We were protecting humans.

"You are in disguise," I trembled.

"Aren't we all?"

"How many people have you killed?" I inquired, she looked back to me as if the question didn't surprise her.

"Have you ever asked your daddy that question?" She bit. I bristled, and my heart rate quickened. She noticed my reaction, smirking softly. "Thought you weren't afraid of me."

I swallowed the lump in my throat.

"I'm not," I lied.

"I'm going to tell you a secret, little Hunter, and I need you to promise that you'll never forget it, ok?" She moved until she was sitting up on her knees with her hands gripping the bars in front of her, she looked hopeless, afraid, and weak.

"Ok," I agreed. She smiled.

"This world is full of monsters, and not all of them look like me. They're not always so obvious, with large claws and fangs. No, some monsters are hiding in plain sight, pretending to be the heroes," she seethed. "You're better off not trusting a single person besides yourself."

I listened intently to her anger as it poured out of her.

"After all, you're the only one you can trust."

"I can trust my dad," I argued, although a small tremble in my voice gave away my hesitation.

She leaned toward me, a look of pure concern on her features. I felt drawn in. Before I could stop myself I had taken a step. Her eyes scanned my masked face with reverence. It was so disorienting, so unlike anything I expected from a creature like this, that I didn't even flinch when her gentle fingers came up to brush against my mask. When she slowly gripped the edge of the mask, I didn't shy away. When she began to remove it, I didn't stop her. Cool air brushed against my skin as Evangeline studied my bare face. The *way she looked at me was so motherly, so caring. I didn't realize how much I craved that until it was dangling in front of me. "Little Hunter, you can't trust anyone."*

She moved faster than I'd ever seen a creature move. Suddenly my body was pressed up against the bars and my arm was pulled into the darkness. My eyes had barely adjusted to her speed when the pain radiated from my wrist. A scream erupted from my lips as I looked down my arm to the woman who had sunk her fangs into my skin. Her kind blue eyes were gone, replaced with a violent bright red. Her hands wrapped around my wrist and held me in place as she drew my blood into her mouth. It stung, like a thousand hornets attacking the exact same part of my body. I tried to pull away from her, to retreat behind the safety of the red line I had foolishly crossed, but her hold was steadfast and impossible to break free from. I pushed against the cage which she was holding me to, swinging aimlessly into the darkness within. My vision slowly started blackening along the edges, as she drained the very life from my veins.

I had almost given up, my escape attempts becoming weaker and weaker the more blood was stolen from me, when a metallic clang sounded through the hallway. A rush of air brushed against my face as the ax swung, barely missing me. Something cold and wet splattered across my skin. The force against my wrist receded, but the pressure of the fangs on my skin did not. When I looked down at my injured wrist, I saw the severed head of Evangeline. I didn't register the rag that was thrust in my face until it had wiped the substance from my skin.

"Don't fucking taste any of that shit, clean your face."

I barely recognized my Dad's voice, I was still frozen in fear, unable to tear my eyes from the head attached to my wrist.

"Archer, snap the fuck out of it."

I wasn't breathing.

"Jesus Christ," he said under his breath before a bucket of water was tossed onto my face, drenching me and washing away the remnants of whatever it was that had gotten on me. The cold shock of the water finally brought air back to my lungs. The world was technicolor again. Tears fell down my cheeks as I tried to pull my arm back through the

bars, but the head attached was too wide and when it hit the bars, the fangs ripped at my tender skin. I screamed in pain again. My panic was so vivid, I knew I would never be able to wash this memory from my mind.

My dad's hand clasped around my arm, above where the head was attached, quickly, he helped relieve my wrist of its new accessory, sending a few jolts of pain up my arm. Finally, I was able to pull it back from the darkness of the cage, cradling the bleeding appendage against my chest. As I stumbled back to behind the red line, I watched as my father slammed a wooden stake into the chest of the headless form on the floor of the cell. He stood a few moments later, pulling the stake from its place, and turned to face me, I saw the dark black mask covering his features. He looked calm if a little out of breath, but I knew my father well enough to know that this was him when he was angry.

He gripped my shoulder and led me quietly out of the hallway, away from Evageline's corpse. He didn't speak to me until we were safely locked behind his office door. He pulled his mask off with a grunt and turned back to me with disappointment oozing from his pores.

"I'm sorry," I whispered, knowing it wasn't enough.

"What the hell were you thinking?" He asked, his voice eerily even and restrained. He moved to his desk and took a seat on the ledge.

"I wasn't," I replied, timidly. My father nodded to himself.

"Clearly."

He ran a hand through his soft strawberry-blonde hair and sighed.

"Show me your arm," he demanded, holding a hand out for me. I winced as I extended my tender wrist toward him. He studied it in silence for a few moments before grabbing a small white box from his desk drawer. The liquid he poured on the wound burned, but it was like a pinch compared to the fire of Evangeline's fangs. Once it was wrapped and the gaping red wound was no longer in my eyesight, I started to feel the shock wear off. Tears stung my eyes.

"Don't cry," my father scolded, but I couldn't help it. "That's part of being a Hunter. Look." He slid off his suit jacket and began rolling up his shirt sleeve to reveal *several white raised scars in the shape of vampire bites littering his skin.*

"Why did you cross the line?" He inquired, as I memorized the way the scars looked against his pale skin.

"She felt safe," I answered, quietly. I was ashamed of how I acted.

Reaching behind him, my father grabbed the bloody stake from the place where he discarded it. Taking a rag from his pocket, he wiped it down, although I don't think the nearly black blood of the vampire would ever truly be gone. It would stain this wood, the way this scar would stain my skin, and this memory would stain my soul. "You need to understand that you are only ever safe in this world if you fight for your safety." He held out the stake for me, and I grabbed it with shaky hands.

That was my first day as a Hunter.

The Wanderers had been here, but they were long gone. I slid the forever-stained wooden stake back into my waistband and locked the door.

I walked Athena to her friend's house and watched the door from a distance for a few hours waiting for their arrival. Eventually, I determined The Wanderers either didn't care enough to kill her…or maybe they cared too much. Watching the front door, I thought about the fiery redhead inside. The night I walked into her store I was simply following a feeling. I felt their presence, it led me there. I half expected to see the vamps inside, that's how strongly I felt their influence, but instead, I ran into an innocent human. The ease of our chat was a breath of fresh air for my morally corrupted lungs. It'd been so long since I just talked to someone, in fact, I got so caught up in the feeling of normalcy I hadn't even thought to interrogate her on if she'd seen them. It wasn't until she mentioned the paint on my hands that I remembered just why I shouldn't be making easy conversation with her.

It was another stroke of fate that she found me at the lighthouse. There was something so familiar about the hollow look in her eyes. A kindred spirit. Just as terrified of what she'd seen as I was. As I still am. She's brave though, I have to give her that. And I can't say I hate the companionship of our conversation.

She and I could have been friends in a different universe I think. If there weren't monsters out there if I wasn't hunting them. But as I staked out the house she was staying in, attempting to protect her from the creatures of the night, I knew there was no chance of us having a normal friendship. Nothing about any of this was normal, so despite the briefest glimmer of a blossoming friendship, I had to keep my distance. I'd be gone soon anyway. With four vampires in tow, hopefully.

The next morning, I watched the house for the majority of the daylight hours, and a good portion of the evening. At night, I went back to the store and tried tracking them, but whatever trail they might have left was long since cold at that point.

The next day, I checked in periodically between canvassing the entire town.

The third morning, when I was sure no one was going to venture to the house where Athena was staying, I made my way back to the pale blue and white lighthouse and climbed the solitary staircase to the top. This town looked even smaller from this vantage point. Those monsters were out there somewhere. As I leaned my arms along the railing, looking out over the crashing waves, my fingers absent-mindedly traced the scar on my wrist. The bite mark was a constant reminder of what I had to lose if I ever let my guard down again.

Ring. Ring.

I pulled my phone from my pocket and glanced at the name. With a groan, I answered.

"Bennett."

"Progress report?"

I rolled my eyes, leaning further onto the railing of the lighthouse.

"Hello to you too," I joked.

"There's no time for jokes, son. You need to make a move and you need to make it soon. They're going to discover The Wanderers are settled in that town any day now and Galvin will send the Hunters. Your chance will be gone." He sounded desperate. A far cry from the usually put-together calm leader he was.

"I know," I sighed. "I have a lead. I'm following it." There was silence on the line for a moment.

"Good. See to it that you get this done, kid." I nodded, although I knew he couldn't see me.

"I will. Hey, you ever gonna tell me who your contact was that knew they'd be here?" I couldn't help but feel curious. I'd walked around the town quietly studying each face wondering if they were the ones who had told my father. Wondering who knew about the monsters under their noses?

"It's just an old friend from another life," he said, solemnly.

"Are they a Hunter?" I asked.

"Don't worry about that," he dismissed me. "Just get the job done." The line went dead. I held the phone to my ear for a few moments longer, not sure what I was expecting to hear.

Just as I was devising a plan to draw them out of hiding, my phone buzzed with a text from Athena, and suddenly the plan created itself.

An hour later, after greeting Athena, and engaging in a verbal sparring match with her firecracker of a friend, we were at her bookstore.

She was starting to trust me, and truth be told, I was starting to enjoy her company too. She was smart, had great taste in music, and her bravery was inspiring. I've seen some Hunters take longer to recover from an encounter with vampires. She was growing on me. And I can't deny that it felt good to have someone to talk to again.

If she was going to be the bait for this plan, I was going to protect her. No harm will come to Athena Landry. Not while I'm alive.

ORPHEUS

FIVE

I've had the unfortunate pleasure of enduring torture three times in my life.

The first time was rather early in my second existence. I was still quite young and without a guide or mentor to show me the ropes of how to survive in this new reality that was thrust upon me. I was struggling to maintain control over my bloodlust. Three elder vampires caught up to me somewhere near Moldova and chained me up in a bunker, claiming I was 'soiling' the vampire name, and drawing unwanted attention. They were right, of course, but as a young fresh-turn with little to no regard for anyone's safety, including my own, I didn't take that new development lightly. They took on a sort of 'educator' role, promising to let me go once I learned to control my instincts. Their methods were brutal, savage even. Before I had gone through the proper ritual to survive in the daylight, they'd set me up in a chair just in front of a window and slowly pull back the curtains, inch by inch. They did this every day. For two years. The light scarred my flesh, permanently in some places, and their lessons were drilled into my mind. They let me go once they were sure I was 'trained'.

I have always appreciated what they did for me, teaching me how to control my emotions. It certainly made it that much more satisfying when I found them again years later and spent three months prolonging their violent and painful deaths.

The second time was just a few years back when Nameless got their fucking hands on us. We had been evasive up to that point. Careful, of course, but we weren't implementing anywhere near the level of countermeasures I put in place in recent years. It was a trap, of course, it was. I should have fucking seen it. It isn't often that our coven runs into other vampires. We'd avoided meeting in large numbers after the Hunters grew to be a more serious threat, but that night we had been invited to a night of vampiric debauchery, mirth, and above all…blood.

Silas had met a woman while out in the town early in the evening, just as the sun set. She was a gorgeous temptress. She promised him a night of sex, blood, and mindless passion.

Silas fell for it. Hook, line, and sinker.

But then again, so did I.

The mansion was dark when we arrived, we weren't tipped off to that though. Of course, they would try to hide their party from prying eyes. Nameless could be anywhere, right?

Right.

That sensual female vampire sold us out to the Hunters, making a deal with them that they would let her go if she delivered the elusive Wanderers to their doorstep.

She fulfilled her part of the bargain.

And they staked her through the heart.

They held us for months. I don't understand why they didn't just kill us and get it over with at first, but after a few of their 'interrogations,' I realized quickly that they were running out of leads. They were so desperate to find more blood-sucking vamps that they were reckless enough to leave us alive.

Although 'alive' is definitely not what I wanted to be. I had endured everything they threw at us before. It wasn't any more painful than my time with my 'teachers' in Moldova, but my companions hadn't. The torture wasn't unbearable because of what they were doing to me, it was unbearable because of what they did to *them*. My family. I felt every second of their fear, their agony, and their desire to die. Their emotions were so potent, I was choking on them. Each day, their screams were knives in my chest. Their burnt skin was acid on my body. I was the reason they were all vampires, after all. It was my doing that they were forced to withstand this. It was my fault.

The torture of knowing their pain was my doing was worse than anything Nameless could do to me.

The third time I suffered through torture was in the days following the shocking revelation that Athena Landry, a human from Maine, was my mate. The two days when my body, and the bodies of my coven, burned through blood faster than they had in our entire second existence. The two days when we had to hunt more frequently in order to fucking survive. When we were moving around the house like zombies, with sunken eyes and hollow cheeks, our dead hearts aching with each phantom beat. Our bodies desiccated from the inside out the longer we fought against the mate bond.

The torture of watching my family start to fall apart and knowing there was nothing I could do. The torture of realizing my soul belonged to someone and discovering she wanted nothing to do with me.

I've never felt this helpless, this lost. This torture was agonizing.

Just yesterday, I walked past Silas' room and saw her frame peeking out through the crack in the door. Her long red hair and her soft innocent face looking back at me from the floor length mirror. I nearly sprinted in and wrapped her in my arms. It took me a few moments to recognize it was Silas using his gift in order to see her again. He stood there in front of the reflection and studied her face, her eyes. Wanting to feel her near him. I understood the urge.

Luckily, or unluckily, I could feel her. Even from this distance. Her fear was so fucking potent. It ebbed and flowed, though, as if she would suddenly remember our encounter again after a moment of reprieve. But the emotion I felt that sent me into a spiral of agony was her pain. She had lost connections she started to cherish. She felt their loss nearly as strongly as I felt hers.

I'd lived a long life. I've endured things that would test even the strongest of constitutions. But this. This torture had the potential to kill me.

"We can't keep this up for long," Laz said, plopping down into a chair in the office I'd commandeered for research. I glanced at them over the top of the laptop screen. Their usually tanned skin had lost some of its luster. Despite feeding this morning, they looked hungry, but that was becoming a constant state for all of us. A flask of human blood, which used to sustain us for weeks, was now barely getting us through the next few hours.

Silas and Samara had left the day before to hunt. They had tracked down a trafficking ring in a city a few hours from here. After setting the women free, they had their pick of the predator buffet. They brought back an entire cooler full of blood. If my current calculations were right, the blood they brought would only sustain us for three more days. We had to find a solution by then, because even though there was no shortage of evil people in this world to feed our bloodlust, Nameless would be looking for that exact sort of hunting pattern. And since we were going to be here for as long as it took to convince Athena that we were hers, we needed to be careful. We couldn't be careful if we were hungry.

"I know."

"We need to go to her," they said, quietly. I leaned back from the screen, letting my hands rest behind my head.

"I know."

They groaned and ran their hands through their sandy blonde hair. Their emotions were overwhelming. I felt every ounce of want and desire they did, which only increased my own tenfold. But I also felt their despair, their fear. It was potent. Sickening. "I've never felt like this before, Orpheus."

I nodded my agreement. They were right. I'd never experienced this either.

"I feel so incomplete. I need her," they whispered.

I've never needed anyone. Truly never. I'd been taking care of myself for as long as my mind can recall. And yes, I love my coven, and I'd die for them, but their companionship was purely a selfish thing to combat my growing loneliness. I didn't *need* them. But, Athena? I now understand why Silas and Laz were so desperate to stay. They had recognized the connection first.

I should have.

The way her eyes met mine as we walked into the bar that night. The way she held me captive in her gaze and I had to force myself to look away. The way I so eagerly jumped at the chance to destroy the man who dared to put his hands on her. The way I was so drawn to her in her bookstore.

Fuck.

I spent so long trying to keep my coven safe that I didn't dare indulge in the sinfulness that was Athena Landry. I ignored all the signs because I couldn't accept the truth. While Silas and Laz were basking in her attention, I was always watching. And now, I may never get the chance.

"What did you find out?" Laz asked, indicating to the computer.

"Not much, you can imagine how many hoops I had to jump through to get to any real information." It was essentially a nightmare trying to wade through hundreds of unsubstantiated claims from thousands of 'believers' to even find some truth among the tales.

"What I do know is the longer we wait, the harder our thirst will be to control."

They nodded at that, and already I saw their fangs slightly elongated.

"We either need to accept and complete the bond, and soon… or…" I paused, afraid to continue. As if by speaking the words, I'd be speaking the possibility into existence.

"Or?" Laz prompted.

"Or we can reject it."

Laz growled, their eyes reddening. Long fingernails dug into the arm of the chair.

"Never," they snarled. Their fury hit me in the chest like a brick wall. I put a hand up to calm them, and steady myself against the onslaught of anger radiating off of them.

"I know, I can't stand the thought either…But-"

"There is no 'but.' She won't reject us." Their voice was full of fury, but I recognized the fear that trembled behind the facade.

"If she doesn't accept us…" I started, hating the way the words felt on my tongue.

"She will!" They stood, their voice booming. I heard Samara and Silas making their way upstairs.

"But if she doesn't," I repeated, standing to meet their gaze. "We need to know how to reject it so we can survive."

"I won't survive without her," they spoke with such conviction, and their emotions flooded with a deeper sadness than I could even comprehend, that it made me pause. A small part of me, the logical part which used to be the most dominant, wanted to argue. Tell them we've made it this long without her, we could do it again. But the rest of me, the part that belonged to Athena, the part that was hand-crafted by whatever fates there were to be hers, wanted nothing more than to agree.

"I don't know why you're even bothering with this argument, Orpheus," Silas interjected from the door frame. "She is ours. She'll realize it soon."

"Maybe not soon enough," I sighed exasperatedly. "We are running out of time, I won't lose a single one of you because of her fear." I didn't care how much my heart yearned for her, or how much my body craved her touch. I refused to lose my family. If she doesn't want to be a part of it, she doesn't have to be.

But fuck. I need her to.

"You're acting like you don't fucking care if she accepts the bond. What kind of mate are you?" Silas challenged and I saw Samara place a warning hand on his chest, slightly angling her body to fit between the two of us.

"I'm trying to think realistically here, Silas! There is a strong chance she will reject us. All of us."

He growled and stepped forward, but Samara's hand kept him from crossing the threshold into the room.

"You're weak, Orpheus," Laz spat.

"Somebody has to protect this family!" I screamed, feeling my hands balled into fists at my side.

"Athena *is* a part of our family!" Laz glowered. I heard Silas grunt in agreement, and I glanced slightly over to Samara who had been quiet this entire time. Come to think of it, she had been pretty subdued for most of these past few days. Her emotions had been a mix of desire and guilt. Overwhelming, agonizing guilt.

"Not if she doesn't want to be," I replied, calmly, fighting against the devastating flood of feelings that were pouring out of my coven. Laz stormed off toward the door, to join the others. They paused just before venturing out into the hall and turned over their shoulder to glare at me.

"I'd sooner die than reject her. And if you can't say the same then you don't deserve her." With that, Laz pushed past the others and disappeared down the hall. Silas shook his head, and a cloud of his emotions surrounded me.

His disappointment was suffocating. "By the way, the cops called me about the douche from the bar. We're expected at the station in an hour."

Shock colored my expression, but Silas was gone before I could respond.

When Samara and I were alone, I placed a hand on my chest and forced a few steadying breaths, mentally begging my gift to give me a moment of reprieve.

"Overwhelmed?" She asked from her spot across the room. I nodded, afraid my voice would come out breathless should I attempt to speak. I sunk into the office chair and let my head fall back and drew a few shallow, anxious breaths. I heard Samara crossing the floor to me, but I didn't look up to meet her gaze.

"I was getting a little stifled myself, I can only imagine how it felt to *feel* it all," she offered, meekly.

A few moments passed before I regained enough control to turn my face to hers. Samara's guilt was still potent enough to invade my senses but felt like a calming balm compared to the volatile nature of Silas and Laz's anger.

"I'm just trying to keep my family together," I admitted, quietly. My strength was not a front, I wasn't some hard-shelled monster with a secret soft interior. I was strong. I was tough. The way I show my love and dedication to someone wasn't through soft embraces and meaningless words of affirmation. It was through action.

It was ok with me if they couldn't see that now - if they weren't hearing what they wanted from me, because I would do whatever I had to in order to protect them, whether they liked it or not.

"Yeah," she mused, timidly. Her eyebrows furrowed as she took a deep breath.

"Are you ok?" I asked, scanning her face.

"Huh? Oh, yeah. Just hungry." It wasn't a lie, per se, I could see the tell-tale signs on her face, in the redness that was slowly permeating her eyes, but there was more to it. I felt it. She looked up at my face and must have seen the look on my face because she sighed. "I don't know why I ever try to lie to you." She chuckled softly, without any real humor behind it.

I remained silent, allowing her the space she needed to formulate her response. She toyed with her fingers in her lap, mindlessly picking at the skin around her nails. "I don't think I can do it," she admitted, finally.

"Do what, Samara?"

"I can't move on from her." A tear slid down her dark skin, painting the surface of her cheek with a single path of pain. "Alora was my chosen, Orpheus. She was my wife. My everything. My life. I stood beneath the stars and the moon and I promised my heart to her and her alone. If I accept this mate bond, I am breaking my promise to her." Tears flowed more freely now although her face remained stoic.

With my particular gift, it's easy to comfort others by saying 'I know how you feel' because it's true. I do. I feel it all, I understand intimately how they feel. But I've learned an important caveat to my gift in my many years of existence.

I may know how they feel, and be able to experience it for myself, but never in my lifetime have I or will I be able to truly understand the depths of their emotions as intimately as they can. No matter how much I wish I could, I cannot save them from the cages they forge for themselves.

Samara's affection for Alora grew over time, building each day. I could see it, but it didn't take my gift to acknowledge the budding love between them.

"What brought this on? Just a few days ago you were smitten, following her into sex shops and kissing her at her store?" I asked.

She groaned. "A few days ago she was just an attractive stranger whom I would have enjoyed spending an evening in bed with."

I looked at her, questioningly.

"Now she's… it's just, it's too much," she whispered, before taking a shaky breath. "We talked about it once," she continued, "what would happen if we found our mates."

I leaned forward, watching her face as she spoke.

"We swore to each other that we would reject it," she choked on the word like it felt painful even to utter it. "We promised each other. It was us, and only us. Till the end." She maintained control of her outward display of emotions despite the wave of guilt I felt coming from her.

"It was," I said, calmly. She glanced up at me through moistened eyelashes, inquisitively. "It was you and her till the end, Samara."

A sob wrenched from her chest, but she was quick to regain composure.

"Just because her end and yours are not the same doesn't mean you didn't keep your promise to her."

She nodded, but I could tell she wasn't buying into it.

"I feel like I'm being ripped apart from the inside. Athena's kiss felt like coming home, but Alora *was* my home." She wiped the backs of her hands across her face to catch the stray tears.

"Those can both be true."

She scoffed, letting me see the slightest bit of hidden emotion behind her walls. "How do you reject a mate bond?" She asked, straining against the question.

"Samara I-"

"How do I do it, Orpheus?" She asserted again. I sighed, running my hands down my face.

"Ok, so let's say you reject it. You sever this fate-given tie and cast your feelings for Athena aside."

She whimpered at the thought of it.

"Let's say you do all that, but Laz and Silas manage to complete the bond. What then? Would you stick around, seeing your coven reap the benefits of a mate bond with the one you let get away?"

Her facade broke for a moment and a cry nearly escaped her lips. She shook her head. "I'd have to go."

"Go where?" I demanded, quietly.

"Anywhere!" Her careful grip on her emotions was slipping with each passing second.

"And leave your family?" I argued, my voice raising slightly.

"Alora was my family!" she screamed as she stood, once she recognized her outburst, her hands clenched at her side and she took a few slow breaths to calm herself.

It wasn't working.

"How do I do it, Orpheus?" She begged, her wet eyes pleading with me.

"You have to transfuse with someone else," I whispered. The act of sharing blood was how someone of our kind was created. I've turned a few vampires in my life. It's a slightly intimate process, depending on where you decide to take the blood from, but the pain overshadows any romantic undertones rather abruptly.

A human must drink from a vampire at the same moment a vampire drinks from the human. It activates the venom in our blood, sending it catapulting through their veins to their heart, suspending it in lifeless animation. "In order to reject a mate bond, you have to create a new vampire." Samara's eyes were wide, and I felt the disgust filter into her emotions.

Vampires didn't have an organized 'government' body, just the royal family, who are more for show than anything else, but there were some unspoken rules that the monarchy liked to agree on.

Don't expose our kind to humans.

Don't sell out our kind to Nameless.

Close the wounds after feeding. Regardless of if the victim is alive or dead.

Don't create new vampires, unless necessary.

If our population were to grow too exponentially, we'd have a harder time avoiding breaking rules one and two. So for the most part, turning a new vampire was reserved for life or death, or mate purposes.

"Damnit," she exhaled. "So if she doesn't accept us, in order to survive we'd have to double our numbers?"

I nodded curtly. We'd each have to find a human and condemn them to a half-life.

She absorbed that for a moment, her eyes glazed over as thoughts I could never hope to understand flitted through her mind. Then she stood, the only indication of her discomfort was the hard line of her jaw, and the way her fingers wrestled with themselves. She nodded once, before moving to exit.

"Samara," I interjected, as she paused by the door frame with her back to me. "Talk to her first." She didn't respond. "Just promise me, before you go making irreversible choices that you will talk to Athena first." Her shoulders rose and fell with quick breaths. "Please."

She glanced over her shoulder at me, and I saw her raw unfiltered expression for a brief moment. "I don't make promises I can't keep." And she was gone.

I fell back into the chair with an exasperated sigh.

That was a problem, an issue I'd need to address soon… but first, we had to go make a statement at the station. We needed to feed and get our story straight.

Shockgrove was proving to be a significant problem, and for the first time in my entire existence, I had no idea what to do.

SAMARA

SIX

Walking into the police station was like finding a source of fresh water after days of traversing the dry desert. We had each swallowed down a bottle of blood from our reserves before leaving the house ten minutes ago and while the hunger wasn't ravenous, it was there. Like a pit in my stomach that was noticeable and slightly painful. Orpheus was right to be worried. If we run out of blood before they accept the bond there could be an accidental bloodbath on its way to Shockgrove, Maine.

It didn't matter to me. though. I had already made up my mind.

I had to reject the bond. I made a promise and I wasn't going to go back on my word.

The station smelled like stale coffee and body odor, but that stench wasn't enough to mask the scent of mouth-watering fresh, warm, blood. Even so, I tried to focus on the displeasing aroma to avoid focusing on the other, more tasty smelling one. Several people milled about the bullpen with various levels of urgency. When we approached the front desk, the secretary smiled at Silas and Orpehus with stars in her eyes. So I rolled mine.

"How can I help you today?" She gushed, twirling a strand of light brown hair around her index finger.

"I was called by a Detective Barnes," Silas offered, tight-lipped, without an ounce of flirtation or cheekiness. It was an odd thing to see from my normally very sensually forward friend. She didn't get the message, because she giggled flirtatiously and reached for a phone to call the Detective.

A few moments later, we were ushered into an office at the corner of the bullpen. The room was bright, sunlight poured in from the several windows that lined the walls, my skin felt tender under its warmth. The burn was manageable, but I found myself tilting my body away from the window nevertheless. Awards and certifications decorated the free space between each window and a large mahogany desk sat near the back wall.

The four of us each grabbed a seat in the open black leather armchairs and waited for the Detective to arrive.

It was silent and tense. I've never felt such a distance between my family. Even when Alora died, we came together in the wake of the tragedy, supporting each other through the loss. But this, this was tearing us apart.

Something I never thought could be possible. We'd been through so much together, and came out the other side stronger that I had truly thought our bond was impenetrable. I glanced over my shoulder at the bullpen behind us. Along one of the walls there was a small holding cell, and I felt my body tense as unwanted memories overtook my senses.

I'd lost count of the days. From our cells, we could not see the sky. We had no indication of time passing down here. The torture seemed to come at various times and lasted for varying lengths, but I could be mistaken. Things tend to blend together when you're a prisoner.

"Don't fall asleep, Samara." Alora. After weeks of being separated, with only their voices drifting from adjoining cells to keep me company, I was beginning to forget the nuances of her face. All of their faces. The exact shade of their eye color. The shape of

their noses. The memory of my wife and my coven was starting to fade at the edges. A taunting vignette with the ability to eclipse the pieces of me that made me whole. It was reminiscent of the way my human memories had slowly begun to slip from me, not nearly fast enough, but similar nonetheless. Orpheus said it was a side effect of the hunger. Without blood, our hearts forgot to beat at all and slowly our minds started to think we were dead. Well, really dead. It had been weeks since we last even scented blood and that was only when Nameless used it to torment us. We hadn't tasted the life-giving elixir for so long that I couldn't remember the way it tasted, or the way it slid over my tongue and warmed my entire body, setting it alight.

"I'm not asleep," I whispered with what little energy I had.

"You have to stay strong, baby." Her lilting voice had a hard edge to it. Fear, maybe? Orpheus would know better than I would. He was fortunate, or perhaps unfortunate in this case, enough to have a gift that traversed distances. Me? I had to lay my hands on the wounded person to help them. For the first few months when I would hear my wife and my coven scream in agony - sustaining injuries that were vicious and painful - I knew I could heal them if only I were granted a moment, a single moment to touch them, I could alleviate their suffering. But I couldn't help them.

"Why?"

I'd been fighting for months. Spending each and every day grasping onto my sanity with every ounce of strength I had left. Holding out hope that if only Nameless let their guard down for a moment, we could all escape and return to the life we deserved, the life we fought for. As each day passed, that hope waned like the very memories in my heart.

"Because, I'm going to get us out of here," she whispered. I didn't have the energy to be shocked or surprised. And it wasn't like I hadn't heard it before from Silas, Orpheus, and Laz as well. Hell, I'd even uttered the same words myself a few times over our tenure in these cages.

"Heard that before," I heard Laz whisper from their cell a little way down the dank hallways. Their southern lilt seemed to deepen and become thicker the hungrier they got.

"Alora…" I started, but I heard her shush me softly.

"Samara, I mean it." She was whispering so quietly that I knew the guard down the hall couldn't hear her. Our advanced hearing certainly made it easy to hold private conversations, although that particular gift had started to fade as well with our faltering strength. Eventually, I wouldn't be able to hear anything at all. *"I drank blood."* I sat up as quickly as my frail body would allow me to. I heard the others perk up as well.

"What do you mean?" I asked, trying to reign in my curiosity.

"When?" Silas asked, eagerly.

"Who was it?" Orpheus interjected.

"The last torture session in The Room." I shuttered at the label we had given the site of our 'interrogations'. It was a small metallic room with walls of pure aluminum, silver chains were reinforced into the cement floor. That's where they put us. The room was rigged with a sprinkler system. A toxic mixture of what Orpheus theorized as holy water and garlic concentrate would spray down from the ceiling dousing us in acidic torture. Horrors beyond what I could comprehend had been given out to us in that room as if they were earned. *"They were cleaning up after their most recent scenting taunt. They must have thought I was passed out, which I nearly was."* I cringed, my whole body tensing. I hated the thought of Alora in pain. *"They spilled the blood."* I pulled my knees to my chest and held them close. Just the thought of the red liquid crawling across the floor toward me made my mouth water.

"How'd you manage to drink it?" Orpheus asked, eagerly. He was starving, we all were.

"It wasn't much, barely a mouthful, before they dragged my body out of there." I growled at the image.

"Did they see you?" Silas inquired.

"No, and it wasn't enough to quench the hunger, but I have some of my strength back. I can take the guard. I know I can," she promised, and for the first time in a long while I felt the glimmer of hope.

I should have known not to trust it.

The door to the office swung open and two individuals waltzed in. A taller slender woman and a shorter man with graying hair. They both looked rather haggard, and tired.

"Hello," the woman began as she crossed to the desk. "My name is Detective Barnes, this is Detective Argent. Thank you for stopping by." Orpheus, ever the frontman, reached a hand forward for the both of them to shake. I avoided breathing in their scent, although not entirely appealing, blood was blood and I was hungry.

"My name is David Green," Orpheus offered, and Laz and I exchanged a quick, imperceptible glance.

We had used aliases for a century. It helped us hide from Nameless, but we had never been questioned by the police, so we never had to use an alias for something so formal and so prone to an investigation. If the police chose to look into that name, they would find the very fragile cover we implemented, but it wouldn't take much to look deeper and find the falsified records. It was enough for a rental company…but the police? That was an avenue we'd never tested before. Before I could even begin to think of the name I would offer, Orpheus continued.

"This is Cal Freeman, Haven Jones, and Marcie Phillips." I schooled my reaction, smiling and tipping my head slightly toward the detectives whose eyes were scanning us.

"Heard you're just passing through town. Not staying for the season?" I watched Orpheus handle their questions expertly, like the leader he was born to be. He offered clear and concise information that sounded invested enough to give a reason for our continued presence in town, but nothing in-depth enough to raise any questions. He was a masterful protector.

"So, where did you say you saw him go?" Orpheus looked toward Silas to allow him to offer the answer.

"He went down the street, sorry, I don't really know the names- " Silas began. The Detective nodded before urging him on. "He went toward that gas station though, down the street from the bar. Didn't watch long enough to see if he went inside though." Silas was the one who wore Louis' image into that gas station. He would have been seen on cameras all over town on his way out. That was his job, and he was good at it.

Detective Barnes seemed to accept the information, but I noticed the suspicious look brewing on the man's face.

"Why'd you follow them out?" Argent asked, his eyes narrowing on all of us.

I felt Silas and Laz tense next to me, the memory of why we followed them outside fresh in their heads. I waited a moment for Orpheus to answer, but when I glanced at him he was still, taking a deep breath to calm himself.

I spoke up, quickly demanding the attention of the Detectives. "It was my suggestion actually." Barnes and Argent turned to look at me, patiently waiting for me to explain. "I guess it's a force of habit. If I see a woman who may be drunk being led out of a bar by a man, I tend to keep a particular eye on that just in case she needs any help." I saw the respect flash across Detective Barnes' face while Argent nearly scoffed and was just short of rolling his eyes. Bet he was the kind of guy who said 'not all men'.

"Do you think he's ok?" I asked, feigning platonic worry.

"We have no reason to suspect anything to the contrary at the moment," Detective Barnes answered diplomatically. "Well, thank you for taking the time to come down and talk with us." Orpheus shook their hands, and soon enough we were back out on the sidewalk in the open air.

Silas and Laz both exhaled, deeply. Their eyes were tinted slightly, but I could tell they still had a grip on their hunger.

"Let's head home," Orpheus offered, beginning the trek toward our rental. We had to pass the pier to get there, and on the way here, the four of us were silently walking past with our eyes fixed on the slightly aged red awning of The Maine Plotline. We stared at it like lovesick fools. I mean, they were the lovesick ones. Not me.

I couldn't be lovesick. There was no love here.

The walk there was painful, a sort of invisible string was drawing us to that small bookstore cafe. The walk home was worse.

The first flash of red hair in the wind had each of us coming to a stop. Our feet were glued to their spots. My heart was racing at the sight of her. She was wearing a blue shirt, showing off her creamy shoulders, and tight blue jeans hugging her curves. She sat on the park bench that was outside her store, a book in her lap. Her hair swirled around her face as she read.

She was stunning, and breathtaking, like a wonder of the world. For a brief moment, I forgot.

I forgot I planned to reject this fated bond between us. Forgot I made a promise that I will not break. Forgot I couldn't have her.

"Athena," the soft, pained and longing voice was Silas'.

"She's perfect," Laz added.

I hated that my heart wanted to agree.

Laz and Silas took a step forward, but Orpheus was quick to put his hands out, blocking their trajectory.

"We can't go over there, you'll scare her." Orpheus, ever the realist.

Silas grabbed his phone from his pocket, without ever removing his eyes from her form. I shook my head. He had been trying to call her several times a day since the night she blocked his number with no success. But that didn't stop him from attempting.

He dialed her number and held the phone to his ear.

"Holy shit, it's ringing," Silas exclaimed, barely containing his excitement. Laz and Orpheus were turning to him quickly.

"Speaker, now," Orpheus demanded, and Silas obliged, holding the phone out for us all to hear. The ringing felt like a lifeline. We'd been adrift in the open water for two days with no sight of land, but here she was, giving us a reason to keep swimming.

Our gazes traveled down the pier to where Athena was resting. She closed her book, sliding it onto the bench next to her as she shimmied enough to grip her phone from her pocket. Her free hand came to rest on her chest when she looked at the screen. I could see her shoulders rising and falling slightly faster, but the same fear we saw in her that night wasn't present.

A glimmer of familiar torturing hope bloomed in my chest.

It rang again, and again. She didn't leave her spot. She didn't answer. She didn't even move. It was like she was stuck.

"Come on, bookworm, answer the phone," Silas whispered. His voice was full of a type of pleading I'd never witnessed from him.

Another ring.

Then another.

With each ring, I felt my confidence waiver. She was fighting a battle inside her own mind, I could see it from here. Could feel her turmoil, her struggle. I wanted to tell her it was ok. Tell her we would never hurt her. That we would protect her.

Another ring.

She pulled the phone to her chest, and sighed, her shoulders slumping as she exhaled. Her chin lifted and she looked to the sky as if she could find the answer in the clouds.

She pulled the phone from her chest, staring once more at the screen.

Then she answered.

The dial tone ended, making way for the sort of buzzing silence that told us she was there.

My heart beat once, hard and strong. Renewed energy filled me and even the constant hunger waned for a moment.

"Athena," Silas said, his voice low and sultry, his eyes never left her form. "Thank you for answering."

She sighed, and even her soft breathing felt like a soothing balm on my burning chest.

"I want to explain everything, we all do." Laz and Orpheus were nodding along. Orpheus was wearing his usual charcoal suit, but the collar was slightly crumpled, not the pristine sharp edge he was used to sporting. His grip on himself was slipping. He needed her to hold onto.

"You are safe with us, I swear that to you, darlin'," Laz interjected softly. Their eyes shining with unshed tears as they watched her sitting on the bench.

"We know we scared you, and I'm so fucking sorry about that," Silas exclaimed, running a hand through his hair, pulling a few strands free from the tie at the back of his head.

She breathed, softly, calmly, still not responding, but still not hanging up. That was enough.

"Athena," Orpheus started, his usually calm, collected voice wavered slightly. "We owe you answers. And we're going to give them to you." I watched as she wiped a tear away with the back of her hand. "What we're going to say will not make any sense to you, and it will sound like we're lying, but I need you to promise that you'll keep an open mind."

I glanced over at him, breaking my concentrated gaze on Athena for the first time. His face was contorted with a strained emotion. Orpheus has only ever told four people about what we were. And three of us were here with him now.

It wasn't a secret he offered up freely. It wasn't something we go around advertising. Especially not over the phone. But we may not ever get the chance again if we didn't take it now. I knew it, so did he.

I looked over at the gorgeous woman who was intently listening to the call. Her chest heaved with labored breaths, her eyes watered with tears of confusion, her red hair gently swayed in the wind. She hadn't seen us yet, so we were seeing her in all her natural beauty. She was stunning, but it was more than that. She was powerful. She was strong. She was a woman who had been beaten down by the world, by the people who were supposed to protect her and when she came out the other side, she crawled her way through the impossible to put herself back together as well as she could. I understood that. Watching her, I felt my chest burn with want. My hands begged to touch her. My lips yearned to brush against hers. I wanted Athena. I needed her.

But I couldn't have her. It was going to kill me, but I was going to reject this bond. This connection that was making me feel alive, that had me nearly thinking I would be able to move on. I had to turn away from it. I tore my eyes from the object of all my joy and turmoil and looked at my friend, Orpheus. His frame was now blurry, from the tears that had started to gather in my eyes.

Despite the protest in his mind, Orpheus spoke the next words carefully… like a promise.

"There is more to this world than anyone realizes, things that may be considered myth to one person, could be another's very existence." He swallowed the lump in his throat. "It is imperative that even if you feel like what I tell you is false, you keep this truth close to your chest."

Silas and Laz were locked on Athena, their gazes somewhere between forlorn, and hopeful.

"We are not human, although I can assume you've already put that together." She inhaled sharply on the other side of the line. I didn't dare look back at her to see how her body reacted to that revelation. "We have been called many things throughout history, Night Walkers, The Undead, Damphir…" He took a long breath. "But most commonly we are called Vampires."

I couldn't resist. My eyes involuntarily searched for her again and I watched as she let the phone fall from her hand onto the bench. Her hands cradled her head and she shook it back and forth. We stood there, at the edge of the pier, watching her compose herself after hearing what we had to admit. But still, no matter how much we yearned to comfort her, our feet remained steadfast. Silas was holding the phone in his hand so tightly he was close to breaking the device. Laz was as still as death, their eyes glued to her, their hands rigid at their sides. And Orpheus was watching her like he was seeing his future. He could hide his affection, mask it behind his protective nature, and it might even work for Laz and Silas. But I saw it. Every painful ounce of it. He was drowning in his desire for her. It was changing everything for him. It was changing everything for me too. I wish I could embrace the change. Embrace this new chapter. Move on. Athena might be the future I was promised by whatever fates there are, but if I dive headfirst into a new future, I'm betraying the one I promised to Alora.

Athena was a worthy partner. Anyone would be lucky to share in her wisdom and kind heart. It just couldn't be me.

She rocked back and forth for a moment longer on the bench, while we watched. Then she gripped the phone in her hand, her sweet sighs sounded so desperate.

She prepared herself, taking several long breaths. Finally, with the phone pressed firmly against her cheek she spoke, in a voice that sent a shockwave directly to my heart, a second beat. I was shocked, feeling how lively my heart had become. The second in just a few minutes. More than the one beat an hour I was so accustomed to. She was doing that to me.

"Tell me everything."

ATHENA

SEVEN

I felt their eyes watching me, my skin burned under their gaze, but I refused to acknowledge them. I wasn't ready to invite them back into my personal space, but I would hear them out. I wasn't sure what I was expecting to hear, but nothing could have prepared me to hear those words. "...we are called Vampires."

I was stunned. Speechless. I waited for the punchline that deep down I knew was never going to come.

It was impossible.

It was a lie.

It was make-believe.

Although, even as my objections rattled inside my brain, the truth behind the confession rang true above it all. Their bright red eyes, the long fangs, the claws, how they reacted to my blood. The most insane of explanations was the sanest thing I had heard in days.

My first instinct was to react in fear. It's a conditioned response to 'monsters'. After a long deep breath, I let my body sway back and forth as if bouncing the information around my brain would help me absorb it.

They could have killed me.

They didn't.

There was a lot I didn't know, and I wasn't naive enough to believe I didn't need to know it, but I was ready to let them control the conversation.

"Tell me everything," I demanded.

Several shocked inhales sounded over the call. I knew if I looked toward the end of the pier and saw them standing there, they would take it as an invitation to come to me, and I wasn't ready for that. Not until I heard it all.

I also wasn't sure I was ready to see their faces, the ones I had come to care for, and longed to see.

"I was turned first," Orpheus began, his voice even. "I lived in Romania, well it wasn't called that back then, but that is what you call it now." I nodded, knowing he could see me. Could they see everything? I knew they were far away, but how good is their vision? If I breathe can they see my chest rise and fall? If I sweat will they see the bead run down my forehead? Maybe that's why it felt like they truly saw me. "I was ill, with no cure in sight. The healers had considered me a lost cause. They'd given up trying." My heart tensed almost painfully at the thought of Orpheus being abandoned to die alone. "I don't know who turned me, I don't remember it. But I spent the first several decades of my new existence learning how to control my thirst." I swallowed the lump in my throat. "Many, many years later, I found Samara."

I heard a whispered conversation beyond the phone that I couldn't quite make out, there was a slight shuffle and then I heard Samara's melodic voice. "Orpheus saved my life." I could hear the reverence in her tone. Her pride at knowing Orpheus, at being a part of his group. "He gave me a chance at a life where I could make choices for myself." Her voice cut out to make way for a muffled sob, I nearly turned to look at her.

"The others all joined our coven when they needed to escape most," Orpheus continued. "For one reason or another, we all had been dealt pretty shitty cards in our first life. This existence, this transformation. This was the escape. The second chance." I nodded my head. I could understand the urge to escape. Honestly, I can't even say what I would have done had I been given the same choice in those few months after going to the police about my stepfather. When the entire department and the town turned me into a liar and a whore.

Desperate people do desperate things, like begging to become a vampire.

"We've been a coven for a very long time," Silas interjected. "The closest thing to a family most of us ever had." I smiled softly at the fondness with which Silas spoke about them. I felt similarly about Davia. I had a wonderful mother who worked tirelessly to make sure I never felt like I was missing anything without having a father figure in my life. However, without any siblings, sometimes I did feel that tiny twinge of loneliness, at least I did until Davia filled that space with all her loud-mouthed glory.

"We take care of each other, we fight for each other…we would die for each other." The conviction with which Silas uttered those words nearly took the breath from my lungs.

"You would *kill* for each other," I whispered, shivering from the cool wind as it blew my hair around my face.

They were silent on the other side of the line for a few moments and I tried not to read into it. I told them I wanted to know everything, and I did. Even this. Especially this. I needed to understand, in order to decide what I would do next.

"Yes," Orpheus spoke the single word as if it shamed him. Which loosened the fear that was attempting to grip at my heart.

"You have to understand something very important about us, darlin'," Laz's sweet accented voice was breathy, they sounded desperate. "In order for us to survive we must consume human blood-"

I inhaled sharply at the admission of what I already had believed was true, and they continued quickly, "but we will only hunt those who deserve it," they continued. I couldn't help but scoff.

"Who decided you had the right to choose if someone deserves to die?" I bit, with more malice than I was anticipating. I've seen the news stories and read the papers. Every day people are being killed because someone 'decided' they deserved it. Women all over the world are being killed because men believe they "deserved" it. I couldn't help but feel disgusted at the notion.

"Louis deserved it," Orpheus seethed.

I stopped breathing.

Somewhere, deep down, I had considered that unbelievable and terrifying possibility after seeing their true faces, but even then, I didn't know if I wanted to hear the truth. To know Louis was dead, because of me.

"Don't you dare, Athena," Orpheus growled. It was such a demanding tone that I couldn't stop myself from turning my head in his direction. There they were, the four of them, the vampires. Standing steadfast at the end of the pier, huddled around a phone. All eyes trained on me.

I was locked in their gaze, unable and unwilling to pull my eyes from them.

They looked how I remembered them, their beautiful features prominently on display masking the inhuman creatures within.

Despite all the fear, and the logic telling me to cut ties, to run, to find Archer…there was this undeniable connection sizzling between us like a piece of paper over an open flame. Beautiful, powerful, deadly. I didn't stand a chance of staying away from them.

"You will never feel guilt over that scumbag's death, do you understand me?"

I heaved, breathing erratically as I watched Orpheus take a step forward. Just a single step, but it lit my core with electric energy. The others followed behind as he took slow deliberate steps toward me. "Never again will you blame yourself for the actions of another. Never again will you let their wrongdoings cause you pain. I can feel your guilt, Athena, and he does not deserve it."

I found myself nodding at him as he approached, the others hot on his heels with equally ravenous looks on their faces. I wanted to tell them to stop. Wanted to keep my distance, but their pull was just too strong.

"We kill monsters, Athena. Evil people who hurt others, who take what doesn't belong to them as if it is something they are owed."

My shaky breath comes quickly.

"We are not heroes-" he stated, as they breached the halfway point. Now that they were closer, I could make out more of their features. Their eyes, their lips. Things that have simultaneously haunted and comforted me. "We are not villains."

I inhale sharply at the hungry look in their eyes, and not a hunger that scares me, but one that excites me and has my core tightening in anticipation. They're close now. Twenty feet or so, I can nearly feel the cold radiating off of their bodies. Orpheus hung up the phone and spoke directly to me.

His voice was clear and intoxicating. "We are yours."

I put my hand up.

They stopped their approach, watching me for signs of distress, no doubt. Worried expressions cross their faces. Their stunning, handsome faces.

They paused to look at me as if they adored me. Their eyes scanned my form and I felt so secure under their watchful gaze. And even as my body longed to bridge the gap between us, to welcome my strangers from the bar back into my life, I knew I could not confuse those people with the ones standing before me now. I had to be careful, and smart. Logical. And logic was telling me to keep my distance until I knew everything.

"You turned into vampires in my store. Your eyes, your claws... You looked like-" I started, feeling like I was rambling and unable to contain it.

"Monsters." Laz finished for me.

I nodded.

"You chased me, I felt it. I thought you were going to…" I swallowed, putting a hand on my chest as I stood to face them fully. "I thought you were going to kill me."

They all simultaneously growled, in anger, but I wasn't afraid.

"We would never hurt you, Athena." Samara was the first one to speak, her eyes full of care, adoration, and sadness.

"But-" I began.

"No." Silas bristled. "No buts, bookworm."

My heart leapt.

"We would all rather die than to see any harm come to you, by our hand or another's." Silas looked like he wanted to reach for me. I almost let him.

"When you were in the store, you all said something," I started slowly, trying to make sense of my thoughts. "You said 'mate.' What does that mean?" I saw Orpheus and Samara exchange a quick glance and more emotions than I could ever perceive past through that one look.

"It means you are our fated mate, Athena. We were crafted by the stars to belong, mind, body, and soul to you." Laz wiped a tear from their eye as they explained it to me. "And you were forged to be ours."

I'd read a thousand books featuring the concept of a 'fated mate', and it was a beautiful story device used to give readers hope. To mimic the silly belief of soulmates. Had I grown up wishing there was someone out there who was perfectly tailor-made to love me? Of course, it was nothing but a childish dream.

"That's not real," I stuttered, taking a single step backward.

"Neither are vampires," Orpheus claimed. "And yet, here we are."

My heart began beating faster, as if it may just up and jump out of my chest onto the pier at my feet.

"I don't understand," I stumbled. Silas took a tentative step forward and I raised my hand again to stop his approach. His honeyed eyes softened with a mixture of pain and want.

"Mates are a powerful thing to our kind," Samara began, her face twisted as if it physically pained her to be in my presence. She wouldn't make eye contact. "It's like this intense draw, this string connecting your soul to theirs." She tilted her head toward the others. I noticed Orpheus toss her a forlorn look, but didn't have time to analyze it further.

"When someone is mated, their connection only grows stronger," Silas added. "They're stronger, faster, some say that any power they have before is enhanced after they complete the bond."

"What do you mean, complete the bond?" I asked, and watched as the four of them shared timid glances. "Whatever it is that you're thinking about hiding from me, don't." I smoothed the hem of my shirt idly, letting my hands fall to my side. "I said I wanted to know everything, and I do."

Orpheus stepped forward, but this time I did not retreat.

"In order to complete the bond," he began, his eyes darkening as he watched me. Inside I felt like cowering under his intense stare, but outwardly I stood my ground. "We need to taste you, Athena." A blush crept across my face, heat spread through my lower belly.

Orpheus smirked darkly, as if he could tell exactly what I was feeling.

"What?" I stammered.

"Your blood," he clarified, in a low husky timber. "We must taste your blood to complete the bond."

That admission did strange things to me. At first, I felt disgusted, but quickly that small tug at my heart tightened in anticipation. My heart soared. As if that was exactly what it wanted, exactly what it deserved. What it was made for.

"Would that kill me?" I whispered, afraid.

"Of course not," Laz growled between clenched teeth.

"You will always be safe with us, bookworm," Silas pleaded.

"What happens to me if you drink my," I lowered my voice, "blood…do I become.." I trailed off, timidly. A wave of uncertainty blanketing the rush of desire that had previously been there.

"That's not how it works," Samara explained sadly, a tenseness to her tone.

"How does it work, then?"

I watched as they exchanged yet another hesitant glance.

"Don't lie to me, please," I begged.

"In order to transform, you would have to drink from us as well," Silas whispered, just loud enough for me to hear. I glanced around the pier for any listeners, but there was no one close enough to overhear. Over my shoulder I tossed a glance back at The Maine Plotline and saw Archer sitting at the front counter, he was holding a book, but I could have sworn his eyes were watching us.

"What happens if you don't complete it? The bond," I asked, quietly. I heard a few soft whimpers from them.

"If you don't accept the mate bond, we will need to either reject it…or we'll die," Orpheus explained, his calm demeanor was undercut by a barely restrained anger.

The thought of any one of these people standing before me dead was making me feel physically ill, like I might lose my balance and pass out. The blood rushed from my face and I felt dizzy.

"Are you feeling ok?" Laz asked, anxiously.

"Yes, I'm..I'm fine. Just…processing," I rambled. They watched me cautiously for a few moments, ready to intercept me should I fall. I could make heads or tails of what I was feeling. What I was considering. I needed to understand the whole process and the pros and cons in order to make a logical decision here. I'm not talking about going on a date, I'm talking about solidifying some strange supernatural bond with four literal vampires. A decision like this requires time. And information. "How do you reject a bond?" I asked, quietly.

Silas and Laz let out a soft moan of agony. Laz's eyes welled with unshed tears. Orpheus watched Samara closely, something unspoken passed between them.

"We would have to create a new vampire," Samara breathed, nearly imperceptibly. She still hadn't met my eyes, and I couldn't deny the twinge of disappointment and rejection I felt at that realization. Laz and Silas looked shocked by that admission, had they not known?

Did she want to reject me? Is that why she can't look at me? Is that why Orpehus keeps watching her? Does she not want me?

Why does that thought bother me so deeply?

"Athena, please... don't," Silas begged, a hopeless look on his face. "Don't ask me to reject you, because I couldn't. I wouldn't be able to." Laz nodded their agreement. I couldn't stop myself from glancing at Samara to gauge her reaction.

She quickly wiped a tear from her cheek as she looked out over the railing toward the ocean. What I wouldn't give to understand what she was thinking right now.

"How long.. How long do I have to decide?" Orpheus couldn't hide his wince at my inquiry, but he schooled his expression quickly. The mask of professionalism was firmly in place again.

"The timeline is moving quickly, we will need to complete or reject the bond within the next few days. Three at most, I'd say." I nodded, shocked by how soon I'd have to decide the course of my future. Of all our futures.

"Ok," I started. "Thank you for telling me all this, for trusting me." It was earnest. I may not be able to sympathize with having a secret of supernatural origin, but I do understand a little bit about having a secret so big it could disrupt your entire existence. "I need some time to think. To absorb."

Orpheus, Laz and Silas nodded.

"Take the time you need, darlin'. We're not going anywhere," Laz assured me. I didn't even know how much I had needed to hear those words until something hollow inside my chest felt whole again.

I begin to take a step back, but pause and scan each of them again. They really are impossibly stunning, crafted from marble kind of beautiful. Now when I look at them, I still see the creatures from the store, but there's more to it now. There's more to them. I had just started getting to know them, just started learning about them, and indulging in the sinful pleasures they promised me.

Maybe I needed more to make this choice. Maybe I needed them to help me decide.

"I'd like to go on a date, with each of you, to talk, to spend time together. I want to make sure I make the right choice."

Silas's smile was blinding as he beamed. Laz exhaled in relief and Orpheus smirked again, darkly, in that way that feels so promising. Samara still hadn't looked at me, but I knew she heard me because her chest began to heave with labored breaths. If she didn't want me, I needed to hear that straight from her lush, red-painted lips.

"Name the time and place, bookworm," Silas agreed eagerly.

I nodded, promising to text them, then I turned to retreat into my store. The moment I turned my back to them, I felt a weight settle on my chest, and with each step away from them that weight got heavier and heavier. By the time I was back inside the store, my mind was swimming.

On one hand, the fear that had been looming over me since that night had dissipated. But on the other hand, what they had confessed to me was shifting everything I had ever known about the world, and everything I ever thought I'd want for myself.

Sure, I saw myself growing up and eventually settling down with a partner. Although, I knew I wasn't likely to leave Shockgrove, and the pickings were rather slim in town. But I had never considered multiple partners. Multiple people devoted to giving me care, and pleasure. I blushed, as I leaned against the cool door.

"Who were they?" Archer's voice broke me from the spell I was under. I quickly composed myself and smoothed my hair.

"Oh, just some friends who are in town for the season," I replied, hoping I wasn't appearing as flustered as I truly was.

Archer studied my face casually, then looked over my shoulder out the window toward the pier. His face was tense, his paint-stained hands were clenched at his sides. I narrowed my eyes at him, his body language was guarded, like he was angry at my interaction with them.

"Hey, I'm going to go out and grab some lunch, do you want anything?" He said, nonchalantly, quickly sliding out from behind the counter and walking past me toward the door.

"Uh, no. I'm ok. Thanks." He grunted his acknowledgment before slipping through the door and disappearing onto the pier.

I watched after him as he briskly walked back toward town. Shaking off the strange interaction, I took a seat behind the counter.

I had a lot of information to process, and some decisions to make.

One thing was clear though. I needed to confirm I cared enough about these strangers to agree to being bonded to them for my entire life.

Oh shit. How long would that be?

Were they going to want to turn me? Is that something I even wanted?

Panic was creeping into my consciousness, but I pushed it away, forcing myself to take deep breaths.

Tackle one problem at a time, Athena.

One breath at a time.

One step at a time.

One date at a time.

EIGHT

Her wintergreen scent was even stronger than I recalled. In the days since I had seen her face, or heard her voice, I spent a lot of my time building up this image in my head, trying to remember every small detail about her, on the off chance I'd never see her again. The way she smelled, moved, the way she tasted. The memory of her I crafted was so vivid, so incredibly perfect that a small part of me worried I was putting too much pressure on the real Athena to live up to this indescribable version of her in my mind. But all it took was one glance to know nothing I could ever create would hold a candle to the perfection that was Athena Landry. My mate.

She stood her ground, keeping us at a comfortable distance, but the distance to me was anything but comfortable. I yearned to touch her, to feel her body pressed against mine. I needed her. But despite the pain I was in from restraining myself, the interaction went about as well as I could have dreamed. Well maybe not dreamed. In the dream version of that conversation, she would have accepted us, and allowed us to drink from her right then and there so I didn't have to waste another useless second of my life on living without her by my side.

All things considered, it was a success. She wanted to try. She wanted to think it over. She wanted to spend time with us. With me.

I'd do whatever it took to show her the life she deserves to have with me.

We walked home in a daze, nobody said a word, but I'm pretty sure Silas' smile never faltered. He was on cloud 9, or whatever the supernatural equivalent might be.

We walked in a daze, distracted by the realization of our current situation. We had a chance to convince her. She was allowing us that, and I knew I was going to take it seriously.

When we arrived home, we let out a collective sigh of relief.

"Well, that went better than expected," Silas finally said, breaking the tension. The two of us erupted into soft laughter. Days of worry and fear escaping with every exhale. Things had gotten dark, and while we weren't entirely on the other side of the tunnel yet, there was hope. And hope is something worth holding on to.

"I'm not gonna tell you assholes what to do, but don't fuck up your dates, ok?" Silas teased, but I knew he wasn't kidding.

Orpheus watched Samara with a piqued interest that seemed… odd. There was something they weren't telling us. They were acting strange earlier, and now they were sharing silent loaded glances as if they were having full conversations with their eyes.

"I wonder who'll be lucky number one," Silas mused, resting his head back on the headrest of the chair. His exhaustion was evident. We hadn't been sleeping very well, how could we when our hunger was keeping us up half the night, and our desire for her occupied the other half?

We didn't have to wait long for an answer.

Ten minutes after we arrived home, we were scattered throughout the living room, in a collective state of exhaustion. I don't think any of us had realized just how impactful the threat of losing Athena had been to our well-being.

Silas sat with his head lulled back and his eyes closed, a soft snore sounded from him. Orpheus and Samara sat side by side on the couch, idly watching whatever mindless show was on, they were struggling to keep their eyes open too. I felt the sting of exhaustion, of course, but there was something else pumping, the adrenaline that comes from planning a perfect date.

I was scrolling through my phone, making notes, preparing a menu and finding the perfectly paired wine. Before too long, I had crafted the single best evening. One fit for someone like Athena.

I was swiping through the wine list of a local market when the notification banner appeared at the top of my screen with her name.

My heart thumped loudly once and I felt the toxic blood in my veins rush to my cheeks. If I were alive, I'd be blushing.

ATHENA: Hi, Laz.

A smile spread across my lips at the memory of her sweet voice speaking my name. I was eager to hear it again.

LAZ: Hey there, darlin'.

And because I couldn't contain myself.

LAZ: I've missed you.

I hoped it wasn't too much for her to hear, but it was the honest truth. Even before the bond revealed itself, I felt this draw, this connection to her. I couldn't leave her then, and I sure as hell couldn't leave her now. Not after knowing her.

ATHENA: I'm sorry.

What on Earth did she need to apologize for? This whole thing was our mess. Our fuck-up. We should have told her exactly what we were the moment we could. We waited too long.

ATHENA: I needed time.

LAZ: I know. And nobody faults you for that.

ATHENA: Can we meet tonight? Just us?

I would say my heart skipped a beat, but it only beats once an hour so that's not a very good analogy. My fingers brushed across the screen hurriedly.

LAZ: I'd love nothing more.

That was a lie.

I'd love her more.

I was never one for taking charge. Not in my former life, and certainly not in the coven. We had enough natural leaders with Orpheus and Silas constantly butting heads. I was content being the follower. It wasn't mindless though, my following. I was analytical, I put a significant amount of thought into what I chose to do with my life, and who I chose to spend it with.

When I was first turned, I did feel like I owed Samara a significant debt for saving my life, so I remained with her coven for years in order to learn how to control and adapt to my new reality. When I felt like I had a firm enough grasp on the person I had become, I spent a lot of time trying to determine if being a member of the self-proclaimed Wanderers Coven was what I wanted for myself.

I had to decide if Orpheus' hot headed attitude and strict rules were the kind I could see myself following. I had to decide if I could cope with Silas' recklessness. Hardest of all, selfishly, I had to decide if I could stand to see Samara and Alora living so authentically when a similar expression of queerness was what landed me face down in the streets in a puddle of my blood in the first place.

Before there was even a description for how I felt about who I was, I knew I never quite fit the binary boxes that society labeled for me. I've had intense feelings for men and women alike, faced with so much persecution that I sometimes didn't even know which way was up. There was a certain freeness to Alora and Samara that I couldn't help but resent.

For a while, I wanted to leave. Wanted to get out of there and wallow in my solitude as a person who had enough courage to know exactly who they were, but not enough to become them.

Alora and Samara helped shape me. In their own way. Once I was able to move past the anger and jealousy, it was like looking at a snapshot of what could be.

As time moved, so did the standards, and the terminology.

I will never take for granted how lucky I have been to live through the emergence of this sort of tentative acceptance. I am who I was meant to be, and in every way, I owe that to Samara and Alora.

I may be a follower, but I know what I want, and I will protect my right to have that for as long as I live.

LAZ: Meet me at the pier at 8?

I anxiously waited for her response, watching the bubbles appear and disappear with her thoughts.

ATHENA: I'll see you there.

The next few hours were a blur of nerves and phone calls. I was given an opportunity to prove to Athena that she has nothing to be afraid of with us, and I was not going to mess it up.

After changing approximately five times, and downing a bottle of blood to quench my hunger, I finally descended the stairs to the living room, where Silas was laying on the couch.

"I take it, you're up first?" He asked, eyeing my wardrobe. A soft linen button up, and tight khaki pants with rolled cuffs.

"Yeah," I answered absentmindedly. My mind was racing.

He stood, making his way over to me. His presence had always been thick and intoxicating, he had that kind of effect on everybody, but I couldn't help but wonder if recent activities were affecting the way his presence sent shocks of excitement through me. Or the way my entire body tensed in anticipation as he towered over me.

We hadn't discussed what happened between us with Athena that night. Not really. I wasn't sure anything really did happen. For all I know, Silas could have been swept up in the energy that night, the palatable lust that was rolling off of Athena's body and echoing through her moans. It was Athena he was turned on by, not me.

"You ok?" He asked, tilting his head to study me. My fingers were intertwined in front of me and I fidgeted with them nervously.

"I don't know," I replied honestly. He nodded, agreeing. My breath caught in my throat and I felt my eyes beginning to sting with hot tears that began to fall, freely. Through heaving sobs, broken and breathless, I admitted a truth I had been trying so hard to hide. "I'm scared, Silas."

He watched me carefully as I spoke.

"I'm so scared," I finished.

His honey eyes glanced down at me though his soft black lashes. "She's going to accept us, Laz. I know she will." He spoke with such conviction that I nearly believed him.

"She has to. Or I won't survive this."

Silas' hand clasped around the back of my neck and pulled my forehead to his. We stood there locked in a comfortable embrace for a moment. His breath mingled with mine as we drew comfort from each other.

"Just go out there, show Athena how amazing you are. She'll see it." He put a little more pressure on my neck, pressing me into him. "I know she will."

I let my hands drift up to rest on his hips, gently, not commanding. It felt comfortable, this embrace, like it was something we'd always been doing, although we were not the affectionate type before Athena showed us we could be.

Embracing the affection I had for Silas would not diminish the blinding passion I had for her.

After a few moments, Silas pulled back. His eyes were glossy and sincere. "Bring her back to us, Laz. If anyone can do it, it's you," he pleaded in a whisper. He looked so vulnerable, a way I had never seen before. Not from him. Before I could stop myself, I raised my hand to his face and let my thumb brush against the skin of his cheek.

We've considered each other found family for nearly as long as I'd been undead, but right here, in this moment of vulnerability, this was the most intimate we had ever been.

"I will," I promise. A new determination in my soul.

Silas nodded, leaning into my palm ever so slightly. Just enough to let butterflies loose in my stomach.

When he pulled back, stepping out of my personal space, I felt his absence. Which was a strange, but not an unwelcome, feeling.

With a nod, and newfound determination, I left to prepare for my date.

An hour later, after I was sure everything was as perfect as it was going to get, I made my way to the end of the pier. Despite the chilly Maine evening, the setting sun managed to burn my exposed skin, slightly. Not to the point of pain, but enough to remind me I was alive. Or my version of it.

My elbows rested on the wooden railing as I looked out over the restless sea. Waves crashed against the wooden posts below, lightly spraying my face with a mist. There was something familiar about the ocean. Not in the sense that I spent much time around it, because I hadn't, but this vast open body of water held so many secrets that even those who devoted their lives to studying it couldn't confidently say they really knew it. In some sort of weird way, being a vampire felt like that.

The sun was creeping toward the horizon of the water, sending golden rays scattering across the surface. Fractaling against the blue canvas with glittering reflections. It was not often that The Wanderers stayed in one place long enough to enjoy it, to come to know it. To relish in its beauty. Being on the run has destroyed these sort of calm contemplative moments. This was just another thing Athena was giving back to us.

I wasn't foolish enough to think we would never have to run again, but I was beyond thankful for Athena's gift of a reprieve.

In the time since we arrived in Shockgrove, Maine, we had begun to live again. To stop and smell the proverbial roses. She has inadvertently reminded us of something we had come to forget.

There was more to life than simply surviving it.

Sometimes it's ok to sit and watch the sunset over the ocean. Sometimes it's ok to spend an entire afternoon reading a good book. Sometimes it's ok to let responsibilities and fear fall away.

Sometimes it's ok to live.

I heard her footsteps approaching, but I forced myself to remain calm. Taking slow breaths to counteract the urge to taste her blood. She might not be aware of my sensitive hearing, and I want her to acknowledge me when she's ready. Her scent invaded my nostrils as she neared me, I inhaled shakily, fighting back my fangs. All I wanted to do was sink my teeth into her skin and claim her. I wanted her to be mine. Finally, and formally. I wanted her to wear my bite on her body like a promise.

"Hi Laz," she said with a fair amount of false confidence. When I turned to face her, I couldn't breathe. She had substituted her blue blouse from earlier for a deep hunter green shirt with soft patterns. The sleeves were held together at the wrist by ties and her legs were hugged by dark wash jeans. She was stunning. The kind of beauty that wasn't forced or pressured. Her face was painted in a dark makeup look, very reminiscent of that first night we saw her at the bar and just as she had that night, she was captivating me. Her red hair was bound at the base of her head in a loose bun, tendrils hung in every which direction and danced in the wind.

"Hello, there." I smiled warmly. She was close to me, closer than she had been since the night she ran from us, and my body was reacting in a nearly feral way.

"Thank you for meeting me," she added nervously, her eyes dancing around to the nearly empty pier. There were a few stray people walking around, which probably made her feel safer. The thought sent a jolt of pain to my chest.

"Thank you for giving me the chance."

She smiled, and briefly I saw the warm-hearted Athena who laid in bed beside me that night. It felt like forever ago. "Walk with me?" I asked, offering my extended hand. She eyed it for a few moments, studying the fingertips as if she thought the claws might return at any given moment. Which, I guess they could. I sighed, quietly, careful not to let my disappointment show on my face.

Slowly I pulled my hand back, letting it settle at my side. "Everything is at your pace tonight, ok?" She nodded, relief flooding her face. Stuffing my hands into my front pockets, I smiled and began heading toward the back half of the pier. She fell in step beside me, maintaining a few feet buffer.

"You look gorgeous tonight, Athena." I glanced over at her out of the corner of my eye to find a soft blush creeping onto her cheeks. The rush of blood beneath her skin had my body reacting. Heat coursed through me, warming me in a way only she could.

"Thank you." A soft laugh escaped her lips, and I wanted to capture it with my own. We walked in comfortable silence for a few minutes until we reached the steps that led down to the beach below. The moment we set foot on the sandy shore, I leaned down, slipping my shoes off and gripping them in my hand. She did the same and as she sunk her toes into the soft chilled sand, her body relaxed. I saw the exact moment when her comfort overtook her fear and I could have jumped for joy, but I had a date to impress.

She walked beside me, her smile infectious as I led her to the large blanket and basket I had set here a little while ago.

"What.." she asked, pausing and a small gasp sounded from her.

"Do you like it?" I asked, watching her as she surveyed the scene in front of her. She nodded, smiling timidly.

"It's beautiful," she choked out, holding back a flood of emotions. I moved to sit down. Placing the basket beside me, as a buffer. She settled in, her shoulders were tense and I saw her glancing around to ensure we could be seen from where we sat. I knew she would be worried about that, so I scoured the beach to find the spot that could be seen from the main road behind us, and anybody walking on the pier. She seemed to realize that and with a released breath she relaxed.

"My mom used to take me for beach picnics all the time," she recounted, smiling out at the water. "She would pack us some lunchables and juice, well I would get juice she would get wine," she chuckled softly. "And we'd sit there for hours just sort of talking about anything and everything." The sadness in her eyes wasn't desolate, instead it looked hopeful, like the remembering wasn't as hard as it used to be.

"You speak so fondly of her," I said with a hint of admiration. She hung her head slightly.

"She was my best friend." She sighed.

I reached into the basket and produced a bottle of moscato. She giggled as I popped the cork and poured her a glass. "We are definitely not allowed to drink this out in the open," she warned playfully as she gripped the stem of the glass in her hand. I poured my own glass and felt my entire body shake with laughter.

"If anyone asks, it's juice." I offered her a wink and her genuine smile felt so rewarding. A prize I was entirely unworthy of, but would cherish nonetheless.

"I wish I could have met her. Your mom," I whispered, truthfully. Athena nodded, sipping from her glass.

"I think she would have liked you," she laughed, half-heartedly. "You know, if she could get over the whole vampire thing." I studied her face as she spoke, trying to gauge her reaction.

"Can you?" I asked, she turned her head to face me, and I was struck breathless by the way the receding light painted her face in a warm amber glow.

"Get over the whole vampire thing?" She clarified, and I nodded. With a deep sigh, she looked back over the water, and I had to force myself not to stare at her bare inviting neck. "I'm trying to." It was the answer I expected, but it still gripped at my heart and sent a sharp pain through me.

"And if you can't?" I asked, turning my eyes away from her. Instead, I focus on the blanket beneath me, tracing the checkered pattern with my fingertips anxiously.

"I don't know," she replied. I took a drink of the wine, willing the sweetness to overpower the sour taste in my mouth as my hunger flared. "How did you.." she started.

"Become a vampire?" I finished for her, still averting my eyes.

"Yeah ."

I downed the rest of the wine and set the glass down, digging the base into the sand. I hugged my knees to my chest and sighed. "It's not a fun story," I warned.

"You don't have to tell me," she offered, but I shook my head.

"No, it's ok. I don't mind telling it, but it's hard to hear. It helps to know the story had a happy ending. It just took some time to get there." I heard her shift slightly, turning her body to face me, offering me her undivided attention.

"I was born in 1898." I heard Athena inhale sharply. "If you think that's a long time ago, wait till you talk to Orpheus," I offered, playfully. "I grew up in the south. Texas to be specific. A place where even to this day, it's not safe to be who you are. Especially when what you are is something they've never seen before. Something they don't understand." I saw her head nodding out of the corner of my eye. "I knew I was different. I found passion with men, with women, but that wasn't the crux of it. I never felt like me. Back then there wasn't a word for it, but I knew I had never, and would never, fit their mold. But despite that, I found love. His name was Charles." I paused, breathing deeply, letting the salt tainted air fill my lungs. "We hid our relationship from the town and the world. He wanted to remain hidden forever, he would have been content to live his life in the shadows, but that wasn't what I wanted. I would never tell his secret, but I wanted to tell my own." I wet my dry cracking lips with my tongue. "That angered a lot of people. It started innocently enough, with death threats." I chuckled, it was a humorless and hollow sound. "When it became clear I wouldn't change, couldn't change, they graduated to more violent displays of discontent." I swallowed the lump in my throat, carefully navigating this treacherous part of my history. I rolled my sleeves up, ignoring the sting of the setting sun's rays on the pale skin, to show her the scars that danced along the surface of my arms. So faint that you'd have to know what you were looking for to see them. But the visibility of a scar has no bearing on the severity of the trauma.

Sometimes the deepest scars are the hardest to see.

"Jagged, vicious little slices, given to me by men who decided it was their right to mutilate my body," I seethed through clenched teeth. A tear slipped from my eye, and flowed down my cheek. Suddenly, a soft, warm hand pressed against my skin. Her touch was a salve on a burn, an embrace after an injury. I turned my head to face her, leaning my cheek into her hold, eagerly. More tears slipped through the confines of my eyes as I scanned her face. There was so much empathy, so much care flooding her expression. I had never felt more visible than in that moment.

"One night, those men decided they had had enough of my existence. They decided I would be better off dead." Athena was crying, her hand pressed into my skin as her thumb wiped away the tears as they fell. "For hours, I endured their torture. Hit after hit, slice after slice. I wanted death. I begged for it. Those men hated me because they didn't understand me. They were afraid because I was unknown, but at least I understood it. Their hatred wasn't the worst part.. No, the unbearable part was that it was Charles who struck the final blow." She tilted her head to the ground, her hand fell from my face, a sob wrenched from her throat. "He hated me because he understood me intimately. He hated me because I was an extension of his own guilt and shame. He hated me because he loved me."

Her hands clenched into fists on her lap. I reached a hand out to her face to return the calming gesture. She allowed my hand to grip her chin and tilt her head up, her eyes met mine. Glossy and red, they still looked beautiful. Her skin was a soft canvas, I'd almost forgotten how it felt to touch her, if she'd let me, I'd never forget again.

"Samara found me in the street, she offered me a new life, with a new family, and I took it."

She closed her eyes, and leaned into my hand.

"Because of that, I've lived long enough to put a name to my identity. I lived long enough to see people like me living freer than we ever had before. There is still a long way to go, but the distance we've traveled so far is no small feat. And I got to witness it." I smiled softly. " It was like I had been spending so much of my life walking around in the wrong size shoes. They protected my feet, they got me from one place to another, but they were clunky and I would trip up. I couldn't walk unhindered." I held their hands together in front of them. "Because of this life, this second life...I got to try on new shoes."

A single tear fell down her face. "You found your size," she whispered, and I turned to face her, a rush of euphoria blooming in my chest. I smiled, choked up, holding back a sob. I nodded, letting the truth of those words hit me.

"Yeah… I found my size," I answered. "See? Happy ending." She let out a sound that was somewhere between a sob and a laugh and I smiled sweetly at her.

"How do you do that?" She asked.

"Do what?" I brushed my finger against her chin.

"Find the bright side in something like that." I sighed, letting my hand fall into my lap. "How do you look at those scars everyday and survive?" She trailed a light touch across the scattered white lines on my forearms. "You carry these, but it doesn't seem to weigh you down. My scars are invisible, but they still feel unbearable."

I furrowed my brows and exhaled slowly. "Come with me," I said, standing up and once again extending my hand to her. This time she accepted it. I pulled her with me toward the shoreline, the rush of cold water brushing against my bare feet.

"Where are we going?" She asked, playfully, giggling when the cold water startled her.

I scanned the water quickly, my eyes searching the crystalline water. "What are you doing?" She asked, as I bent over at the waist, reaching my hand into the ocean and finding what I needed.

I turned to face her, holding out the oyster in my palm.

"I don't get it," she said with a slight smile.

I cracked the oyster, opening the shell enough to see the soft-white round pearl inside. Athena inhaled excitedly and watched as I removed the pearl and placed it in her palm.

She studied it. "Did you know only oysters that are wounded in some way can produce pearls?" I said softly.

She glanced up at me with disbelief in her features.

"It's true," I continued. "Essentially, if an unwelcome or outside substance enters the oyster, like a parasite or a grain of sand, the oyster gets to work creating layers upon layers of protective cells to defend itself from the intrusion. Those layers build up and eventually become a pearl. The more wounds the oyster endures, the more pearls are created."

She looked back at the pearl in her hand with an expression of wonder, a tear slid down her face.

"Each scar becomes something valuable. Something beautiful," I closed my hand over hers. Her eyes met mine. "Your pain will always be with you, Athena. But that doesn't mean it can't be a beautiful part of you. That doesn't mean it's not worth carrying."

My hand was resting gently on hers while her chest heaved with labored breaths. I looked down at her lips as they parted slightly. I wet my lips again and her eyes traced the movement intently. A soft inhale was the only sound between us.

Suddenly, her lips crashed to mine and everything around me exploded into vibrant sounds and colors. The world had been a dull excuse of existence, but with her kiss she introduced me to what life can be. Her hands snaked around my neck and held me to her, and I stole kiss after kiss from her willing lips. Euphoria like I'd never experienced before flooded my veins as her soft moans were muffled by our kiss.

My hands tangled in her hair, holding her against me with restrained desire. Her scent was driving me to the edge of my restraint. Hunger pulsed through me. I needed her blood nearly as much as I needed oxygen.

I felt my fangs begin their slow descent, and I pulled back, turning my face from her and rushing back up the beach toward the blanket.

"What's wrong?" She asked breathlessly, chasing after me.

"I just need a second," I answered, through tight lips as I sank down onto the blanket, my body facing away from her. I felt the mindless creature beneath my skin threatening to break free, but with each breath I placed another brick up in the wall between us. I knew my eyes had darkened, and my claws had elongated, and I hid my face from her so she couldn't see me. I wouldn't survive it if she ran again.

Her hand gripped my face and she applied pressure, forcing me to turn to her. I fought it for a moment. "Please, I don't want to scare you," I begged, but she persisted, turning my face to her. The moment her eyes landed on me, I expected her to drop her hand and leave me there, but she didn't. She sat there, her hand exploring the skin of my face. Her eyes scanned my sharpened features as if she was looking for something specific.

"This is still you," she whispered, and I nodded. Entranced by her bravery, her kindness. The mindless need to complete the bond mixed with the mindless desire to please her, and I felt my fangs retract, my eyes returned to their normal shade and she watched with fascination.

"It's me. It's always been me, Athena." Something in her expression shifted then, like a barrier had been breached.

"I know," she whispered before claiming my lips with hers again. Her kiss was soft, but demanding. It felt like a promise, and my heart burst to life.

My hands held her to me, cradling her like the prize she was. I could live a million lifetimes and never earn her affection, but I would spend the rest of my existence trying.

Her fingers danced along my exposed forearms, brushing against the scars as if she was acknowledging each and every one. Her tongue pressed against my lips begging for entry and I opened willingly, letting her in. I would always let her in.

In a flash, her leg swung over my hip and she was straddling me. I was only vaguely aware of the public nature of our reunion, but I couldn't care less. Her heated center pressed against my length, and I felt it harden to a nearly painful point. She slid across me, chasing her own desire through our clothes-covered bodies.

"I've missed you," she admitted against my lips, and I groaned as her center created friction against my eager need.

"You'll never have to miss me again," I promised. She rode me eagerly, her breathing coming in ragged spurts. I met her thrust for thrust, despite the confines of our clothing, I felt her burning heat and knew any intimacy with Athena had the ability to claim me mind, body and soul. She sped up, her hips moving in disjointed quick movements, as she chased her release. I slipped a hand down the front of her jeans, and the first brush of my fingers against her swollen bud was met with an encouraging moan. I slid through the slickness there eagerly, and impatiently. Pursuing her orgasm as actively as she was. She rocked onto my fingers, guiding me lower to her core. I slipped a finger inside of her heat and she cried out, tossing her head back. Her heart beat matched the pace of my breathing. Slow, steady, needy.

"Oh, Laz," she exhaled, and I nearly came from the sound of her voice. My fingers pressed against her center, in and out, sliding easily though her slick desire. Her breathing ramped up as she climbed to the heights of passion. Our bodies were communicating through a language I would only ever be able to speak with her.

"I'll never get tired of watching you fall apart, darlin'," I whispered through my own ecstasy.

When she reached her peak, she let out a scream, I pressed my mouth to hers to muffle the sound. Those sounds were mine and I'll be damned if I let anyone reap the benefits of hearing her scream for me.

She bucked against me, riding the last of her release, and I knew nothing would ever compare to basking in the beauty of her desire. I restrained myself, focused only on her. A feat I would have considered impossible, but most of my energy was diverted to keeping my fangs from sinking into her throat.

When she slowed her movement, and looked down at me, her flushed cheeks darkened with embarrassment. She started to dismount, but I held her in place with a wicked smile, letting my fingers press deeper into her. She moaned at the renewed sensation.

"Don't go," I pleaded. She smiled, softly, laughing.

"I've never done that before. Publicly, I mean," she admitted, shyly. I gripped her hips tightly with my free hand and pressed her down onto me again. She moaned. I let my fingers dance against her clit once more before removing them from the front of her jeans. She sighed at the loss.

"Me either," I agreed, my eyes landing on her neck, I watched intently as the vein pulsed just beneath the surface. Taunting me. Instead of tasting what I so desperately needed to, I slid my finger into my mouth and sucked the sweet taste of her arousal off. The delectable taste satisfied my hunger, for a moment. Her eyes darkened as she watched me, but I couldn't focus on anything but that spot on the column of her throat.

"You are trying not to bite me right now, aren't you?" She deduced. I swallowed, turning my eyes to her and nodded. She bit her bottom lip with a contemplative look on her face. "What happens if I let you?"

I couldn't breathe for a moment as the anticipation of doing just that seized me. "If we accept the bond, then we belong to each other. Forever."

She absorbed that answer for a few seconds before she dismounted, swinging her leg back over mine and sliding down onto her spot on the blanket. She leaned back, laying down so that her gaze was trained to the sky, a sort of wistful look was painted on her face. She raised the pearl I gave her above her eyes and studied it.

I slid down until I too was laying on the sand. Her ragged breathing was beginning to slow, and I hoped regret would not find its way into her mind.

"Your forever, or mine?" She asked, quietly. Turning the pearl in her fingers. I let that question ruminate in my brain for a second before answering the only way I could.

"My forever is yours, Athena. However long you want that to be."

"So you wouldn't want me to become a…like you?" She held her hands tightly against her stomach as she watched the night sky overtake the orange and pink reflections.

"I only want what you want for yourself. This life was the right choice for me. That isn't the case for everyone. I would never take that decision from you." She sighed.

Her phone vibrated and as she checked it, I saw the coy smile form on her lips. "Tell Silas that I said he can wait his turn." She giggled, tossing her phone down onto the blanket.

"He wants to have our date tonight." I rolled my eyes playfully.

"Of course he does," I lamented. She laughed and rolled over until she was resting on her elbows the pearl pinched between her thumb and forefinger.

"Does it not bother you?" She asked, suddenly serious. "Sharing my time, attention …body?" She added, meekly.

"At first, the thought of sharing you with him made me want to rip Silas' head clean off, I nearly did, in fact," I recalled, a slight chuckle ringing in my voice. "But, the more I have gotten to know you, the more I am intimately aware of how much you have to offer. You are everything, Athena. It would be selfish of me to keep that to myself when you deserve every ounce of love you can get."

Her soft smile deepened, a strand of red hair blew into her face. I brushed it back behind her ear and tried to memorize the look she was giving me.

"Go meet Silas," I said. Her eyebrows shot up.

"But I'm with you," she argued.

"And you always will be, even when you're not." She turned her face to the sand and furrowed her brows.

"This is not a selfless act, darlin'. The sooner you have your meetings with the others, the sooner you make your choice and the sooner I get to claim your pleasure and make you mine." It was a bold claim, but one I was positive in making.

After the way she looked at me, the way her body sought her ecstasy from mine, I knew it was only a matter of time. Athena was mine. She knew it too.

Her face darkened with a blush, and she leaned forward to brush her lips against mine.

It was a vow.

As she got up, dusting off the sand from her clothes and slipping the pearl into her pocket, I stood to meet her. "You have no idea how much today has meant to me," I stated, earnestly. She smiled, unhindered and freely, a stark contrast from the looks of fear she was harboring at the beginning of the evening.

"I think I might," she offered before pressing her lips to mine once more then turning to head back to the pier.

I watched her walk away, but this time I was confident she would come back.

ARCHER

NINE

If you would have told me a week ago I'd be tailing a coven of extremely powerful and dangerous vampires through a small New England town, I would have called you a fucking liar. But here I was, following two of the four creatures across town. When I saw them earlier, it was like a time machine had captured me and forced me into my worst memories. The several months where The Wanderers were prisoners of Nameless were infamous in our line of work. I had never seen them, but I knew who they were the instant my eyes landed on their forms on the pier.

Once the shock of seeing them, right there, out in the open, during daylight no less, had worn off, I focused on Athena's reaction. She was frightened and hesitant, that much was clear from her body language, but there was a familiarity there I had not expected. She knew them. Intimately, I'd wager based on the way they respected her boundaries. She put her hand up, and they paused. Keeping their distance from her. That wasn't a quality I expected from these blood-thirsty monsters.

I studied the interaction through the lens of a Hunter. Or at least I tried to. I couldn't help the way my palm itched to grab my stake and move to protec

Athena from their vicious nature. But I knew I had a job to do and I was not going to be able to do it without the benefit of my anonymity.

That's why I haven't used the paint yet, haven't made the mark, and haven't let them know I was here. They would figure it out eventually, I'm sure, but with any luck, I'd be dragging their asses to Nameless by the time they pieced it together. And then it'll be too late for them.

I sprinted after them initially, but I lost their trail. I spent the better part of the afternoon trying to pick it back up. I cursed myself for getting so close, and being unable to follow through. I could practically hear my father's voice calling me a disappointment. A few hours later, as luck would have it, I saw two of them emerge again in town. This time I was determined not to lose the trail.

I haven't spent much time in the field, but I know how to tail someone. The tall one with the suit looked around him, and checked his surroundings a few times, a habit I can guess he picked up after his encounters with the Hunters. The woman with him, the only female left in the coven after my dad killed the other, walked dazedly, staring forward. A few times, Suit Guy glanced in my direction, but I schooled my reaction and willed myself to remain calm. I couldn't let my own fear get in the way of completing this mission. From protecting Athena, and all humankind, from these monsters.

I followed them through the streets, silently begging them to lead me to their den. Wherever it is they're calling home base for now. If I can find that, I'll be able to get the jump on them. Just as I started to feel the bloom of hope in my chest, I saw Suit Guy's eyes catch on something off to his left. He whispered something to the woman who carefully gazed over her shoulder in that direction.

My eyes followed theirs to see the most obvious undercover cop car I'd ever seen. Through the darkened windows, two individuals sat stoically. I couldn't make out their features, but their forms were obvious enough. Without slowing their walk, the vamps turned and headed in a new direction.

Damnit.

The car remained still. Turns out, I wasn't the only one hoping to get a peek into the secret life of these creatures. As they turned down a new street, heading back toward town, I silently cursed the cops for their incredibly pathetic attempt at remaining inconspicuous. Now, who knows how long it'll be until they lead me to their den? They certainly won't go there while they're being followed.

I remained a few hundred yards behind them all the way to the diner at the corner of town. They slipped inside, Suit Guy ushered the woman inside first and offered a quick scan of his surroundings before following her in. The neon sign read 'Dale's,' and the moment I stepped inside I felt like I had been transported to the 50s. The diner had charm, the kind you don't really find in big towns. I can see why a quaint town like this attracts so many people during its season. It's got quirks. I could probably be happy here if I was allowed to.

The vamps took up a booth in the corner of the diner, and I thanked my lucky stars it was crowded enough in there to justify my sliding into the booth right behind them. The hair at the back of my neck stood at attention, everything in my entire body told me not to put my back to them, but if I wanted to hear anything in this loud place, I needed to be close. Sliding on a pair of headphones to give me an outward reason for ignoring the world in favor of listening, I strained to hear them.

"Of course, they're tailing us," Suit Guy exclaimed, quietly seething.

"They're hoping we make a mistake," the woman replied. Funny, I'm hoping for the same thing.

"We won't." Suit Guy was very resolute, it was almost admirable. Almost.

"What are we supposed to do, Orpheus?" The woman asked. Orpheus, a fitting name for a creature of the underworld. I made a mental note of that as he replied.

"I wish I knew." He sounded defeated. An attribute I hadn't expected from the fearsome and ruthless leader of The Wanderers.

"We can't stay here long," she stated.

"What can I get ya to drink?" I jumped slightly at the voice. Glancing over at the petite older woman wearing the baby blue dress with a pad and pencil in her hands.

"Coffee? Decaf." I say, and she smiled, jotting it down. I try to focus on the continued conversation behind me but some things were lost to me in the loudness of the encounter.

"Sure thing, sweetheart. Be right back." I expected her to head away, but she slid down to the booth behind me.

"Anything to drink today?" I awaited their answer eagerly. I had no idea if vampires could even consume human sustenance.

"Any chance you have a mimosa?" The waitress giggled, no doubt finding herself enamored by the lead vamps charms.

"No such luck, honey. But I can get ya orange juice, what you do with it once it's at your table is your business." Orpheus offered a soft chuckle.

"Just a water then, Maureen." My eyebrows rose. The big bad evil vampire took the time to learn the waitress' name and address her as such. "And you, sweetie?" The waitress, Maureen, asked.

"I'll have chocolate milk." After the waitress assured them she'd be right back, I heard Orpheus let out a low choked laugh.

"Shut up," the woman exclaimed playfully. "Chocolate milk is delicious and you know it." I couldn't quite wrap my head around the fact that I was listening to the so-called 'most dangerous coven of vampires' joking about chocolate milk.

"Do you think she'll accept?" the woman asked, quietly, nearly too quiet for me to hear. I heard Orpheus sigh. Accept what?

"I couldn't possibly fathom a guess. She was so afraid of us, Samara. You don't just forget that kind of fear." The woman, Samara, took a deep breath.

"You know why I can't do it, don't you?" Do what? Fuck, I wish they'd stop speaking so vaguely.

"I know that's what you're telling yourself."

"I'm going to do it… reject the bond." Bond? I leaned back, trying to ensure I didn't miss a single second of their hushed conversation.

"You know what that means, right?"

"Of course, I do. I'm not making this choice lightly, Orpheus." Samara raised her voice briefly before calming herself again.

"So what is your plan then? Run away with your fresh turn? Start a new coven? You would leave your family?" My head was spinning. None of this made any sense to me, but I made mental notes on each and every moment, each word.

"I can't stay and watch you be happy."

"Then stay and be happy yourself!" There was a silence then that was only broken when Maureen came back to drop off our drinks. She started at their table this time. Asking for their order. Orpheus coldly asked for a few more moments to decide. When she came to my table, I ordered the very first thing my eyes landed on from the menu. She sauntered off to place the order and I retrained my focus.

"I can't."

"No, you can. But you're deciding you aren't allowed to. You're placing this arbitrary restriction on yourself. Nobody else is forcing this on you. Not me. Not Silas or Laz. Especially not Alora."

Samara sucked in a sharp breath.

"Don't be an asshole, Orpheus." She exhaled on a long slow breath.

"Do you truly believe you cannot accept this bond?" He asked and I heard the tension in his voice.

"I know I can't."

Maureen dropped my food, a Belgium waffle apparently, onto my table and then made her way to the vampires again. "Just the drinks for us today, Maureen." I started scarfing the waffle. I'd need to be done before they left if I wanted to continue following them.

"Ok," Orpheus finally said after a few moments.

"Ok?" She asked.

"Ok, I promised you once that you'd never have to give any more of yourself than you were willing. And I meant that. If you can't accept the bond. I won't either." He sounded confident in his statement, but something about the way his breath hitched told me he was anything but.

"I would never ask you to do that," Samara offered exasperatedly.

"I know, you don't have to ask me. I'm offering." Orpheus continued. "You are my family, Samara. I spent centuries suffering in agonizing loneliness. Until I found you. Nothing, not even a mate bond could make me forsake the bond I've created with you." I heard a soft sniffle. Samara must have been crying.

"But she's your mate." My heart rate quickened. Were they talking about Athena? Was Athena this vampire's mate? Holy shit.

"And you're my sister."

"What about Laz and Silas?" The other two, I noted.

"They will have each other…and her." He sounded strained as if the very thought of it was painful.

"I can't let you…"

"I'm not asking you, Samara. If you decide you cannot accept the bond with Athena, then neither will I. This is not some sort of trick, this is not my way of pressuring you. I mean every word I say. No matter how much it will hurt. No matter how much of my soul I'll be leaving behind with her, I choose you."

A strange emotion stirs within me - something vaguely resembling empathy, but I quickly stamp that out, finishing the last bite of my waffle.

"But if you're going to reject her, she needs to hear it from you." Orpheus challenges, and I heard Samara wipe away a few tears.

"And you? Will you still meet with her?"

"I will," he answered.

"Thank you, Orpheus," she whispered, so vulnerable, so full of love. I had no idea how these people were considered villains.

"No need to thank me. Especially not until we do what we have to. We can't do it in this town, there's already so much heat surrounding the missing guy." My ears perk up.

"I know. I don't suppose you think we have enough time to find someone willing?" Fuck, are they talking about…

"We have maybe two days tops. It took weeks for me to explain the nuances to you, for you to fully understand what you were in for. We won't have the luxury of that kind of time."

They're going to make another vampire.

They're going to kill someone. Someone who's not willing.

Fucking monsters.

They slid out of the booth, and after dropping a twenty on the table, I followed suit. Far enough behind that I could just barely see them in the distance, but it was enough. With this newfound determination I felt brewing within my chest, I tracked them all the way to a white beach house just off the beaten path. They filed inside and I crouched in some brush outside a house across the way.

These creatures nearly made me feel sorry for them. Showing me a type of humanity I didn't think they were capable of.

Every new thing I learn about them makes them more confusing. Maybe this is how they've brainwashed Athena, by charming her. She doesn't know the real monsters behind their skin. I would show her the truth, I would protect her from falling into their trap. I would save her.

ATHENA

TEN

Walking away from Laz, with the slick evidence of my arousal between my legs, I struggled to make sense of just how quickly desire for Laz overcame my fear. It felt like my soul was seeking something it could only find in their arms. Was it mindless lust, or was it this mate bond? I wasn't sure. But one thing was clear. I wasn't afraid anymore. I don't know when it happened, but it did. There wasn't a doubt in my mind that these people were not going to hurt me.

But even with that obstacle out of the way, I still had a decision to make. A life-altering decision. Just because I'm not afraid, doesn't mean I want to bind myself to them for the rest of my life.

Does it?

The thought of waking up early and spending a lazy Sunday morning filling out the crossword with Laz certainly does sound like a dream come true. But all dreams end, and I need to be sure I'm willing to survive the nightmares before I get lost in the dream.

SILAS: Follow the roses.

Before I had a chance to text back, asking what he had meant, I arrived at the top of the stairs to the pier and instantly understood. Scattered across the wooden walkway were hundreds of pink rose petals. Tears tickled my eyes, but I held them back. The wind was relatively still, but the slightest breeze had their delicate forms dancing along the ground. There was a clear direction, leading directly to The Maine Plotline. I swallowed the lump in my throat and followed the path.

Guilt seeped its way into my mind. Was it wrong of me to accept the pleasure they were offering me without giving them an answer about the bond? Should I refrain from getting physical with any of them in order to keep my mind clear enough to make an educated choice?

Probably.

But the moment I entered the open store and felt Silas' presence envelop me like a lust-filled cloud, I knew I wouldn't be able to resist.

"Silas?" I called out, my voice heady. "How'd you get in here?"

Then, venturing around one of the stacks was Mr. Tall-Dark-and-Sinful himself. His torso was covered by a tight white t-shirt that accentuated his biceps and showed off the intricate black serpent tattoos on his alabaster skin. Dark black jeans hugged his thighs, and a silver chain hung from one of the pockets and dangled against his leg. Black hair hung loosely in his face and down to his shoulders, and that delectable lip ring glistened in the light. Fuck, he was sex on legs.

"Bookworm, if you don't stop looking at me like that, we're going to have to skip all the important stuff I had planned and skip right to the after-party." My core tightened at that idea, remembering the way he dominated my body at the drive-in. What could he do to me when we were in the privacy of my store?

"Hi, Silas," I whispered, carefully avoiding scanning my eyes across his chest again.

"Hi," he replied, the sweetest little smirk spreading on his lips. I was dazzled, utterly and completely. He was stunning. "I'm sure you have questions, and I know Laz probably answered several of them, but I want there to be no secrets between us. No walls. I want you to ask me anything, and I'll answer it."

I nodded, thinking about the wealth of information Laz had offered me. There were plenty of questions I still needed answers to, and I know it's important for me to understand everything there is to know, but looking at him and seeing the inherent sadness between his eyes - the sadness I put there with my fear and indecision - I had only one thing I wanted to say.

"I'm sorry," I spoke into the emptiness between us. The air felt charged.

"I'd be a liar if I didn't admit that these last few days were some of the most painful I'd ever experienced."

I winced, and he must have seen me because he stood from his relaxed state and took a tentative step forward.

"But you don't have to apologize to me."

I shook my head. "Laz said the same."

"Laz was right," Silas stated, confidently. He stood his ground, keeping several feet between us. A buffer that was simultaneously clouding my mind with lustful thoughts and allowing me to breathe.

"But I am sorry," I offered, eagerly.

"Stop apologizing." He commanded.

"Yes, sir." The word slipped out as if it was the most natural response in the world. Silas' eyes darkened sinfully, and his tongue ran along his bottom lip. A delicious-sounding groan rumbled from his chest and seemed to hit me directly in my core.

"Fuck, bookworm," he sighed, running his hands along his face in agony. "You are trying to kill me aren't you?" I smiled innocently, and his hands clenched at his side. I took a step forward. "I'm trying to be a gentleman here," he groaned.

"Uh-huh," I replied, continuing my trek toward him.

"I wanted to answer your questions, give you context and information… conversation.." He was stumbling over his words, clearly battling against his desire for me and his desire to respect my boundaries.

Fuck my boundaries.

When I came to a stop just a foot from him, I felt the cold roll off of him in waves. It felt like the brisk morning air. Comforting, welcoming. I looked up at him through my dark eyelashes and was once again awe-struck by his beauty.

"I do have questions. A lot of them." I brought a hand up to his chest, letting it settle against the material of his shirt there. He inhaled sharply and nodded while his eyes tracked my movement. "But I think we have some lost time to make up for first." He looked shocked for the briefest of moments until I added. "Sir."

Then it was all over for me.

His demeanor switched from the relaxed and sassy Silas I had come to enjoy, to the dark and dominant lover, I'd come to burn for.

"So, my baby girl wants to play, huh?" I nodded arousal flooding between my legs. "Words, baby girl, use your words."

"Yes, sir." He hummed darkly, taking a slow step back.

"I'm going to give you everything you want, but first…" he smirked wickedly. "I want to read with you." A thrill shot through me at the idea of what he has planned for us. If our 'reading' last time is any indication, I know it's going to be sinful and delicious.

"Stay here, do not move until you are told. Do you understand?" I swallowed the lump in my throat, pushing away the smallest threat of memory from that night so long ago, when I was told a very similar thing. "Answer me," he snapped.

"Yes, Sir," I squeaked out.

Silas let his eyes travel over my form once more before stepping away and disappearing into the stacks of books. I stood silently for a long while, listening eagerly for any sign of his plans. Finally, he spoke.

"'She stood cautiously at the edge of the room,'" I heard his voice echo sexily from somewhere deep in the belly of the store. "'Desire flooded her lower core. She knew if she went to him, she would be lost to the lust he was promising.'" I smiled. "Hmm, this book sounds interesting. Time to lock the door, baby girl. Do it now." I turned and locked the door behind me, smiling at the irony that just a few days ago I was locking this door to keep him out, but here I was locking myself inside with him. "Good, now come and find me, come read with me." I followed his instructions eagerly.

"'With each step, her core fluttered with anticipation. One thing was abundantly clear.'" His voice was getting louder as I ventured through the stacks. The fairy lights cast a soft glow over the aisles. The dark-painted walls and cozy velvet furniture scattered throughout only added to the torturous temptation that surrounded me and set my skin alight. I tensed as I peeked around every corner, trying to follow his beckoning call.

"'She wanted him to find her, wanted him to claim her in every way a man can claim a woman.'" Excitement danced across my skin. Was it wrong? Maybe. Did I care right now? Not one bit.

I turned a corner to see Silas lounging on a dark green velvet loveseat, his body lazily sprawled across the furniture.

He held a book in front of him, but his coy smirk told me he knew I was there.

"'She wanted him, nearly as much as he wanted her.'" He looked up from the pages, and his honey eyes met mine directly. My heart skipped a beat. He laid the book down on the cushion next to him and stood slowly.

I remained glued to my spot, watching him with careful eyes.

"He needed her forgiveness," he continued, the dialogue from the book long forgotten as he spoke from his own heart. "He needed her to know she was safe with him."

"She wasn't afraid anymore," I added, and I watched as the worry drained from his face, replaced with dark eagerness.

"He would go to the ends of the world to satisfy her." He took another step forward, his presence overwhelmed me in the way only he could.

"She was working on letting him," I whispered, venturing into his space. His lips were inches away, and the taste of his breath on my mouth was sweet and intoxicating.

"He wanted to kiss her." He whispered, and I felt the brush of his lips against mine.

"She wanted him to fuck her," I pleaded against his lips.

Silas' shocked laugh was the kind of dark sound that sent a flood of desire to my core. I groaned. "Ask politely," he taunted darkly.

"Please, sir."

His mouth was on me in an instant. Our kiss was a violent display of passion and need. My hands gripped the base of his shirt and pulled it up, breaking our kiss for only a moment, but his lips claimed a place on my bare neck and he ran his tongue over the vein there. His fingers made quick work of the buttons on my jeans.

I was suddenly lost to my base urges. My hands moved where they wanted, searching for some sort of relief. His lips brushed against my chin, and then the space just below my ear, and finally finding the column of my throat. My pulse quickened. His mouth found mine just as his hands pushed my pants down my legs.

"I can sense your arousal, baby girl. You want this cock don't you?" I nodded, whimpering against his mouth. "Say it," he growled.

"I want your cock, sir."

My hands gripped his waistband and he helped me relieve his perfect body of his clothing. His thick length sprung free and pressed against my bare skin. The chill his body gave me at our point of contact had me shivering in anticipation.

Then his palm came to my throat, closing around the column eagerly. A move he'd done before, but this time, ever so briefly it wasn't Silas there. A flash of perfect hair and an unassuming all-American smile had my body seizing. "Blood," I whispered.

Silas' hand was gone from my throat in an instant. "Athena, hey. Are you ok?" I nodded, softly, but ashamedly. "Where'd you go, just now?" I wiped a tear away from my cheek.

"I'm sorry, It's not you. I just.. Fuck. I hate that he still has this much power over me." Realization crossed Silas' face.

"The one who hurt you" He stated, and I nodded.

"My stepfather." His eyes burned with heat and anger I'd never seen in him before. The corners of his eyes darkened to a deep red. But still, I couldn't find the good sense to be afraid. "He... He held me like that. He told me to stay still. Not to move. He commanded me." He instantly understood.

"Bookworm, you should have told me. I never would have…"

I stopped him by pressing a quick kiss to his lips. "I wanted you to do it, Silas. I wanted you to make me forget him. I wanted the memory of your hands to replace the feeling of his." Was it fucked up that I wanted Silas to dominate me when that was the crux of my very trauma? I don't see it that way. I see it as allowing myself to heal by regaining the agency he stole from me. "I want the last person to do those things to me to be you, not him." There it was. The broken truth. Silas leaned his forehead against mine and our breath mingled.

"I will erase every kiss he ever stole from you. I will wipe away every memory of his selfish hands on your body. I will eclipse his hold on your soul, Athena. Because you are mine. Mine to worship. Mine to command. Mine to protect." He growled the words, like some sort of primal beast, and I felt my arousal return with full force.

"Erase him, Silas. Please." He kissed me again, with more passion than he'd ever displayed before. There was a deeper meaning to this kiss, the way his hands encircled my waist, and dug into my bare skin. His length hardened against my stomach, and I rubbed my body against him with reckless abandon, seeking the cathartic passion he was offering me.

His hands snaked up my back, and slowly made their way to my throat. His eyes settled on mine, a silent question. I nodded.

"That's my fucking brave girl." His praise had me nearly buckling my knees. "Does my hand on your throat make you wet? Are you eager for me?" His fingers dipped into my folds, running through the slickness there, eliciting a moan from my lips that he eagerly swallowed with his mouth on mine. "Fuck, you are soaked for me, aren't you? Because you know how safe you are with me, don't you, baby girl?" I nodded, whining against his mouth as his fingers circled my clit. "You love following my commands, because you know you have all the power, isn't that right, baby girl?" His fingers slipped inside, and my hands went to his shoulders in earnest. "Answer me."

"Fuck!" I exclaimed as his thumb pressed down on my clit and his fingers curled to hit that spot so deep inside. "Yes! Yes Sir!" He smiled against my lips. My hips moved, riding him excitedly as he expertly worked my body to orgasm. I detonated around his fingers, feeling my walls pulse around him.

"I need you," I exhaled, riding the last of my release, my hands snaking down his chest searching for his thick cock.

"Ah ah ah," he teased, pulling his fingers from me and pressing them against my lips. I opened them wide and willingly and he slipped them inside. I let the taste of my arousal flood my tongue and I moaned around his fingers. He groaned as if in pain before withdrawing his hand from my lips. "Good girls ask nicely to be fucked. Say that magic word, baby girl."

I smiled at him, his lust-filled eyes revealing just how hard it was for him to hold himself back. I had that effect on him. Then I whispered our little phrase, the one that was so deeply ingrained in the facet of who we were. Words I once spoke in this very spot. I hadn't meant them nearly as viscerally then, but now it was a vow, a promise. A declaration. "Fuck me, please."

He moved quickly, gripping my thighs and hoisting me, my legs circled his waist and I felt his length hard and ready pressing against my opening. I gasped, clutching his shoulders. With one hand, he held me there with ease, and the other slid between us, brushing ever so slightly against my sensitive clit.

His cock was notched at my opening and I couldn't contain my eager breaths. The mask of this dominant Silas was slipping, giving way to the breathless, handsome man who utterly adored me. His eyes held mine as he lowered me down onto his length. I felt each glorious inch as he stretched me. When I was fully seated, we both let out a long delicious sigh.

"Holy shit. You were made for me, Athena." His breathless admission felt so personal, so full of passion that I felt my heart tighten with a new emotion. "You were made for *us*," he added, with a grunt as he withdrew entirely only to thrust himself inside of me again.

The truth hit me like a ton of bricks. I *was* their mate. I *was* made for them. Despite whatever I planned to do with that truth, the fact remained the same. And I think I was starting to like it. The idea that I was crafted to fit someone so perfectly. Four someones.

"Does my girl like that?" His hands were on my hips and he lifted me with ease, bringing me slamming back down onto his cock. I cried out with each thrust. "You like the idea of belonging to all of us, don't you? You want to know what it feels like to take us all at once don't you?" I whimpered. "You'd take my cock in your cunt, and Orpheus would take your ass. We'd stretch you so full, but you wouldn't be able to scream because your mouth would be buried in Samara's pussy or choking on Laz's length." I cried out as his hips slammed against my thighs.

"Yes, please!" I begged, but I wasn't sure what I was begging for. Was it him, or this fantasy he painted for me? Either way, my body was tightening with anticipation as I climbed closer and closer to my release. Without breaking his pattern, Silas pressed my back up against a bookcase. The wood creaked under the force as it bounced against the wall. He released my hip and pressed his fingers against my clit again sending me tumbling blindly into a euphoric orgasm. A few books fell from the shelf behind us from the force of our bodies. "That's it, oh shit. You're so tight." He gasped as he chased his own release. His body stilled as he rode out the last of it and his head rested on my chest. Our heaving breath was the only sound for a long moment. Soon, too soon, he lifted me off of his length and helped me set my feet back onto the ground.

Despite the cold radiating off of his body, I felt like I was on fire. I leaned into his hold, my cheek pressing against his bare chest. My heart was beating quickly, violently, and as I focused on it a thought seeped into my mind.

Pulling back quickly, I looked up at Silas. "I can't hear your heart beating," I exclaimed worriedly.

Silas smiled, holding my chin gently in his cold grasp. "A vampire's heart beats so infrequently it's nearly dead." I gasped, but Silas turned my eyes to his. "Before you came into my life, my heart would only beat once every hour." I couldn't wrap my head around that. "But the first moment I kissed you, and every moment after that, it's been more alive than it's ever been." I pressed my ears against his chest and we stood silently, nakedly embracing, as I listened for his heart.

Thump.

I started counting. A minute passed. Then two. Then three.

Thump.

"Three minutes," I stated.

"For me, that's racing." He kissed the top of my head.

He took a step back from me and began sliding his jeans back onto his body. I followed suit until the two of us were fully clothed and resting on the velvet loveseat.

I leaned into his hold and we sat comfortably together as if it were the most natural thing in the world. As if we'd been doing it forever.

"Do you have anything else you need to know, bookworm?" He asked, a bit of trepidation in his tone. I traced the ink on his forearm.

"Why snakes?" Silas lifted one of his arms, showing off the swirling designs of scales that decorated his body.

"Snakes are misunderstood. They're not aggressive creatures and they won't strike out of malice, they don't go looking for trouble. But if they, or anything they care about, is threatened, they'll defend themselves till their last breath." He spoke so reverently. I smiled.

"That sounds just like you," I mused. He chuckled.

"I also have an affinity for wrapping my body around anyone who's brave enough to get close." As if to demonstrate, he tightened his hold on my waist. I sank into his hold eagerly. A few moments later, I shifted in his arms, slightly uncomfortable due to the question I wanted to ask.

"Why did you choose to become a vampire?" I asked, the word still feeling volatile on my lips.

"Has anyone told you about Alora?" I shook my head. "Alora was once a member of our coven before she died." His voice wavered with a thick agony. I sighed, and a brief flash of shock bloomed in my chest. Another member of the coven? Was she my mate too? Did I lose a piece of myself before I even knew it was missing? A sadness blanketed me, and I felt Silas' arms tighten around me. "She was my best friend growing up, back when we were humans. I had lost my parents pretty young, too young, so Alora and her family took me in. She was my family. My sister." I squeezed the arm that was encircling my waist, thankful my back was to him so he could not see the tear that slid down my cheek at the longing and pain which was evident in his tone. "We were freshly adults when Alora's parents died. But it still hit her pretty hard."

"I'm so sorry, Silas." He sniffed, and I felt his body move as he breathed.

"For what?"

"You lost them too." His arms tightened around me.

"Yeah. For the majority of my life, they were the only thing between me and the foster care system. Which was not exactly cozy and comfortable in the 1890s."

I took a slow breath, letting the new information about Silas sink in.

"After they died, Alora and I moved out to Los Angeles, trying to make a new life for ourselves, and we did. For a while." His voice shook, slightly. "In 1910, we were walking downtown together, enjoying the weather when we walked by the LA Times building."

I listened intently, a soft alarm going off in my head.

"When the bomb went off, we were on the street out front." His hold tightened on me.

I gasped, tears falling down my skin.

"The reports have fluctuated from a gas leak to a widespread union conspiracy. But it didn't matter. The two of us were fighting for our lives in a hospital bed for days, I could care less how we got there. It was a blur, really. I couldn't tell you what all they did to us to try and bring us back. But all I remember the whole time was begging them to let me see Alora, and they wouldn't. I spent those days in pain, not knowing if I'd lost the last member of my family."

I felt his pain as if it were my own then, my chest tightened.

"One night, I snuck out of my room. Ignoring my broken bones, and pushing past the pain from the injuries. When I got to her room, she was in a coma. I nearly lost it." His voice quivered. I gripped his arm in my hands and squeezed it reassuringly. "Orpheus slipped into her room to find me crying. I didn't find out until much later that he was robbing the hospital of blood bags, and it truly was just luck that he found me. I don't know if it was the meds or the pain, but I was so vulnerable that I just spilled my entire life story to this stranger. When I was done, he offered me a chance to live, a chance to save Alora."

I was suddenly so thankful for the chance encounter that Orpheus had all those years ago.

"Twenty-one people died in that bombing. Twenty-three if you count Alora and I joining the legion of the undead." He chuckled.

"You almost died," I choked out, and suddenly Silas rearranged himself so he was looking into my face.

"I didn't. I had to survive so I could make it to you."

I nodded and leaned forward pressing a kiss to his lips.

"Tell me you're mine, bookworm," he whispered against my lips in a soft plea.

I felt like his. All of theirs. I wanted nothing more than to be the mate they wanted me to be, but despite the outpouring of love I've received and felt, I couldn't make this choice yet.

"I want to be, I do."

He sighed, but I saw the understanding on his face.

"I need time," I whispered.

"I've waited a century for you, Athena. I'd do it again."

With Silas' arms around me, I let him tell me more about the first years of his second life, my decision getting closer and harder with each passing second.

ORPHEUS

ELEVEN

Silas and Laz returned last night with content smiles on their faces, and despite the ever-present hunger in their gaze, they looked satisfied. A twinge of jealousy flashed within me when I looked at them. While they assured me Athena had not accepted the bond yet, that they hadn't had the distinct pleasure of sinking their teeth into her perfect skin and drinking the blood that coursed in her veins, I couldn't help but feel like these two had once again surpassed me. Their relationship with our girl was leagues beyond where I stood with her. And that was my fault and my fault alone. I had only indulged in her once, that kiss. The way her trembling body calmed when she looked at me made me feel like I was her anchor. The one thing keeping her grounded. Her lips met mine in a desperate comfort-seeking way and I was lost to her. I always would be.

Even if I had to leave her.

Samara was the first member of my family. The first person to combat my loneliness and win. If she had to leave, I couldn't let her go alone. No matter how fucking painful it was going to be to turn my back on my mate.

I slept like shit last night, tossing and turning, knowing most likely Athena was going to request a meeting with me today, and I'd have to look at her in those perfect emerald eyes and tell her the truth.

That I wanted her more than anything on this Earth, but I couldn't have her.

By four a.m. I knew trying to sleep was futile so I got up, threw on a pair of jeans, and made my way down the stairs. After downing a blood bag to curb the hunger, and pouring a coffee with entirely too much sugar in it, I pushed through the glass doors and found myself leaning on the railing overlooking the beach. The water was peaceful this morning as the moon began its slow descent to the horizon. Breathing a lungful of the crisp salty air felt like a calming embrace. Fuck, it felt good to have a place that felt familiar.

It had been so long since we'd felt 'settled' in a single place. Mostly because settling meant getting sloppy, and getting sloppy meant getting caught.

I was worried about that happening here.

What were Laz and Silas going to do if they saw the Nameless mark in this little town? Something tells me they're just reckless enough to ignore it. Without me there to bark orders at them, they would try to fight, and they would lose. And chances are Athena would be caught in the crossfire.

My chest tightened at that thought. My free hand, not holding the mug of coffee, gripped the railing with inhuman strength. The reason we survived for so long, and were able to avoid being captured by Nameless again is because we didn't make mistakes. And yet, since the moment we arrived in Shockgrove, mistakes are all we've made.

How long did we have until they found us?

The sun began its slow climb to its perch in the sky, casting a warm amber glow across the dazzling water.

My shoulders had just started to relax when my phone vibrated in the pocket of my jeans, effectively erasing all instances of calm I had been feeling.

The name on the caller ID made it worse.

"Detective Barnes," I answered coolly.

"Mr. Green." Her voice was relaxed. I tried not to let my frustration over finding them tailing us yesterday seep into my response. I had the eerie feeling that someone was watching us, and sure enough there they were.

"How can I help you?" I heard her clear her throat on the other end of the line, and I waited with bated breath for her to play her hand. Whatever that might be.

"I wanted to inform you that we have closed the missing person case for Mr. Dells."

I bit back the sigh of relief that nearly fell out of my mouth.

"Was he found?" I asked, with false eagerness.

"No, but camera footage confirms he left town on his own accord. We've reached out to neighboring towns to keep an eye out for him, but without any threat, the case is closed," she answered quickly. *Thank you, Silas.*

"I'm glad to hear that he seems to be safe," I replied, diplomatically.

"Yes, well." She paused, waiting for me to offer something else. I didn't. "I apologize for concerning you in this matter."

"Not at all, you were just doing your job." After a brief goodbye, I hung up and felt a small weight lift from my shoulders. Another potential threat dodged effortlessly thanks to Silas' gift. I couldn't help the silent dread that began to fill me at the thought of trying to survive on the run without his power.

We all worked so well together, it kept us sharp and prepared. Without our united front, were we just biding our time until it all comes crumbling down?

I heard the door creak open behind me and I tossed a quick glance over my shoulder. Silas sauntered out, his broad, bare chest on full display. Only dark jeans hung low on his hips.

"You're up early," I said, returning my gaze to the ocean. His satisfied, content, lust-filled emotions were vibrant and powerful.

"Had a sex dream, had to wake up and take care of business," he teased, leaning on the railing next to me.

"Please refrain from informing me of that ever again," I replied, nonchalantly, but jealousy was roiling within me. The cup in his hand smelled of blood.

"How is your hunger after engaging in intercourse with her?" I asked, attempting to make the act seem as clinical as I could in my mind so I couldn't picture the way her body stretched to take him, or how well she would take me.

"Intercourse?" Silas asked, raising an eyebrow. I nodded, and he chuckled softly before it died out. "Worse," he finally stated, taking a sip of the red liquid in his cup. "Definitely worse."

I groaned. If the timeline was accelerating this quickly we would be out of blood by tomorrow.

"And Laz? Same for them?"

Silas nodded, and I peeled my eyes from him again and watched the tide rush in, then out.

"You and Samara need to make a good impression, I think she'll accept us. I know she feels this bond too. She just needs to give herself permission to."

I didn't respond. How could I? Was it my place to tell Silas what Samara's plans were? What I was planning to do with her. Maybe not, but he deserved to know, nonetheless.

"Right," I said, absentmindedly.

"What is it, Orpheus?" He asked. I couldn't seem to look at him.

"Samara is intending to reject the bond," I whispered, but I knew he heard me because he nearly dropped the cup of precious blood from his hand.

"What the fuck," he exclaimed. "Why would she do that?"

"I think you know the answer to that, Silas."

That calmed him slightly, his frantic breaths returned to normal, and he leaned forward on the railing again, this time burying his head into his arms.

"Fuck, of course. I can't believe I didn't even think about that." He was in pain, I could feel it. "I can't imagine how she feels right now."

Alora had been Silas' best friend. They were attached at the hip for their first few years in The Wanderers and still were even after Alora found something special with Samara.

"She's going to reject her mate because of Alora," he whispered to himself, not as a question, but as an answer.

"Yeah, she is."

"So what, she'll just sit there and watch us fall in love with Athena every day? That'll hurt like hell. Even if she rejects it."

I didn't answer, I didn't turn to face him. His eyes burned into my profile, a quiet realization.

"She's not going to stay…is she?"

I shook my head.

"Did you try to talk her out of this?" Silas asked, his voice raising slightly.

"Of course, I did," I answered.

Silas groaned.

"I've told her she's allowed to move on, but she will never be able to until she believes it herself." I shook my head, ignoring the guilt building in my chest.

"If she goes out on her own, Nameless is going to find her." He downed the last of his blood and set the cup down on the railing. "She'll never survive alone."

Again, I stayed silent.

His questioning glare deepened.

"You already know that, though," he accused. I didn't give anything away despite the pit of despair forming in my stomach. "You're going with her." It wasn't a question. He knew.

"You said yourself, she'd never survive alone." I tried to hide the traitorous emotional crack in my voice, but of course he caught it.

"Orpheus," Silas whispered, the sound was full of the brotherly love we had created together. "Athena is your mate." He was angry. I ignored him. "She is your mate!"

"You think I don't know that?" I snapped, turning my molten gaze to him.

"You think I'm not intimately aware of what I will be losing here? Because let me promise you, I am."

He just stared at me. "Then why?"

"Because Samara is my family," I whispered, feeling Silas' anger and sadness roll off of him, enveloping me in a blanket of his agony.

"What about me?" He screamed, a tear sliding down his face. "What about Laz? Aren't we your family?"

I choked down a sob. "Of course, you are," I assured him.

"Then why the fuck are you planning to abandon us?" He was yelling now, it was only a matter of time before Laz and Samara were aware of our conversation, if they weren't already.

"You'll have each other and…Athena," I added with a pained whisper.

"You're a coward," he seethed, quietly. "You both are."

I turned to follow his gaze to see Samara had arrived and was standing at the threshold of the glass doors. Her eyes were glassy with unshed tears.

"Silas," she started, but Silas only stalked off onto the beach. My eyes darted to Laz who stood motionless behind Samara.

"Tell me that's not true," Laz begged. "Tell me, you aren't doing this."

Samara shook her head, unable to give them what they wanted. Laz nodded to themselves a few times, shock and betrayal coloring their emotions. Samara reached for them, but they pulled back violently.

"Don't." They pushed past Samara and followed after Silas.

"Fuck," she exclaimed under her breath and I felt her guilt rear its ugly head again. "Why did you do that?" She cried.

"They deserved to know," I replied, letting my mask of indifference slip away entirely.

"Our family is falling apart," she lamented, watching after Silas and Laz.

"They'll be ok," I lied.

"I thought Silas would understand. He loved Alora, shouldn't he be glad I'm taking my vow to her so seriously?" Her voice cracked with sadness.

"I was there that night," I stated. "When you and Alora made your promises to each other."

She wiped a tear from her cheek.

"Do you remember what she promised you?"

She nodded. "Every word."

"She promised you would be happy, content, and loved," I reminded her. Samara sniffled. "Look at you, Samara. You are anything but happy and content right now."

She sobbed.

"Have you considered that by keeping your promise to Alora, you're breaking her promise to you?" I whispered, I didn't want my words to hurt her.

Her sobs continued and I almost couldn't stand to be in the presence of that much pain

My phone vibrated with a text from an unknown number.

UNKNOWN: Hi, Orpheus. This is Athena.

My heart beat once. That single text had injected a sort of hope in my veins I hadn't felt in so long, while also seizing my heart in a sort of dread.

ORPHEUS: Hi, Athena.

UNKNOWN: Meet me for lunch today?

ORPHEUS: Of course. Just tell me when and where.

She sent an address for a crab shack just down the pier from her store. After issuing my agreement, I pocketed my phone and turned to find Samara in her state of distress.

"I meant what I said, if you're out, then I'm out."

Samara looked up at me through wet eyelashes.

"Are you out?" I asked, attempting to mask the hope I had that she would change her mind. There was a slightly longer hesitation in her response, but then she nodded, effectively dashing what little hope I had.

"Ok, I'm going to go get ready. I'm meeting her in a few hours." I began walking away but then Samara's meek voice stopped me.

"What are you going to tell her?"

"The truth," I uttered as I retreated into the house.

Silas and Laz had not returned before it was time for me to leave, and Samara had not come out of her room since locking herself inside after the confrontation.

I wore the same burgundy suit I wore the night we arrived in this little town and our life was turned upside down. Call it a full circle moment, or maybe I just wanted to feel her eyes on me the way I did that night before I ruined everything that was growing between us.

I pulled open the cooler of blood and winced at how little remained. One flask each. We weren't going to survive without more soon. It had been a few hours since I drank my four a.m. fix, but the hunger wasn't unbearable. I could probably keep it under lock and key while I have this conversation. I can't imagine she'll want to drag it on for very long anyway. Not after hearing what I have to say. I closed the cooler without taking another flask.

I was at the pier a few minutes later, ignoring the sense of dread that was settling over me with each and every step toward my mate. Mostly because I knew that every step I took toward her was only a step I'd have to take away from her.

The crab shack was empty when I arrived except for a few employees who sat around making themselves look busy. Boredom rolled off of them.

I grabbed a table near the window, overlooking the water and I found myself once again entranced and watching the sun glistening on its calm surface.

I felt her the moment she entered the restaurant. Her nerves were screaming for me. I felt her emotions so fucking clearly, like I truly couldn't tell if it was her or me feeling them. I stood as she arrived at the table. She was wearing the same grey T-shirt dress she wore the day of our tour. The day I felt her panic so clearly I nearly was brought to my knees. I should have known right then what she was to me, but I couldn't see what I didn't want to.

"Hello, Athena," I said, coming around the table to hold her chair out for her. She blushed deeply and I had to suppress a groan at the look of her delicious blood blooming beneath her skin. She nodded her thanks and sat down.

Settling back into my chair, I found myself admiring her. Her strength, her bravery. There was a twinge of fear threading through her emotions, but her courage and determination were front and center. Driving her.

"I've already done this twice and it doesn't get less awkward." She giggled and I wanted to bottle the sound to keep with me when I left.

"Do you mind if I start?" I asked and she shook her head, gesturing for me to continue. "I wanted to first and foremost apologize to you, Athena."

She looked at me curiously.

"For everything that occurred at your store that night. From the moment I sent you tumbling into your worst memories, to everything that happened after."

She furrowed her brows at that, tucking a strand of her soft red hair behind her ear. "Everything?" She asked, timidly. A soft bloom of lust broke into her emotions. My fangs bit into my bottom lip as they tried to descend. A deep breath managed to force them back. Here it was. The moment of truth.

"Yes."

Shame, and rejection. Both emotions flooded my senses.

"Wait, allow me to clarify. I do not regret the moment we shared, Athena. In fact, your kiss was the single best moment of my entire long existence."

She smiled, blushing again. "Laz did mention that you have been…around for a while."

I nodded. Just then, a waiter came to the table and took our drink and appetizer order. All the while, I didn't remove my gaze from her.

"A 'while' is a bit of an understatement," I replied once the waiter had left. She waited for me to continue. "I was turned in the mid eleven hundreds."

"Holy shit," she exclaimed loudly, before clasping a hand across her lips. "Sorry, I just…wow. That's. Laz wasn't kidding."

I smiled sadly at the wonder in her gaze. It was such a stunning sight. Her amusement. I could spend my entire life showing her new things if only to be blessed with that look again.

"And in all that time, you've never had anything better than our kiss?" She asked, tentatively, but I could feel the spark of jealousy. She thought I was lying. She was considering the other women I might have passed time with. If only she knew how little those women mattered, how insignificant and forgettable their touches were.

"No matter what pleasures I've experienced before, nothing compared to the moment you claimed my lips with yours."

She released the slightest moan, the sound hitting me directly in my core.

"However," I started, noticing her nerves return to the forefront. "I should not have indulged until you knew the truth about what we were."

She nodded. "I agree, but I can't fault you for guarding your secret. You had no idea who you could trust."

Here we go.

"I also should not have indulged until I knew what my decision would be." I tried to keep my tone even and steady.

She studied me.

"A mate bond is sacred, I'm sure the others have explained that fairly effectively."

She nodded.

"And I should have withheld my affection for you until I was positive I could accept the bond."

She tilted her head, watching me. Her emotions settled calmly, a quiet storm. "You don't want the mate bond," she stated.

"Fuck yes, I do, " I snarled before I could contain it. My nails dug into the table.

"I don't understand," she said, shaking her head. The coldness in her tone sent icy jolts through my heart.

"I want you more than anything I have ever wanted in this existence. I want to sink my fangs into your perfect skin and mark you as mine and mine alone. My body fucking burns for you, Athena."

She gasped, her lust enveloped me instantly, driving me absolutely fucking crazy.

"You've barely said ten sentences to me," she added, breathlessly.

"And yet, my eyes were the ones you could not look away from that first night," I replied, darkly.

Her tongue darted out to wet her bottom lip and my eye tracked the movement hungrily. "So you do want this bond?"

I shook my head. "I do, but I can't."

"So why are you meeting with me if you don't want-"

I raised my eyebrow.

"I mean, *can't* do this?" She asked, watching me with the same fervor I watched her. I tried to ignore the strands of disappointment that were threading through her desire.

"You deserved to hear it from me," I offered her, with my attempted mask of indifference in place. Her cold eyes were full of fearful rejection.

"Well thank you for your candor," she snapped, contritely. A bite behind her words was hidden behind a mountain of sadness. She pushed back from the table and tossed a twenty-dollar bill down before turning to leave.

"Athena, wait," I nearly begged. It couldn't be done yet. I wasn't done yet.

"You've made yourself very clear, Orpheus. I am not expecting anything from you. You are not obligated to fulfill this bond any more than I am. You're free."

I felt anything but free as she stalked away from me. Her pain danced around me, invading my senses like a nightmare would invade a dream.

The moment she exited the restaurant, I expected a reprieve from the torture of her agony, but it never came. If anything the burning pain grew more intense the further she got from me. I stood from the table, offering my apologies to the waitstaff through clenched teeth, and raced out of the building after her. Her red hair was blowing in the wind as she stalked down the pier toward her store.

So I ran. My feet pounded the wooden planks below me as I flew across them. My heartbeat caught me by surprise. It was violent, vicious, pounding against my ribcage as if it were actually alive. She made me feel that way.

My hand grasped her by the arm and pulled her into an open alleyway between two buildings. The brick structures offered a slight shield of privacy from the pier's walkway, but the ocean was still visible over the railing near the back of the buildings. I turned her so she was facing me, backing her up against the brick wall until she was caged between it and my form. Her gasp was so delicious I nearly bent down to taste it. Heat rolled off of her, and fear laced with want danced around her in a taunting cloud.

"What the fuck, Orpheus?" She exclaimed, but I couldn't answer her. My chest heaved as I stared down at this perfect creature. This fucking goddess. She was my Eurydice. The woman I was destined to love, but destined to lose due to my own selfish distrust. But even the tales of the beautiful nymph goddess of nature paled in comparison to this stunning creature before me.

"I…" How could I explain this? How could I prove to her how desperately I needed her, and how no matter that, I couldn't have her? Suddenly, my breathing came in ragged spurts, my heart beat again to my surprise, and utter torture. It was such an unfamiliar feeling, but so fucking wonderful all at the same time.

"Orpheus," her voice pierced through the cloud of despair. Her hand came to rest on my cheek, fire against the ice of my skin. "Talk to me."

"I made a promise to Samara." I had made the decision that it wasn't my place to divulge her secrets to Athena, but I needed her to understand. I needed Athena to know why I was doing this. I couldn't bear the thought that she might think I didn't want her. "If she goes, I go with her." Athena absorbed the new information.

"She's going to leave too?" It wasn't an accusation, and her emotions weren't full of rejection this time. Just pure worry.

"She had a chosen once, not a mate, but their connection could rival some of the more powerful bonds out there."

Athena inhaled deeply, feeling the weight of my confession. "It was Alora, wasn't it?"

I wasn't even shocked that she knew her name, not after having her conversation with Silas. I nodded.

"She doesn't think she can allow herself to commit to this bond. Not after losing Alora." To Athena's credit, she seemed to be taking all of this rather calmly.

"And you're going to leave with her," she continued.

"She's my family," I said again, although, after Silas' interjection this morning, I could admit it felt slightly less noble of an admission.

"That is the most selfless thing I've ever heard, Orpheus." Her emerald eyes watered slightly as she looked at me with adoration.

"Fuck. I want to be selfish with you, Athena," I added, stepping forward until her breasts were pressed against my chest. Her arousal invaded my nostrils and I groaned, burying my nose in the crook of her neck. I didn't allow my skin to touch hers, instead hovering just above making contact. The space between us was electric, charged with something I'd never had the fortune of experiencing.

"I'm not ready to give you up yet," I whispered, it was a soft, broken sound.

"So don't." I pulled back and looked at her questioningly. "You can't stay, but we can have today." I stared at her, feeling her words wash over me with a hope I didn't dare feel. "Be selfish, Orpheus."

That was all the permission I needed. My lips captured hers and I pressed her body into the brick wall behind her by driving mine into hers. She moaned at the friction. Her kiss was not gentle, and neither was mine. We were ravenous hungry creatures who were soaking up every ounce of pleasure they could before the moment ended. Her fingers threaded through my cropped hair and pulled my face to hers. My tongue danced with hers, an exchange of promises we weren't able to say aloud. I tore my lips from hers and began kissing my way down her perfect skin, stopping briefly at her throat. The smell of her blood was so powerful now that I had gotten a whiff. How had I missed the clear indication that she belonged to me? It was as obvious as the sun in the sky now. Hunger flooded me, and I paused a moment, resting my forehead against the skin of her neck, sucking in spurts of cool ocean air to stave off the monster that was threatening to rear its ugly head.

"How does it feel?" She asked, breathlessly, her chest heaved, and brushed her pebbled nipples against my chest. "Drinking blood," she clarified. I moaned, my length strained against my slacks.

"Fuck, Athena. You're trying to make me lose control," I exhaled a slight chuckle.

"You won't hurt me," she asserted. How far she's come in these few days. How brave my girl was.

"Never," I swore, despite the agonizing need to taste her.

"How does it feel?" She asked again.

"Blood from the vein tastes like the most delectable thing on the planet. It's euphoric and earth-shattering. It fills you with a sense of power and longing."

She shivered under my touch where my nose nestled against the column of her throat.

"Now, when someone drinks from you, it's an aphrodisiac. You'll feel heat and arousal flood your core. You'll be so close to a release that you might just beg for it."

She sighed sensually, letting her head fall back against the brick behind her.

I kissed her neck, the spot where I would have marked her had things turned out differently. My tongue slowly slid over the exposed skin and she released a guttural groan, her desire was so potent I was drowning in it.

"I wish I could have you," I whispered against her skin, feeling her shiver under my touch.

Her hands danced along my back, leaving trails of electrified paths in their wake. When her hands disappeared from my body, I growled my frustration, but it was quickly replaced with desperate whimpers when her hands gripped the hem of her grey t-shirt dress and lifted it slightly. Her eyes scanned the surroundings. Looking down toward the opening of the alleyway. From where we stood, nobody could possibly see us. I could do whatever I wanted with her in this alley and only she and I would know. I was on my knees before I could take my next breath.

"You want me to devour you, little nymph?" I looked up at her from my position and was struck by just how beautiful my Athena was. Her dress settled around her waist, giving me a perfect look at the soft white panties that covered her core. I pressed my lips against the fabric letting the first taste of her arousal brush against my willing and eager lips. She sighed, resting her hands on my head.

"Yes, Oh god, yes," she cried out, quietly.

"The gods aren't here right now. It's just you and me." She whimpered, pressing my head into her hot center.

I pressed a kiss to her core, feeling her slick wetness soak through the fabric barrier between my lips and her folds. "Taste me, Orpheus," she pleaded, and if I thought I was hard before, I was sorely mistaken. My cock was pressing painfully against my pants, but I didn't dare relieve my ache until her needs were well and truly met.

"Your wish is my command, little nymph." It took minimal strength to rip the fabric from her body and reveal her wet hot center. I wasted not a moment of time before burying my tongue inside of her, eliciting pained passionate moans from her delicious lips. Her taste flooded my mouth and I knew no matter how long I lived, I'd never taste another thing this sweet. Her hands worked my head, pressing me further into her, and I let her drive me. She rode my face with reckless abandon, seeking her every desire. I let her use me the way she so desperately needed to. I was her plaything, perfectly molded to make her every wish come true. Her satisfaction was mine.

I slid two fingers inside of her as I offered special attention to that exquisite bundle of nerves at the apex of her perfect cunt. She bit her bottom lip to avoid releasing the scream I knew she was teetering toward. Her breathing ramped up, and her amped-up heart rate only made the blood under her skin pump faster, sending me into a frenzy of epic proportions. My hunger was rivaled only by the desire for her.

As my mouth ravaged her, I felt my fangs elongate, but I couldn't stop them. When the sharp point brushed against her clit, I heard her gasp. I hadn't turned entirely, but I felt small qualities of the creature inside of me venture to the surface. When I looked up at her, I knew what she was seeing. Nearly blood-red eyes, and elongated fangs. A monster feasting on her center. I readied myself for her to push away and keep me from finishing my task, but instead, when I looked into her eyes I didn't see fear. I saw curiosity.

And all I felt was lust.

She rode my face harder, holding my head to her. I was careful not to let my fangs break the skin, but the soft gasp she released every time they brushed against her was too damn delicious for me to resist. Her walls tightened around my fingers and her hands held me to her center as she found her release. I hummed my appreciation and watched her come undone from my rightful place on my knees before her.

Her body settled with heaving breaths and satisfied sighs, all while I remained in my spot tracing lazy brushes of my tongue against her sensitive core.

"If we were mates, I would never leave my knees," I whispered, pressing my forehead against her stomach.

"We are mates," she returned, breathlessly.

I glanced up at her and saw a gaze filled with admiration and care. It was nearly too much for me to handle.

"I know," was all I could say.

She sank down to her knees in front of me and took my face in her hands. Her eyes searched mine, and I wondered if she found what she was looking for in their black depths. "If you're going to ask me to say goodbye to you, I want you to make me scream it." Her hands fumbled with my belt, and then the button on my slacks. When her delicate fingers managed to free my length from its confines, she marveled at my size. She hiked her dress up and straddled my legs. I felt her heat slide against my cock as she climbed into position, pulling a groan from both of us.

"Anything you need, little nymph."

She positioned her slick entrance over the head of my cock and didn't waste a single second before slamming down on top of me. Her perfect cunt swallowed my every inch expertly.

"Oh, fuck, Athena," I gasped out and she began swirling her hips teasing me, and forcing friction against her clit. I helped her, bringing my fingers to her center and sliding them along that bundle. Her head leaned back, exposing her throat to me.

I kissed the skin there again, reverently.

"Take it all, Athena. I'm yours. Use me." I had never been a selfish lover, it wasn't in my nature. I got pleasure from my partner enjoying themselves. If their body was brought to a beautiful, explosive climax, I never needed to even be touched to feel accomplished. Not that I didn't fucking love the feel of Athena's pussy strangling my cock, but I didn't need it. All I ever needed was her pleasure. I could never have sex again, and the memory of the way her face twisted in desire would sustain me for the rest of my existence.

I tried, unsuccessfully, to forget that this could be mine - if I didn't have to leave.

Athena bounced harder, using my shoulders for stability, her walls tightened as her climax neared. I let my other hand sneak around to her tight hole and I felt her curious surprise as I slowly circled it with my index finger. I watched her face, memorizing the way her lips fell open as she moaned, the exact color of her green irises, and the way her hair flowed down her back. My mate was perfect, and I would never forget it.

"Say it, Athena," I growled through clenched teeth.

"Goodbye!" She screamed as I pressed a finger through the ring of muscles. Filling her completely.

When she orgasmed, she cried out and buried her face in the crook of my neck to muffle the sound. Her teeth bit down on the skin of my neck and that was all I needed to topple over the cliff of passionate oblivion with her.

I held her there longer than I needed to, as I rode out the last of my climax, but I couldn't help but remember that once I removed myself from her, I'd never feel this kind of euphoria again.

Luckily for me, she didn't seem like she was in much of a hurry to leave.

"Will I ever see you again?" She asked, a tiny flash of hope blooming in her emotions.

"I don't think I could survive watching the others reap the benefits of a bond that should have been mine."

She nodded as if it made perfect sense.

"If I can't have you, Athena, I can't see you. I'll only be reminded of what we could have been."

She plastered a fake smile on her face but a tear slipped through her eye and I had to refrain from darting out and licking it. "Thank you for this. It was the perfect goodbye."

"It was," I agreed.

She hesitated to stand and withdraw from our joined position, but she knew, as I did, that our time was up. When she stood, I felt something inside my chest crack. My heartbeat pulsated loudly and more lively than I'd felt in my long second life, and I suddenly hated the feel of it in my chest. The wretched organ came back to life just in time to break.

We righted ourselves, smoothing our clothes and hair in silence, an attempt to prolong the farewell that was acidic on our tongues.

"Goodbye, Orpheus. I wish you every happiness."

I didn't have the heart to tell her I was leaving my every happiness behind with her.

"Goodbye, Athena."

She left first, something I was thankful for because I wasn't sure my feet would have allowed me to take one single step away from her. When she disappeared around the corner and back toward the main pier, I let the full force of her pain hit me. It held my soul and my nearly dead heart in such a grip I almost hoped it never let me go.

Would I still feel her emotions this powerfully after rejecting the bond? I didn't think so. So even though this pain was violent and agonizing, I wanted to feel every single second of its sting, because the moment it ceased would be the moment I lost her.

ATHENA

TWELVE

I was well and truly past being afraid. Now, the only thing I was worried about was keeping the fragments of my heart that belonged to my wanderers from shattering into a million little pieces. Samara and Orpheus were going to leave. They didn't want this bond with me.

A pain unlike anything I've ever felt struck me each time I thought about it. I felt like my chest had been flayed open and I was going to lose myself entirely. I'd been trying to figure out if the way I felt about them was the bond or simply a school girl crush, but nothing about the way I felt knowing two of the pieces of my soul weren't going to stay screamed 'crush'. Since the moment I left Orpheus in that alley, I felt a tidal wave of misery crash over me, and I haven't been able to come up for air since.

It was only going to get worse.

There's a special kind of torture in finding your soulmate only to lose them.

The afternoon shift at The Maine Plotline moved by in a blur. I hadn't yet texted Samara, and I debated if I even could bear it. I knew what she was going to tell me, and I didn't know if I had the strength to hear it.

Archer stopped by for a few hours, and thankfully he didn't inquire about my near zombie-like emotional state. He made me laugh, which was like a bandaid over a bullet wound, but it was nice nonetheless.

When he left, he promised he would call me later. I still wasn't sure what he was up to in town, but his companionship was too nice to question.

A few minutes until close, I sat by the counter with my phone opened to an empty message history with Samara. I had gotten her number, and Orpheus', from Silas the day before. He eagerly gave them to me, urging me to meet with them as soon as possible. I knew he wanted to complete the bond, although he didn't pressure me.

I was lost in a daydream, staring at my phone, when a loud crash jolted me from any semblance of peace. The glass of the front window shattered violently, flying in every direction. I turned my head to avoid the assault of the tiny sharp shards, but I felt them pelt against my skin leaving tiny cuts. I cried out as something heavy and pointed caught my shoulder. A sharp pain permeated through my entire body. I winced and stammered backward into the wall. Shock was all I could feel as I looked down to where the offending object sat. A dark red brick, sitting amongst the shattered glass, with white painted lettering.

'Lying Bitch'

Tears flowed from my eyes and blurred my vision, and I shivered from a combination of the pain in my arm, and the cool night air flooding in from the now open front window. My unhindered hand pressed against my shoulder, feeling the sticky warm blood there. I winced again at the tenderness I found. My blood slid down my arm and pooled on the floor near the brick.

White-hot, blinding pain seared through my arm, and I looked out through the window, but all I could see was the quiet Maine night sky.

I reached for my phone, and a sob escaped my lips at the exertion. I held it in my bloody grasp, my entire soul begging me to call them, but all it took was a glance at my blood that was spattered on the floor and crawling down my arm to remind me that they should not be anywhere near this mess.

The phone rang.

SILAS

I answered before I could think otherwise.

"Athena, are you ok?" Silas asked frantically. I heard rustling behind him. And it sounded like someone was wincing in pain in the background.

"What - how did you-" I started.

"Are you hurt?" He pleaded.

"I'm ok, just…I'm ok. Can I call you back?" I asked, trying to hide the pain from my voice.

"What's going on, Athena?" Laz's voice came through the phone.

"I'm going to call you soon, ok?" I assured them.

"We're on our way," Laz asserted.

"No!" I yelped.

"What do you -"

"Just give me a little bit of time, ok? Don't come here!" I begged. I heard them inhaling sharply on the other end of the line. I leaned my head back against the wall, feeling the blood pour out of my arm. I needed to call someone, and soon.

"Athena-" they started.

"I am bleeding all over the fucking place and you being here will only make it worse, ok?" I exclaimed through the pain. "Just give me a little bit of time to fix this and then I will call you. Please." I waited for their response.

"I'm calling 911 now," I heard Laz say. There was some slight rustling and a hushed conversation. "They're en route, Athena."

"Thank you," I said, weakly. Feeling the effects of the blood loss.

"Call us the second you're safe," Silas commanded.

"I promise." I hung up, knowing they wouldn't be the ones to end the call, but I didn't want to worry them any more than they already were. I took shaky breaths and leaned into the wall for support. The world was getting foggy, I needed someone.

I sent a quick text to Archer asking him to come to the store and I felt calmer the moment he responded that he was on his way.

I'd come to trust him, and as far as I knew, my blood wasn't going to send him into some weird frenzy. Archer arrived first, he must have been close. His eyes were wide with worry as he hopped through the open window and beelined directly for me.

"Holy shit, Athena. What happened? Are you ok?" He didn't seem to care about getting his hands or clothes dirty, because he gently pulled me against him, careful to avoid aggravating my shoulder. I couldn't explain it, but the moment I was in his hold, I felt comfortable. Safe. Protected.

"Somebody threw a brick through the window," I stuttered, feeling my body shake as the shock began to wear off.

"Who did this?"

I shook my head, although now as my mind cleared from the initial jolt, I could think of someone who might consider me a 'lying bitch'. Especially with the timing of the phone call from Detective Barnes I got this morning, it wasn't that unreasonable of a guess.

"I didn't see anyone, but.. but.." The sound of a back door swinging open had both of our heads snapping in that direction. I whimpered, in fear and pain as Archer situated me behind him. His hand went to his waistband and I saw the top of a weapon hidden there. It wasn't metallic like a gun, but instead looked wooden, like a blunt end of a club or something.

We waited with bated breath for something to arrive through the door, but nothing came. Eventually, the calm night was disturbed by distant sirens and echoed shouts as the police and paramedics made their way down to my store on foot from where they parked their vehicles at the mouth of the pier. Archer didn't leave my side as the police took my statement, not exactly stating Greg's name outright, but alluding to my recent case involvement with Detective Barnes, and the paramedics checked my wounded shoulder.

They assured me I would only need some stitches, and the bleeding had already begun to stop.

They called me lucky.

Archer squeezed my good arm that was looped through his when they said that. As if he knew how unlucky I had felt at that moment.

There was a sort of wicked irony about the whole situation. My vampires had protected me from Louis, but in doing so they created a threat in his unstable friend. And now, if I didn't want to force them into a potentially painful situation, I couldn't even call them.

The paramedics were adamant I get taken to the hospital, and I told them I would once my grandma arrived. She got there about twenty minutes after my call and walked straight over to me, pushing past the hordes of people analyzing the scene.

"Oh my god, you beautiful thing. Are you ok?" I nodded, letting tears slip through my eyes. She hugged me close to her chest. "Shh, shh, it's ok." Her warm voice was like a cooling balm against the painful burn in my chest.

Only after she assured me, multiple times, that she would take care of the shop, did I allow the paramedics to take me.

Archer had a soft exchange with my grandma and although I couldn't focus on what was said, the two seemed chummy, comfortable with each other. After he said goodbye to my grandma, Archer accompanied me to the hospital and sat by my side as they patched up my arm.

Once whatever pain meds they had given me started to take effect, I started crying softly. Archer reached forward, gripping my hands in his.

"Hey, you're ok, Athena. You're safe now," he whispered. His eyes watched me carefully, without an ounce of pity, but with all the worry in the world. "Do you want to talk about it?" He asked, and I shrugged, wiping tears from my cheek. "You told the police it might have something to do with another case you were involved in?"

I nodded.

"Are you in danger?"

I motioned to the bandages on my arm that now covered the seven stitches I had to get. "Apparently," I teased, and he cowered at that.

"Fuck," he leaned back in the pale blue chair. It creaked under the shifted weight.

"Hey, um, thank you. For coming when I called."

He held my gaze as I continued.

"Davia's still out of town, and anyone else I could have called is well, a little squeamish with blood."

His eyebrows furrowed the slightest bit at that. "Hey, I know I haven't been here long, but I'm glad you felt like you could call me. I guess I am sort of getting used to your company, and I would have hated it if you had died," he said with all the delivery of a joke, but the solemnity of the truth. It felt nice.

"Last week, there was a guy at the bar who was kind of coming on too strong."

Archer listened intently.

"I didn't like the vibe I was getting, so I told him I was going home. He walked me outside." I paused. Wondering why I suddenly felt the urge to tell the truth, the *real* truth to him. After the momentary lapse, I continued. "We went our separate ways, but apparently he never went home." This statement felt more toxic now that I knew without a doubt what had happened to Louis. He was ripped away from me before he could violate my body any more than he already had, and he was killed. Probably drained of his blood by my vampire mates.

That thought didn't scare me as much as it did before.

"His friend thinks there's more to the story. He's getting a little aggressive," I added.

There was a tick in Archer's jaw that indicated his anger, but his face remained void of any clear indication of his feelings. "Has he tried anything like this before?" He inquired and I swallowed the lump in my throat, sitting up and wincing at the slight pain in my shoulder. Even dulled by the meds, it was one hell of an injury.

"He came to my store and confronted me. He was aggressive, but I didn't think he'd go to this length."

Archer was fuming. I could see the urge to go find Greg dancing behind his eyes. I needed to ensure my wanderers didn't go after him or else we'd have another body on our hands.

"The missing persons case was dismissed today, so that might have something to do with the snap."

I groaned as a thought occurred to me.

"What is it?" Archer asked.

"I just realized that I have to tell Davia about this. She was sleeping with the guy."

Archer reached for my phone at the same time as I did and held it in his hands. "Allow me," he offered. I raised one eyebrow. "I will gladly tell your incredibly attractive best friend that her previous, sub-par, lover is a psychopath and she needs to find someone else to spend her nights with."

I rolled my eyes, but ultimately let him find her number and input it into his own phone and step into the hall to make the call. She was gonna give me an earful for giving 'a stranger' her number. I would talk to her soon, but I was so tired, and I secretly was thankful I didn't have to answer her million questions right now.

I grabbed my phone which Archer had sat back down on the bedside table and sent a message to my grandma asking how the store was. She sent back an answer quickly telling me the money was secured, the insurance company already called to start a claim, and Mr. Harley from the hardware store brought a bunch of his buddies down to help board up the window until it could get replaced.

I felt a weight lift off of me. I don't know what I would have done if there was irreparable damage done to that place. It was my home. It meant everything to me.

Archer was still in the hall, and I faintly heard him verbally sparring with my best friend in a playful, yet annoyed manner. They'd be good for each other if he was planning on sticking around Shockgrove.

Suddenly, my phone buzzed with an incoming phone call.

I smiled and answered.

"Hi, Silas. I'm fine now. I promise."

I heard several exhales of relief on the other end of the call. My heart did a little flip wondering if Orpheus and Samara had also been worried about me.

"Holy fuck, bookworm. You worried the shit out of us," Silas exclaimed.

"Are you hurt?" Laz interjected.

"Who the fuck did it?" Orpheus. His demanding tone was so different from the sweet, and attentive lover he was, but it turned me on just the same.

"I think it was Greg." I heard a loud growl and a crash as if something was thrown against a wall.

"That douche's friend?" Samara asked, and a slight pain stabbed my chest at her voice. I hadn't talked to her yet. She might not know that I know she's planning to leave me. It colored this encounter with a somber tone.

"I can't have you going to avenge this," I whispered, keeping an eye on the door. "I mean it, you cannot retaliate." Silence. "I'm not kidding. If you hurt him, I can't accept the bond. I need to know I can trust you."

"He hurt you," Silas whined.

"Yes, he did." Another growl. "But if we retaliate, the cops will be all over you." There were a few hushed words exchanged on their end, and no matter how I strained to hear them, I couldn't. "Promise me," I demanded, when I heard nothing, I repeated myself with more fervor. "Promise me."

"Ok, we promise," Laz finally said. "Are you sure you're ok?"

"I'm a little banged up, but a few stitches and I'm good as new," I tried to interject a little bit of cheeriness into my tone to mask the pain that still radiated through me despite the drugs.

"We should have been there," Silas whispered, sheepishly, and my heart nearly shattered at how broken and betrayed he sounded.

"I was bleeding all over the place and I knew that was going to be an impossible situation to put you through," I admitted.

"We could have handled it," Silas claimed, but even I knew that wasn't true.

"How did you know I was hurt? Was it a mate bond thing?" Again there was a slight pause.

"We can explain it all soon, but you should rest," Orpheus finally answered, his voice tense.

"I'm sorry I never got to schedule my date with you, Samara," I said, nonchalantly, trying to hide the quiver in my voice.

"You were understandably preoccupied, Athena." Her smooth tone was simultaneously a comforting embrace and a sharp stab.

"Come over to my house tomorrow morning? I'll make us breakfast." I tried my best to sound calm. If she was going to tell me what I think she was and break my heart, I'd prefer to fall apart in private. "Wait, do you even eat breakfast?" I thought back to the last time I saw them at Dale's. They had food on their table and I think I recall them picking at it.

"We can eat human food, although its benefits are in taste alone," Samara responded. That was a small reminder that my vampire mates were hungry for more than scrambled eggs. "But, you were just injured, you shouldn't be cooking anything for me," she interjected.

"I'm injured, not dead." I attempted to make a lighthearted joke, but I should have known better. Several low growls sounded through the phone. "Tomorrow morning, ok?"

She sighed, and I could imagine the look she was exchanging with Orpheus at that very moment.

Finally, she replied. "Tomorrow morning," she agreed.

After the others made me promise to give them updates, I hung up, just moments before Archer returned, a smirk on his face.

"Not many people can go a round with Davia Adams and live to tell the tale," I joked. "How did it go?"

He sat down in his chair again and offered me a smile. "She's going to call you in five minutes."

"I thought you said you'd take care of it for me?" I laughed, but secretly I did want to hear her voice.

"I bought you five minutes, that was monumental," he removed his baseball cap and ran a hand through his dyed black hair. The flashes of blue looked dull in the fluorescent lighting.

"I guess you're right," I sighed. "How'd she take the news about Greg?"

"She mumbled something about 'good dick always being attached to assholes.'" He mimicked her tone, and I found myself belly-laughing, then wincing at the movement.

"She demanded that I put you on the phone."

"But you bought me five minutes," I added. He smiled, then a look of accomplishment on his face.

"Impressive, huh?"

I smiled at my new friend, a warmth blooming in my chest at the friendship and camaraderie I had found with him.

"Revolutionary."

Archer reached forward then, resting his hand on the exposed forearm of my good arm.

"I'm really glad you're ok, Athena." He looked at me the way a friend would. I nodded, willing the stinging tears to stay put.

"So when do I lose you?" I asked a soft pang in my chest at the thought of losing Orpheus, Samara, and Archer.

"I'm not sure," he said, weakly and I felt a cloud of sadness blanket us. "But hey, maybe when I'm finished with this current job I'm on, I can come back. I think I'd like Shockgrove during the tourist season."

I beamed brightly at him and gripped his hand in mine. "Shockgrove would be lucky to have you."

He smiled at me, unfiltered and unrestrained.

The moment was interrupted by the ringing of my phone on my lap. Archer leaned back, rolling his eyes. I laughed, gripping the phone in my hands.

"I'm pretty sure that was only three minutes," I teased. Archer stood, grabbing his backpack from the ground at his feet and slinging it over his shoulder.

"Well I'm not a miracle worker," he added before offering me a nod and exiting the room. I smiled after him, and mentally prepared myself for the coming onslaught of questions.

I answered the phone and answered all of Davia's questions, as thoroughly as I could, including the biggest question of why I gave her number to Archer. By the end of our conversation, I had a sneaking suspicion she wasn't as upset about that as she was pretending. I loved my best friend, and I felt how much she cared for me in every single word, every single threat to kill me for not calling her first. I had to remind her she was hours away at a summit, and she scoffed, saying, "As if that's enough to keep me from you."

She promised she would be home tomorrow, despite how I begged her to stay put, telling her I was fine.

When she finally let me hang up, and the doctors signed my discharge papers, I felt a weight lifted off of my soul. Greg was out there, and he was angry, but I had never felt more loved and protected in my life than I did at that moment.

Four vampires willing to kill for me, a new friend who sat by my bedside as I recovered, and my best friend in the world leaving her important work event early just to make sure I was ok.

I'd been through a lot of pretty horrible things in my life, but if it all led me here, to these people. I couldn't help but be thankful for the sunshine that peaked through the clouds.

Even if tomorrow morning it'll be eclipsed by the looming goodbye.

For now, I was going to soak up that sunshine because god dammit, I deserved to.

SAMARA

THIRTEEN

"Will you stop breaking shit?" Orpheus exclaimed again when Silas threw something at the wall of our rental and it shattered onto the floor in broken wooden splinters. "She's ok."

"That fucker deserves to rot for what he did," he seethed, his eyes reddening by the second.

"I agree, obviously, but you heard her," Laz interjected, putting their hands on Silas's chest. A strangely intimate look passed between them as Silas allowed Laz to invade his personal space. "She doesn't want us to retaliate. And we have to respect her wishes." Silas groaned but did not pull away from Laz's touch.

I understood the urge. I wanted nothing more than to rush to her side and heal her of this pain. To take it away from her so she doesn't have to suffer because of our hasty actions. It wasn't lost on me that we were the reason this Greg guy lost his friend, and therefore somehow blamed Athena for it.

But she had asked us not to.

And we needed to listen.

"Go get some sleep," Laz offered quietly to Silas, their eyes locked in an intimate expression of something. They'd never been that touchy-feely before. It kind of shocked me to see it. I glanced over at Orpheus to gauge if he was noticing the same thing I was, but he was too busy running his hands through his hair, his own control slipping rapidly.

"We all should get some sleep," I offered. They glanced in my direction. "Tomorrow, Athena will have talked to us all. She very well may decide to accept your bond tomorrow night." I said to Silas and Laz, who bristled at the mention of it.

"I can't believe you're still thinking of rejecting her," Silas said, his anger about Greg replaced with his ire toward me. It had been frosty at best around the house since Orpheus revealed my intention this morning.

When Orpehus arrived home from his lunch date with Athena, I hadn't expected to scent her on him so strongly. For the briefest of moments, I thought he had gone back on his word to me and decided to stay with her. Which he would have every right to, but it stung all the same.

But one look at his dejected, lost expression told me all I needed to know. Whatever moment he and Athena shared was not a celebration, but a goodbye.

"Please, just try to understand," I whispered so my voice could not betray me.

"I can't. I can't understand it at all," Silas roared.

"Silas," Laz warned, holding onto his arm.

"Tonight is the last night we will ever be a family," he started, a quiver in his lip. "Do you realize that? If she accepts the bond tomorrow, and you two idiots reject it. You'll run off with your new vampires and we will never be a family again. Never be The Wanderers again. Don't you get that?"

My chest tightened.

"Of course, I know that! It's all I can think about, Silas." I was crying, tears streamed down my cheek.

"Don't you care?" He asked, his eyes glassy.

"I care more than anything. This is breaking my fucking heart. I know that by rejecting this bond, I'm not just losing her," I choke out, unable to even say her name. "I'm losing Laz, and I'm losing you. The last living person who loved Alora as much as I did."

Silas glared at me, pain and suffering burning behind his gaze.

"You know what she believed in above everything else?" He asked, his voice an even, low tone, full of hurt. "Family." He finished before I could respond and I nodded, knowing that. My wife had valued her family more than anything on this Earth. "And here you are about to shatter her family."

I gasped, a painful stab in my heart.

"She would be so fucking ashamed of you."

The words found their purchase in my heart and I fell to my knees, tears pouring from my eyes. Laz had pulled on Silas, whispering "Silas…That was low," just as Orpheus ordered, "Get him out of here."

A few moments passed and I knew Silas had retreated from the room with Laz, leaving me alone with Orpheus. He knelt down in front of me, and my blurry gaze found him.

"He's just afraid of losing you," he offered, quietly. I nodded. "You should get some rest, tomorrow is going to be a hard day." He helped me to my feet and then slowly wrapped me in an embrace.

I excused myself to my room, and there in the still of the night, with the soft moonlight flooding through the cracks in my blinds, I mourned. I mourned for my wife, for my mate, for my family.

I mourned until I had no tears left to cry, and then and only then, did sleep finally take me.

*

The morning came sooner than I would have liked, something about the way the sun peered through the blinds and cast painful streaks of light across my skin felt appropriate. I found myself sitting there absorbing the pain for longer than I should have because deep down I felt like I deserved it. I rolled out of bed and donned a soft pink sundress with a keyhole neckline and long bell sleeves. The color was a bright contrast to my dark skin, and I spent a few silent minutes applying makeup to my face, doing my best to hide the red-rimmed eyes that were evidence of my despair last night.

I considered waking the others to discuss last night, but as I passed their doors, I couldn't bring myself to cross the threshold. Instead, I slipped out of the house quietly, after downing half of the last blood bag in the cooler, and headed to Athena's house around the corner.

The walk to her little cottage was brief, but each step felt like it dragged on. I found my feet making a detour before my head caught up. I slipped inside the market and smiled briefly at the cashier before purchasing a bouquet of pink roses. The flower that, at one point, meant nothing to me, but now would forever be a reminder of the love I could have had.

Their sweet aroma enveloped me as I returned to the streets, heading to her.

Turning down her driveway, I felt my heart in my throat, unbeating, but in pain nonetheless. I could barely stop the shake in my hands to knock on the door.

When she answered, the wave of her scent crashed into me, followed soon thereafter by the worry at her current state. She had done her makeup this morning, painting her perfect features with a soft bronzed glow and darkening her eyelids with a deep brown that made her green eyes pop. Her hair was left down to fall in gentle waves down her back. But it wasn't her beauty that gave me pause, nor did the slight white powder that seemed to be dusting her face and clothing. It was the dark bruise that marred her perfect skin, poking out from beneath the gauze bandage on her arm that I could see from underneath her t-shirt sleeve.

My eyes landed on that bruise and I couldn't see anything else. Her pain. Her injury. It was our fault. That was a fact I simply couldn't get over.

"Are you in pain?" I asked, and I saw her eyes follow mine to where her arm was covered. She shrugged.

"It's better than it was." I knew she was covering up the full scope of the injury in order to appease me, and that only made me angrier.

"Come in," she offered, stepping aside and welcoming me into her home for the second time. She must have had a similar thought because she followed up by asking, "Do you have to be invited in?"

I smiled, softly, passing her to enter her living room, trying to tear my eyes from her injury with little success.

"Yes, but you've already invited me in. The first night."

She nodded, processing that as she closed the door behind me.

"Well, um, thanks for coming. I've got a few things going." She brushed past me and headed to the kitchen, the minty scent of her skin mixing with the deliciously sweet aroma of her blood had my body tensing against the urge to indulge in her. A flash of hunger exploded in my throat.

Once I had composed myself, I turned to follow her. To say the kitchen was a mess would be putting it lightly, flour was dusting nearly every surface of the kitchen, and suddenly the powder on her clothing made sense. Cracked eggs sat on the counter, waffle batter sat in pools across the counter, and a slight sizzle came from the stovetop where pieces of bacon were being fried beyond recognition. She cursed under her breath and rushed to remove the pan from the offending burner. I watched her carefully as she favored her good arm, holding the other close to her frame. Fury seethed through me again. She struggled to set the pan down and turn the burner off with just one arm. I rushed forward, helping her.

"Here," I said, switching the burner off. Ignoring the way her breath hitched when I brushed against her skin. I stood still in that moment, soaking up her sweet heated gaze and the way her heat rolled off of her. Her eyes held mine captive, and I wasn't sure I'd be able to step away if the world ended.

It took nearly every ounce of my willpower to step back from her orbit. Clearing my throat, I safely put the kitchen island between the two of us. She composed herself and slowly turned to face me. Her soft breathing was strained.

"Sorry, I um, didn't realize how hard it would be to cook with only one good arm."

I nearly stepped forward to heal her right then and there, but I wasn't sure the intimate connection would be a very good idea at the moment, so instead I offered, "Let me, please?" I indicated toward the waffle iron, and she followed with her eyes.

"You don't mind?" She asked sheepishly, shame coloring her face.

"Not in the slightest," I said, moving around the island toward the cooking station. To my relief, Athena countered my movement and kept her distance. I felt like I could breathe and think when I had this space between us because when I was up close and personal with her I wanted to throw caution to the wind and lose myself in her. "How is your store?" I asked, keeping my gaze on the work ahead of me and stirring the eggs. The less I looked at her, the better. I was likely to throw myself at her if I stared at her too long.

"The insurance company is going to pay for a new window, thankfully. We should be getting it by the end of the week." She spoke with such pained worry. I knew she was mourning the destruction wrought upon her bookstore, and I knew she felt responsible.

"It's not your fault, you know," I murmured. I heard her sigh behind me.

"It's not yours either." I paused, pouring the batter into the waffle iron, and turned to face her. She was leaning against the island with her good arm, and staring directly at me. Her eyes seemed to delve all the way into my soul.

"Except that's not true," I tossed out, peeling my gaze from hers. It was safer not to look at her. When I looked at her, I saw things I shouldn't see, like a future. "He wouldn't be harassing you if his friend hadn't gone missing."

"And his friend wouldn't have gone missing had he not tried to rape me," she said bluntly. I felt my back tense under her gaze, but I focused on continuing to prepare our food.

"I do not regret his death, I only regret that it has caused you trouble," I stated, matter-of-factly, gathering two sage green ceramic plates from the cabinet above the sink.

"I know you're planning to reject the bond, Samara." If I didn't have incredibly quick reflexes the plate in my hand would have shattered across the kitchen floor. My name on her lips sounded like heaven, wrapped in the hell of her words.

"What?" I asked, turning toward her with wide-eyed shock. She simply watched me, curiously.

"I didn't mean to just blurt it out like that, but I couldn't avoid it anymore. You wouldn't even look at me. It was getting awkward." She chuckled softly and I joined her, suddenly relieved it wasn't a painful secret any longer.

"I'm sorry," I said, meeting her gaze and not shying away. There was no way those two words could accurately acknowledge all of the ways I feel I let her down.

"I know," she answered, with a shy smile. I turned away from her and plated the food, focusing on the task so I couldn't drown in the dread of what came next.

I set the two plates of food down on the island and quietly Athena took a bite. She moaned at the taste, and I groaned at how that moan made me feel. My core tightened and I wanted nothing more than to hear that sound again. And again. And again.

I avoided thinking of how I'd much rather spread her wide on this kitchen island and have her for breakfast and took quick bites of the waffle.

We ate in silence, save for a few of those delicious moans. Finally, she cleared her throat. "Tell me about Alora." I stopped mid-bite and nearly choked on the piece of waffle in my mouth. "Sorry," she offered quickly, handing me a napkin. As I reached for it, my fingers brushed against her skin and we both gasped. Her skin was electricity against mine, shocking me with a jolt of magnetic energy that made me feel fucking alive. I instinctively bit my bottom lip, forcing the pooling desire between my legs to calm.

I pulled my hand from her, leaning breathlessly against the island. Guilt flooded my senses. She had just asked me about my wife, and I was being turned on by her mere presence. I hated how weak that made me seem.

"Alora," she prompted again. "She was your partner right?" She asked without a single ounce of judgment. I nodded.

"My wife, my chosen." Athena licked her bottom lip softly, averting her eyes from mine. She took an idle bite of food. "She was the strongest person I've ever known." I felt the tell-tale sting in my eyes as the thoughts of her grew heavy and painful.

My memories of her were so hard to reconcile. How beautiful they were, how horrifically they ended. No matter how I tried to separate the love we shared from the torture we endured, I couldn't seem to.

"Was." Athena noted the verb tense, and although I'm positive Silas or maybe even Orpheus had already told her the unfortunate truth about my wife's demise, she wanted me to tell her.

"Yeah, was," I repeated.

"What happened?" Athena asked, quietly, her eyes scanning my features.

I hated reliving this moment, but if Athena was going to understand why I couldn't be with her, she needed to know why. I took a long, steadying breath, and began.

"She died saving our lives."

"Are you all ready?" Alora's voice whispered from her cell. I tensed, gripping the bars of my cage with a painful grasp. Despite my exhaustion and brutal hunger, I couldn't help but feel a bloom of hope in my chest, blanketed by overwhelming fear.

"Remind me why you think this is going to work?" Orpheus asked, quietly from the cell next to mine.

"Because it will," she asserted, and I couldn't help but smile at the pure optimism of my wife, however misplaced I feared it was.

"It's our only chance," Silas exclaimed quietly, and weakly. We hadn't fed in nearly two months. Our bodies were slowly deteriorating. But Alora had gotten lucky, or as lucky

as a prisoner can get, and managed to get a single taste of human blood. It wasn't enough to quench the thirst, or even offer much strength, but it would have to be good enough.

"When we get out of the cage, we can feed each other," Orpheus offered, excitedly. He had been trying to find a way to get his blood to us since the very first week. Vampire blood, while still delicious and often euphoric, didn't give us quite the same amount of strength as human blood, but a weak vampire could still kill a strong human. We just needed something to stave off the overwhelming hunger. We needed to get out of the cages, and then we could do this.

"If all goes well, we can share a guard for dinner before we get out of here. Just be ready to move. Don't get caught in bloodlust. Ok?" Alora warned, and although I knew the dangers and logically understood a bloodlust trance could mean the difference between life and death, I wasn't sure I'd be able to control myself the moment I tasted blood again.

We waited patiently for an hour or more, I wasn't entirely sure. Time seemed to work differently in the darkness of these cages. Finally, the thick door at the end of the hall opened and a single guard wandered in. He walked down the center of the aisle, firmly keeping his feet on the safe side of the painted red line. His eyes scanned the other cages, although we hadn't had a fellow prisoner in a few weeks. There was an elder vampire trapped in one of those when we first arrived, He'd been there for weeks at that point. He wasn't very good at conversation, and every time Orpheus pushed him for recon or answers, the elder would usher a hopeless response. He seemed to have accepted his death long before we arrived. And a few weeks later, death came for him after all.

The guard scanned the cage next to me, his eyes filled with a sort of disgust and contempt, as if somehow in this scenario we were the monsters when he was starving and torturing us. I glared back at him, tracking his movements carefully. He met my gaze before slowly moving along, His eyes darted to the cage next to mine, Alora's, and his steps faltered.

"Fuck," he exclaimed under his breath. He gripped the walkie-talkie on his vest and pressed a button. "We've got a dead one."

My heart, which hadn't beat in almost three hours, constricted. I pressed my body *against the bars straining for a look at her. She had to be ok, it was her trick, of course. Right? I couldn't think straight, my shift was so close to the surface I could nearly feel it.*

"Bring the cart," he called into the walkie-talkie, and I felt tears stream down my cheek. Please let this be part of the plan.

"Alora?" I couldn't help the cry on my lips. "Alora, please. Answer me!" I was risking the entire thing, but the pain in my chest mixed with the exhaustion won over any logic. "Alora!" I screamed.

"Shut up!" The guard called over to me. "The bitch is dead."

I screamed, a guttural painful sound. "Alora! No," I beat against the bars of the cage with all the strength I could muster, which wasn't much.

The guard got a sick little smirk on his face and leaned toward me just enough so I could see the evil in his eyes. "Be quiet, or you'll join your little girlfriend."

"I will fucking rip you to shreds," I growled at him, he attempted to remain composed, but his face drained of color and he faltered, stepping back from my cage. I didn't even notice then that he had crossed the red line, unaware of the horrors that awaited him on our side of the barrier.

A pair of hands reached out through the cage next to mine and in a blink of an eye, the guard's neck was snapped and his lifeless body fell to the ground in front of my cage. His lifeless eyes looked up at me from the floor.

"Samara, get the keys," Alora's heavenly voice called to me, and I sobbed with relief.

"Alora?" I cried out.

"Yes, my love, I'm ok. Please get the keys." My vision blurred with tears, but I pressed my hands through the bars to the lump of human flesh next to me.

"Good work, Alora," Orpheus praised, but I didn't miss the hitch in his composure. He was just as hungry as the rest of us, and here in front of me was a dead human body, filled with blood. Blood that, if we drank it now, would give us enough strength to fight our way out of here.

"Toss me the walkie Samara," Silas called. I reached for it, unclipping the device from the vest, and slid it down the wall toward his voice. A few moments later, I heard

the voice of the guard call into the walkie-talkie, *"False alarm, the bitch was trying to pull a fast one. All clear."* I smiled, weakly as I searched the body for the keys. Silas' gift had come in handy more times than I could count. His facade might just be the thing that saves us today. My fingers found the keys at the guard's belt and I made quick work of the lock on my cage. When it clicked open, I felt a sort of freedom and hope I didn't know was still possible.

I stood over the limp body at my feet and my shift was so close I couldn't contain it for another second. My fangs elongated and I descended on the body at my feet. Sinking my teeth into his still-warm flesh. The first taste of blood was so impossibly perfect, the world around me fell away until there was nothing but its taste. I drank, and drank, gulping the liquid down like the ravenous starving creature I was.

"Samara! Stop!" The faint scream of my wife was the only thing that penetrated the bloodlust haze. Slowly, logic returned, and shame bloomed in my chest. I pulled my fangs from the body and turned to face my wife, seeing her face for the first time in two whole months. The taste of blood, still fresh on my tongue, was nothing compared to the power I felt from seeing her crystal eyes.

I unlocked her cage, and embraced her, my wife, my chosen, for the first time in too long. Her arms circled my waist and held me close to her frail body. I didn't realize how much her touch meant to me until I couldn't have it.

"Guys, I get it, I do. But get us out." Laz whispered. It took a nearly unbearable amount of willpower to peel my body from Alora's and unlock my coven's cages. When the last cage was opened, I turned to notice Silas, Laz, and Orpheus all latched onto a different part of the deceased guard, stealing what little bit of his blood I had left in his body. Silas, who was now disguised as the very guard he fed from, smiled and the picture was so inherently wicked. Alora set a hand on my shoulder and smiled, turning me to face her.

"You should feed," I whispered, relishing the way her hand felt on my body. She nodded, hungry eyes locking on my neck. She dove in and sunk her fangs into the soft part of the throat. She drank eagerly, and I held her there. Each slow draw of my blood

to her mouth was another reminder of my love for her. She should have drank from the human instead, gathering more than just 'enough' strength. Maybe if she had she would have been stronger.

She retracted her fangs, kissing the spot, her tongue sealing the wounds at my throat.

"Are you ok?" I gasped, scanning her frame for injuries, of which there were plenty.

"I will be," she assured me with a kiss on my lips. I placed my hands on her cheeks and sent my healing power surging through her nonetheless. Finding each cracked rib, each tear of flesh, and fixing them. She let out a sigh of relief. "Why didn't you tell me what you were planning, I thought…I thought for a second there that I'd lost you."

"That's what I was counting on," she replied sheepishly. "I needed you to scare him."

I nodded, hating it had come to that, but thankful I had her here, in one piece in front of me. I brought my lips to hers again, sinking into a kiss that said every word that went unsaid these last few months.

"We need to get out of here, now," Orpheus exclaimed. He looked strong and focused. The little bit of human blood he got was doing wonders at returning our fearless leader to his former glory.

Silas stripped the dead guard at his feet and slipped into the tactical gear he wore. I nearly growled at him, the facade of the guard a vicious reminder of the torture we'd endured.

We slipped through the hallway carefully, Silas leading the charge, the cells lined the space taunted me as we walked past. I would rather die than return to one of these. Alora's hand gripped mine, our fingers intertwined, and I felt grounded.

When we arrived at the thick iron door, the air was filled with unspoken tension.

"We are a coven," Orpheus whispered. "We are a family. And we will make it out of here together."

"But, if someone is lost, do not turn back." Alora squeezed my hand as she spoke.

"Alora," I whined. She shook her head.

"Promise me," she said to me. "Promise," she offered to the others. Silas, Orpheus, and Laz softly agreed, but I shook my head, tears staining my skin.

"It won't come to that," I cried.

"I hope you're right." She pushed a strand of my loose curly hair behind my ear.

"Are we ready?" Silas asked, and his disguised eyes scanned each of us for our acknowledgment. Then he pressed on the door and crossed the threshold.

Nameless headquarters was a dark warehouse, industrial in its design and function. The few times we'd been allowed to see where they were dragging us, we'd seen conveyor belts, and what looked like a weapon manufacturing floor. Normally, it was loud and active in this place, with shouts and machinery. But now, either by a stroke of luck, or a sick cruel sense of hope, the space was quiet. We moved carefully against the wall of the open factory floor with our claws elongated, poised to attack, but nobody came.

We moved at a pace that was slow for our kind, but we didn't dare get caught up in the false sense of security.

We had nearly reached the other end of the factory and a large set of double doors that had to lead outside when a sound echoed across the expanse. We rushed forward, ducking behind the machinery. Alora pressed her head into my chest and I felt her breathing come raggedly. I kissed the top of her head, willing myself and her to calm down. Laz and Orpheus were at our back, their nerves were so palpable I could choke on them. Silas stood up, his guard-shaped form, gazing in the direction of the sound.

"Foster" a voice called from across the space. I glanced at the door, nearly a hundred yards away, but so close I could almost feel the fresh air on my skin. Silas waved his hand nonchalantly.

"Need something, Bennett?" He asked calmly. I cringed at the name of the guard who'd overseen some of our worst torture sessions. How Silas could say his name without seething was beyond me. They had been careless, letting us hear their names. So cocky and confident that we would never escape. But we knew their names now, and have seen their faces. And if we get out of here, we won't let them forget what they've done to us here.

"What the hell are you doing over here?" Silas shrugged.

"I was gonna head outside and get some fresh air, those bloodsuckers smell like shit." I could hear the tenseness in his voice and I knew he was feeling the pressure bubble up. His eyes darted every so briefly to where we were hiding. His head made the slightest nod *toward the door.*

"You were supposed to check in," the voice accused, getting closer. I buried my face into Alora's hair, willing my breathing to slow.

"Jesus, can't a guy have five minutes to erase that stench from his nose?" Silas took a step back toward the door.

I glanced over at Orpheus and Laz, their eyes tracked Silas' movement carefully. He would open the door and we would make a break for it. They readied themselves, getting their feet beneath them and preparing for the race of a lifetime. Alora and I followed suit, my shaking hands pressed against the cement floor.

"Where are you going?" The guard asked an edge of disbelief in the tone. Alora and I shared a worried glance.

"Outside, I just told you," Silas teased again, taking another step toward the door. He was so close now. Come on, open it.

"Freeze," the guard, Bennett, called, and I stifled a gasp. Silas' eyes widened and he put his hands up, no doubt a weapon of some kind was now pointed at him. His eyes flashed briefly toward us.

"What the fuck, man?" Silas said, trying to maintain his cool, but even I could see it slipping by the second. He took a few more careful steps toward the door. "Just calm the hell down, and I'll be in for a check-in soon." He reached the door and as he put his hands on the metallic surface, the four of us in hiding sprinted. With new blood running through our veins, we were able to sprint with the speed we'd so dearly missed these last few months.

"Code Black!" Bennett screamed into his walkie and suddenly a vicious-sounding alarm blared through the air, a bright white and red light flashed, but we were at the door. So close, we just needed to get outside. They'd never be able to catch us out there.

We pressed against the door with all our force, but it didn't budge. Fear and panic seized my heart.

"Fuck, it won't open," Orpheus screamed, his fists banging against the door.

"The door won't open from over there," the voice seethed, angrily, threateningly. "And

Foster would have known that you fucking filthy bloodsucker."

I swallowed the lump in my throat.

"You're trapped, so give up," the guard yelled.

My eyes scanned the area, sounds of running footfalls were echoing through the space, and we would be surrounded soon. We would be dead soon. So close to freedom, and it was all going to end.

"There," Alora whispered through clenched teeth. She nodded toward a panel on the wall near where the guard was standing, we'd passed it on our way here. "There is a key, I bet that opens the door."

"We're too fucking far from it now," Orpheus hissed, his eyes reddening and his claws sharpening.

"We could reach it!" She exclaimed.

"That's suicide, Alora! No," Orpheus snapped.

"What the hell are we going to do?" Silas asked, his form slowly returning to normal now the jig was up. His hands ran along the seam of the door searching for a weak spot.

"We were so close!" Laz cried, digging their claws into the metal of the door with no luck.

We were going to die. The horde of guards was almost there. The one guard held a weapon pointed at us, a dark mahogany stake in one hand, a gun in the other. The gun to slow us down, the stake to finish the job. It was the Hunter's method. That or their garlic and holy water mixture. The guard stared at us, his strawberry hair wild and disheveled as he glared at us with determination.

"Nowhere to run, Wanderers," Bennett taunted.

"We could fight our way out." Silas offered, anger pouring off of him.

"Impossible," Orpheus growled.

"Damnit," Laz lamented. They leaned their head against the door, the barrier keeping us from salvation.

Alora turned to face me, her eyes shining with tears. Her hand gripped my face and I reveled in her touch for a brief moment. Her lips crashed against mine and I soaked up her kiss as if I was starving for it. Her tongue pressed against mine and I let myself fall into her arms, kissing my wife with every ounce of promise and love in my body. Telling her everything I couldn't bear to say aloud. A century of thank you's and goodbyes.

If I had to die, at least I would die with her. At least she would know that I loved her. Whatever afterlife was allotted for my kind, I wanted to enter it with her at my side.

She broke our kiss, her cheeks stained with tears. She looked at me with every ounce of the love we shared.

"I love you, Samara," she sobbed.

"I love you too, Alora."

Then she ran.

For the briefest of moments, time slowed and I couldn't comprehend what had just happened. One second, her soft curves were safe in my arms, the next she was sprinting toward the danger.

"Alora! Damnit!" Orpheus called after her, and the world resumed. My wife was making her way across the factory floor toward the horde of guards, toward the panel on the wall. I took a step involuntarily, ready to follow her to the ends of the world.

Arms circled my waist and held me still. I fought against them. "Let me go!" I screamed, but the arms tightened. I watched in rapt horror as my wife dodged a shot fired from the barrel of the guard's gun. "Alora!" I yelled, scratching at the arms that now acted as yet another cage between my chosen and myself.

"Laz, stop him!" I was only vaguely aware of Laz grabbing a hold of Silas beside me who was nearly as feral as I was at the prospect of Alora heading into the fray alone.

"Fucking get your hands off of me. Alora!" Silas screamed, but Laz grunted, forcing their arms around his thrashing form.

"Samara, stop," Orpheus whispered against my ear, but his voice was nothing but noise. My heart felt like at any moment it would rip out of my chest and follow her itself.

Alora managed to make it past the first guard, but he got a shot off just in time to clip her shoulder. She faltered, crying out in pain.

"No!" I shouted.

"She's ok, she's ok," Orpheus chanted and he held steadfast against my attacks, but he didn't sound convinced.

Blood flowed down her arm, coating the floor beneath her as she made her way to the panel at the wall. The room flooded with Hunters, armed and angry. They converged on Alora. She winced as she pushed through them, but despite their persistence, she managed to knock a few down to the ground at her feet.

She threw herself into the wall, her hands gripping the key and twisting it.

"That's it, Alora," Silas whispered beside me, he had stopped fighting Laz, but his voice was full of fear. I understood it. I felt it too.

The door behind us creaked as the mechanisms whirred to life. Cool air brushed against the back of my neck as the door to our freedom slid open.

"Come on, baby, come on," I cried, watching as Alora began her fight back to me. She pushed past more guards, taking a few more hits. Bullets riddled her body, but still, she fought. Silas screamed just as Bennett plunged his stake directly through Alora's heart, her agonizing wail piercing the air. I stopped breathing. The light in her eyes went dim, she fell to her knees. Her hands came up to her chest to feel for the wound. Her eyes met mine and I watched the life drain from her gaze, before she fell to the floor, unmoving.

"Get up!" I shouted. "Get up, baby please!" My throat was raw from my screaming, but I couldn't hear myself, I couldn't hear anything. There was nothing but her form, lying still amongst the Hunters. There was nothing but her. I pulled on the restraints around my waist. I needed to get to her. I needed to save her. I could heal her. I know I could.

"Samara, stop, she's gone." Orpheus cried, his voice broken.

"Silas, please, help us," Laz pleaded. I raged against the hold, managing barely to break free, but just as I began my sprint to my wife, another set of arms grabbed me.

"Please Samara, I can't lose you too." Silas cried into my ear.

"No! Put me down. Let me go! Let me save her," I demanded through my vicious sobs. "Please, I can save her! I can-" I thrashed, but the arms were already dragging me through the door. My view of Alora's body was obscured as the Hunters rushed forward *toward us. Bullets rushed past us, I heard Silas curse as one hit his skin.*

"We have to go, Samara, please," Silas begged, pain lacing every word, every breath. "If we die, her sacrifice will be for nothing." Only then did I rip my gaze from her. Silas' eyes were red, tears painted his face and I saw the pain I felt so vividly mirrored in his expression. I knew he was right, but dammit, I couldn't move. I don't remember the next several minutes, I might have run, I might have been carried. I don't know. All I could see each time I closed my eyes was her face, the shock, the blood, the goodbye. My wife was dead, and I couldn't save her.

I was crying, the image of her death was so vivid in my mind despite the years that have passed since. It had been so long since I'd let myself fully relive that moment, the moment I lost her.

"Samara." Athena's soft melodic voice gripped my hand and pulled me back from the depths of my darkest memory. I blinked away the tears and let my eyes land on her. She had been crying as well, her glassy green eyes looked even more stunning beneath the wet sheen of tears.

"Words will never be enough to make up for what you went through. What you've seen." She started to reach across the island toward me, but I saw her restrain herself and bring her hands back to rest in her lap. I nodded, wiping the tears away with the back of my hand.

"I've been living a half-life since that day," I explained. "I'm not whole, Athena. I haven't been since I lost her."

She nodded, understanding.

"That's why I can't be your mate. Not because I don't care for you, not because I don't want to, but because you don't deserve someone who's broken." I sobbed, the truth of my pain flowing so easily through my painted lips.

She rushed around the island, and pulled me into an embrace, carefully with her injured arm. Her arms held me together as I fell apart. I cried into the crook of her neck and she brushed my hair from my face. Her wintergreen scent enveloped me, soothing the pain in my chest. I clung to her like the lifeline I wished she could be.

"Being broken does not mean you do not deserve love, Samara," she whispered into my hair.

I pulled back from her hold, putting some much-needed space between us. I shook my head and licked my bottom lip. The salty taste of my tears was acidic, a reminder of the death that followed me.

"Please don't try to convince me to change my mind," I begged. The words *'because for you, I would'* remained unsaid.

"I'm not going to force you to love me," she whispered. "I understand why you feel you need to do this, and I'm not going to stop you."

I furrowed my brows. "You're not?"

She shook her head. "No, I'm not." She moved around the island to the coffee maker and poured herself a cup. I watched her move carefully, favoring her good arm, and carefully maneuvering around with her injured one.

She turned and took a slow sip of her drink before moving back to her place on the other side of the island.

"When my mom died, I thought I was going to die right along with her," Athena said eventually, her voice was even and calm.

"I'm sorry for your loss, Athena," I apologized, softly, settling into a bar stool across from her.

"Thank you," she replied, a solemn smile on her lips. "Basically, I'm trying to tell you that you don't have to explain yourself to me. I know it's not the same thing, but if someone showed up out of the blue claiming to be my fated mother, I wouldn't take that very lightly." I inhaled sharply. I had expected the guilt to soften when Athena understood why I had to reject this bond between us, but instead, it grew. The pit in my stomach was painful. The loss of her was growing nearer and I couldn't find the silver lining amongst the growing clouds in my mind.

"All I'm trying to say is that you don't need to worry about me. You don't need to be upset or afraid that you're hurting me," she spoke calmly, but even I noticed the almost imperceptible twitch in her jaw. "I will be ok."

I sighed, not feeling the relief I had wished would come with those words.

"But will you?" Her eyes bore into mine.

"What do you mean?" I asked, a slight defensive edge to my tone.

"Don't mistake my question, I would never push someone to *get over* their grief. I know that's not how it works," she continued. "But you are immortal, Samara."

I couldn't help but notice how she said that with such ease. How far she's come in such a short time.

"You have, thankfully, a lot of life left to live. Resigning yourself to a loveless existence is torture, and I can't bear to think of you putting yourself through that."

"I can't-" was all that escaped my lips.

"You haven't rejected me yet," she started, her voice caught. She exhaled a shaky composing breath and started again. "You haven't rejected me yet, so I'm still your mate." Tears flowed freely down her face and she forced herself to press on. "And if you can't promise yourself to me, can you at least promise that one day - one day when it doesn't hurt as much when you wake up and you can finally breathe again." She struggled to compose herself. "One day when you can think of her without that stabbing pain, you'll be open to love again. Promise me that you'll let yourself love when the time is right. Even if it can't be now. Even if it can't be with me." Her voice cracked on that word, her careful hold on her sobs slipping.

My heart shattered as her words penetrated the shield I'd so carefully constructed around my soul. In her features I saw the hurt, the type I felt every time I thought about leaving her behind and severing this bond the fates have given us.

I closed the gap between us before my mind could catch up to my feet. I held her face in my hands and she leaned into my hold as her tears flowed. And there, staring into her green eyes, it finally hit me just how selfish I had been. It wasn't just me who would be affected by this rejection. It wasn't my pain to carry alone.

This bond was hers as much as it was mine. While I prepared to carve a piece of my heart out and leave it behind, she was going to let me, despite the torture it would cause her. She would do it, without trying to stop me, not because she didn't want to stop me, but because she loved me enough to let me go. I watched her heart break in real time before my eyes, knowing she would never ask me to change my mind because she respected my decision. My heart hummed to life, a heat blooming in my chest. It beat against my ribcage in a solid thump with more promise and hope than I had felt since the night I lost Alora. A giggle escaped my lips at the shock. Athena studied my face inquisitively.

She watched me carefully, a timid expression on her face, but her eyes scanned my face with what could only be described as hope.

When I looked at Athena when I focused on this powerful bond tying her soul to mine a nearly golden thread of connection, I no longer felt the pain of loss and betrayal, but instead, something deeper thrummed inside of me. A soft glimmer of light and memory dancing through my soul in unrestrained tendrils of blood-red passion and love. I closed my eyes, focusing on the tug of that strand of memory that beckoned for me. Asking for my attention. I shut my eyes tight, willing that familiar warmth in my soul to crest to the surface. Begging it to envelop me in its comfort. A whisper in my ear, clear as day.

'You're allowed to love again, my chosen. It's ok.'

I don't believe in ghosts, which may be a tad naive considering I'm a vampire, but I don't believe in souls sticking around long after their bodies have decomposed, but fuck, at that moment in the cozy kitchen of Athena's cottage, I would swear on my very existence that Alora spoke to me. Tears flowed from my eyes and I felt my body shake with a laugh of disbelief. Years of pain and anger and guilt slipped from my body with each exhale. I felt lighter than I had in years.

'Thank you, my chosen,' I whispered back through the channels of my mind. The warmth of her soul flooded through me like a promise.

When my eyes slid open, I saw Athena with an unfiltered gaze for the first time. Her soft red hair, her caring green eyes. Her creamy skin, and lush lips. The bond thrummed between us with a new vigorous life. I could see that golden bond in my mind so clearly, so vividly. And as I exhaled my fear and my pain, I saw that strand of memory, the piece of me that was Alora's, but instead of dissipating into nothingness, it wrapped itself around the bond. A beautiful display of gold and red, a mix of past and future. A reminder that Alora would always be there. No matter who my heart belonged to, she would forever be a piece of it.

My cheeks hurt from the smile that spread across my face. She studied me with careful curiosity, her fingers brushing against my face.

"What happened just now," she asked, quietly. Without accusation or expectation. Just pure worry and care.

"You just brought my heart back to life," I whispered on an exhaled breath, running my thumb along her tear-soaked cheek.

She looked up at me with love and wonder, a soft smile playing on her lips and I couldn't wait a single moment longer. My lips met hers and I poured every ounce of the affection I had been withholding into the kiss. Words that had gone unsaid, moments that had been avoided. The walls were well and truly down now and I sank into her kiss.

She tentatively kissed back for a brief moment, fear coating her tongue. I pulled back and let my breath mingle with hers.

"Is this goodbye?" She asked, breathlessly with an edge of heartbreak in her tone. I wanted to wipe every ounce of trepidation from her face, I wanted to erase every fear from her soul. I wanted to apologize for the pain I put her through by losing myself in her embrace.

"Athena, I can't leave you. I can't believe I even thought for a second that I could," I whispered, planting a kiss on her throat just above her clavicle.

"What are you saying?" She pleaded, leaning her head back to give me more access to her bare skin.

"I'm saying that you are my mate, and I intend to be yours."

She moaned at that confession, the sound causing my core to clench. "What about Alora?" She pressed on my shoulder with her good arm, putting some space between us. Her eyes searched mine.

"She's always going to be with me, I'll always love her. She's here now, in here," I placed a hand over my heart "She will always be my chosen."

Athena's eyes searched mine for hesitation, or worry, but she wasn't going to find it.

"But, for the first time, I'm ready to love again, Athena." The words were a liberation, the key to the cell that I never truly escaped that night. But here, with my mate in my arms and my chosen in my heart, I finally took a full breath of fresh air.

Her smile brightened as tears continued to flow from her eyes, but they were tears of joy, of adoration. She crushed her lips to mine and kissed me back, passion and promise exchanged through our careful touches and selfish lips. I once compared her kiss to the feeling of coming home, and I realize now, as our tongues press against each other that I could not have been more right. Her kiss is transcendent, comforting, and perfect and by indulging in her I feel like I belonged again.

She went to toss her arms around my neck and she groaned in pain. Her lips pulled from mine and she cursed cradling her injured arm.

"Forgot about that," she lamented, with a soft laugh. I reached for her hand, and with a soft smile on my lips, I helped her stand from the stool.

"Where are we going?" She asked, her lips shimmering and freshly kissed. She placed her hand in mine, and gently I led her through her living room, past the baby blue record player, and headed into her bedroom. Her eyes darkened with lust and I struggled to keep my hands to myself as I helped her lie down. Athena's eager breaths came in quick spurts and she leaned back on the comforter. Her chest rose and fell quickly with anticipation. Her eyes watched me with heat burning within her gaze.

"What are you going to do?" She asked, cautiously.

"I'm going to kiss it better," I promised before slowly unbuttoning her jeans. Her breath hitched as I slid them down her legs, leaving just the thin white fabric of her panties behind.

I hovered over her body, letting my breath trail a path along her skin as I climbed up to grab the hem of her shirt. She gasped as I ripped it in half, exposing her perfect breasts.

"Samara," she moaned, and I nearly lost control right there and forgot my current mission, but the bandage on her arm served as a reminder of the more pressing matter.

"Shhh, I'll take care of you," I urged before planting a healing kiss against Athena's chest. Through the point of contact with her skin, I can feel the injuries and their lasting thrums of pain. I plant another kiss on her shoulder, willing my healing touch to wash away the physical trauma. Athena moaned beneath me, writhing in pleasure as I planted another kiss above the bandage on her arm, then below. My fangs threatened to elongate as my lips grazed so close to the wound. The bandage and stitches did nothing to mask her scent, so close to her blood I struggled to keep myself focused and push the hunger down. But as my lips brushed her skin, I felt the full force of the abuse her body had been through and suddenly nothing mattered more than healing her.

My fingers trailed up and down her stomach, brushing delicately against the top of her underwear and the underwire of her bra. She groaned in frustration each time my fingers changed direction, ignoring the source of her desire.

Kiss. Erase the bruise. Kiss. Close the wound. Kiss. Ease the ache. Kiss.

She moved her arm, tentatively, testing the range of motion. Her eyes widened as she realized the pain was gone.

"How did you…" she began, but my lips brushed against her stomach and her words were lost.

"I think you'll be pleasantly surprised to discover what my lips can do, Athena." I chuckled, kissing a trail down her stomach to the seam of her underwear. She groaned a pleasurable sound that had my hands itching to spread her wide.

I placed a soft kiss on the fabric that separated her heat from my mouth and her thighs pressed against my head slightly as her back arched. I gripped her thighs and pressed against her legs forcefully, letting her fall open for me.

"Samara, I need you," she gasped and I let go of the fragile hold I had on my control. Using my slightly elongated fangs, I ripped through the fabric barrier and then delved into her core. She was soaking wet, her arousal pooling at her center, and it was all mine. I slid my tongue through her folds, eliciting the sweetest sounds. I hummed against her, the vibration had her shaking beneath my hold. She writhed beneath me, her eager body pressing into my mouth as she rode me. I focused my tongue on her clit and pushed two fingers into her heat. She let out a scream as her orgasm snuck up on her. I drank every ounce of her release and her breathing slowly returned to almost normal.

I kissed each thigh before sitting up and studying my stunning mate. She was gorgeous, but there was something so elusive and artistic about the way she looked when she was in the throes of passion. I needed to see more. I climbed up her body again, trailing wet kisses across her skin, pausing briefly to slide the fabric of her bra down enough for me to take a nipple in my mouth and roll it along my tongue. She sighed pleasantly, pushing her chest into my mouth.

"I want," she whispered, stopping to moan as my mouth continued its worship of her breasts.

"What do you want, Athena?" I spoke against her skin.

"I want to taste you."

I clenched, my core tightened and desire flooded between my thighs.

"Anything for my mate," I answer, teasing kisses against her exposed skin. She sat up, pressing on my shoulders until I was lying flat on my back on her bed. She eyed me hungrily like I was the prey. And I kind of liked that.

She let her warm breath dance along my skin as she pushed up my sundress, helping me throw it off. Only my pink satin panties remained, her lips brushed against my skin and she kissed up the length of my leg, stopping just at my apex before kissing up the other. I gripped the bedspread in my fist at my side as I fought against the urge to tangle my fingers in her hair and bury her face in my center.

The first drag of her tongue against my panties elicited a scream from my throat. She smiled up at me from her place between my spread legs and dove into my core again, this time sucking on my clit through the fabric.

Her fingers hooked on the top of my panties and finally slid them down my legs, the air brushed against my already sensitive clit and I shivered as Athena leaned toward my core and let her breath dance along my folds.

"Fuck, Athena, please," I begged, and she placed a gentle kiss on the space where my thigh met my hip.

"Does my mate need my mouth?" She whispered, sinfully. I threw my head back and voluntarily pressed my legs open further.

"Yes, I do. Please." Before I finished, her tongue pressed into my folds. Spearing me. I cried out, my fists twisting in the sheets.

She devoured me as if she was starving, and only my arousal could save her.

"Fuck," I exclaimed as she focused her attention on my clit. She dragged her tongue through my folds, lower, lower until it brushed over the tight ring of muscle. I gasped, but her mouth had already made its way back to my center.

With one finger, she pressed circles against my clit, while her tongue entered me and claimed every inch of my pussy. I was nearly lost to bliss, nothing could beat this feeling. But I was wrong. Just as I teetered over the edge of my own release, with her fingers on my clit and her tongue fucking me, she slid a finger to that tight hole. Circling it, spreading my slick arousal around it. I moaned as she pressed in. Devouring me, owning me so completely. When her finger was fully seated in my ass, I exploded around her. Lights and colors flashed in my eyes and I released a scream. Her tongue traced lazy strokes up and down my core as I rode her face, drawing out my orgasm as long as I could.

My hands released their hold on the sheets and I felt my chest heaving, my heart beat again, harder than before and I smiled at the feel of it existing inside of me as something lively and not a useless organ.

Athena crawled until she was resting over me, her lips glistened with evidence of my arousal, and an earth-shattering smile plastered on her face. I pressed my lips against hers and loved the way her taste mingled with mine.

"I want to lose myself in you," she whispered against my lips, and I felt every crack that had ever been in my soul fill with promise.

"I want that too, you have no idea," I started, pressing another kiss to her lips. She moaned and I captured the sound with my mouth, hoping I'd be lucky enough to hear it forever. "But first, if you're willing…." She sat up, her hair falling down her back in waves, as she watched me. "I think there's a bond that needs to be completed."

ARCHER

FOURTEEN

I was moments away from ambushing the house and enacting the plan when the female, Samara, left the house this morning. I cursed under my breath at the lost opportunity. I wasn't dumb enough to think I could have acted through the night, if I was going to survive this, I needed to do it in daylight when its harsh rays might act as another rope around the throat of The Wanderers.

I watched her leave and swore to myself I was going to do it the second she got back. I don't know how long I sat there in the bushes across the street watching the movement within the house, trying to psyche myself up to go through with this.

The stake on my hip burned against my bare skin, and the smoke bombs, specially engineered to release a mixture of garlic and holy water, felt heavy in my palms. Sweat gathered at the nape of my neck, and fear coursed through my veins just as easily as my blood. I was a Hunter, but I didn't want to be.

I wanted to make music and escape from this world where monsters exist and I'm in charge of killing them.

I wasn't cut out for this. No matter how much my father claimed it was in my blood.

The mid-morning sun was bright, I had to use my hand to shield the glare from my eyes. There was a small gathering of people in the clearing. Several trainees, like myself, stood in a row facing the altar. My eyes landed on my father, who stood at the back of the robed figures who faced us. His eyes were light, and he practically beamed with pride from behind his black mask as I stood there, weapon in hand, prepared to make a pledge to spend my life killing vampires.

The man at the front, Doctor Kline Galvin, stood tall. His face was masked, but his eyes scanned us, disapprovingly. He had a Ph.D. in occult studies and never let anyone forget how well-versed he was in the unnatural. The Galvin line had acted as the head of Nameless for as long as the organization had operated in the dark. He held a metal brand over an open flame, slowly rotating it for maximum heating. My father told me once about the brand. Even showed me his, it was this ugly, violent-looking scar that rested between his shoulder blades. Raised angry white lines to form a disfigured image of the Nameless calling card. The symbol of the Hunters. Two triangles, and a wooden stake. He said it had hurt, but the pride in doing what he was born to do far outweighed the pain. He said it would be the same for me.

One by one, my classmates made their way up to the altar, exchanging whispered words with Dr. Galvin. Then he would lower the heated metal to their skin. The sound was an almost evil-sounding sizzle, it made my stomach churn. But what was worse was the smell, an acrid scent of burning flesh. I forced myself to breathe only through my mouth. A few of my classmates screamed as the brand scarred their skin. Their cries of pain were met with disapproving looks from the council. Then it was my turn.

I begged my hands not to shake as I made my way across the clearing to come to a stop in front of Dr. Galvin. His dark blue eyes passed over me with interest as he leaned forward.

"Your father assures me you will be one of the greatest assets Nameless has ever seen." His voice was rough and textured, and I could almost feel its bass rumbling in my chest.

I couldn't find my voice so I simply nodded.

"Hmmm," he mused, leaning back and scanning me again. "I hope he was not lying." I swallowed carefully, hoping he could not see the fear in my eyes. Suddenly, I was thankful I had a mask on. It hid the way my teeth bit into my bottom lip to keep my whimper from escaping.

"Archer, son of Jacob Bennett, do you swear your oath today to Nameless, and pledge your life to protect this world from the creatures of the night?" He asked in a loud whisper.

I bowed my head, silently begging my voice to remain calm even as I responded, "Nisi nox."

He motioned for me to offer him the bare section of flesh for the brand as he lifted the metal rod from the fire. I swallowed, and slowly unbuttoned my shirt, sliding it off to offer him my shoulder. Right where my father's mark was.

I didn't get a warning before the searing brand made contact with my skin. The pain was so absolute and so overwhelming. I waited, begging for the pride to eclipse the pain the way my father swore it would.

But it never did.

And so I just burned.

Sometimes when I was especially stressed I would mindlessly rub the scar on my wrist, the bite mark I garnered from trusting Evangeline all those years ago. The ugly, raised white lines reminded me so vividly of the brand that sat on my shoulder blade. Yet one came from the villains and one came from the heroes.

How thin was the line between the two?

After an hour or so, I watched as the female vampire returned back to her den, but just as I began to prepare for the attack, I stopped dead in my tracks. Athena was standing next to her, hand in hand. Her face brightened with a smile. The vampire stopped just outside the house, twirling Athena in her arms, and embracing her, pressing her lips against her throat. I nearly jumped out from my hiding space to save her, but she did not scream, she did not cry out. Because the vampire did not bite her, no, she simply kissed her.

My mind swam with questions and confusion. Had Athena fallen so deep into their trap? Or was she seeing something I couldn't? The two of them laughed, and I could hear the melodic sound dance in the wind. It was a carefree, happy sound. Not the sound of someone who was at the mercy of monsters.

They disappeared into the house, and I strained to listen for the tell-tale sound of death and destruction. Waiting for her to scream for help. But it never came.

Minutes passed in silence. I was frozen in indecision. An hour had come and gone before I made a choice.

I tossed my weapons into my pack, and slung it over my shoulder, setting off down the road.

I couldn't very well do the job with a human inside anyway.

But as I walked away, leaving Athena in that house felt like a death sentence, no matter how smitten these creatures seemed. They were still monsters and Athena wasn't safe. She'd never be safe. She was a human amongst monsters.

I stood at the end of the street, the road out of Shockgrove taunting me. I could just leave, leave Nameless, leave Athena, leave this fool's quest to capture The Wanderers. I could start over somewhere far away. Without monsters, without death.

Even as I thought it, the reality of my situation slammed into me. Nameless could track a coven of elusive and powerful vampires, if I thought for even a moment that they couldn't find me if they chose to, I was an idiot. No, like it or not, this was my life, and according to my father, if I didn't act on this task soon, my life very well could reach a rather abrupt end.

My heart clenched and beat against my chest as I glanced back at the house. Athena was inside a vampire den. Her vulnerable human blood was there for the drinking. Something very similar to grief flashed across my emotions. It's only been a few days, but something about her makes me feel like a real person. Her companionship and conversation have brought me more hope and normalcy than I ever thought I'd be able to find. I cared about her, and I cared about her safety.

These vampires looked like they were in love with her. I heard them call her their mate. If that was true, were they going to claim her? Turn her? Kill her? I gripped the stake at my side just as my phone vibrated.

I didn't need to check the caller ID to know who it was.

"Bennett," I offered, calmly, not drawing my eyes from the house.

"What the fuck is taking you so long," he spat. I winced at the harshness of his words. And then sighed at the unfortunate familiarity of the tone.

"This coven escaped Nameless, slipped through the hands of dozens of highly trained Hunters, and you expect me - alone, I might add - to do the job the Hunters couldn't?" I bit back. My father's silence was evidence of how infrequently I challenged him.

A long moment passed before he sighed. "You're right." The phone nearly fell from my grasp at that admission. One I'd never heard from his lips, and doubted I'd ever hear again. "Galvin is getting restless. He sent a group to a nearby town. They are zeroing in on The Wanderers, and I want you to complete this before they interfere." He sounded so desolate, so worried this was the last chance either of us had to set things right. I slid my hand through my hair in frustration.

"I know, I'm trying. Things just…" I glared off toward the house, "got a little complicated."

"How so?" He asked.

"There's a woman here, human. They seem to have taken a liking to her." I hated talking about Athena like a pawn in this long-winded game.

"Are they drinking from her?" He inquired so nonchalantly like he was asking about the weather.

"No," I replied. I had tried not to be obvious or creepy about it, but I scanned all the places on her skin I could see in her hospital gown. There were no noticeable bite marks. "I think."

"Hmm," he mused. "Have you tried to use her to lure them to one place?"

I had to forcibly avoid growling at that concept. I hated that, at first, that had been my intention. Now that I know her, I couldn't imagine using her like that. Shame clouded my senses.

"She is a human, Dad. Or have you forgotten that we are supposed to be protecting them?" I seethed, quietly. Barely containing the anger that bubbled under the surface.

"And you know as well as I do that one human life in exchange for millions is worth it every time."

I let my arm fall to my side, my phone dangling by my thigh as I took a steadying breath. Once I had composed myself enough not to scream at my father, I brought the phone to my ear again.

"What have I taught you?" He prompted. "You -"

"You are only ever safe in this world if you fight for your safety," I finished, dejectedly.

"That's right, son. Don't forget it."

I hung my head.

"When do you think you can make your move?"

I glanced back up at the house. The place where, at that very moment, all four of the remaining Wanderers were inside, undoubtedly distracted by the human that seemed to capture their fancy.

"Today," I whispered, but the word felt like ash on my tongue.

"Then I'll see you tomorrow."

"What about the human?" I asked, careful not to give away how much I had come to care for this particular human.

"If she's dead, ensure you are not implicated."

I winced, the mental picture of Athena lying dead on the floor, her green eyes lifeless, pierced me.

"And if she isn't dead?" I should have talked to her. Should have told her everything. She doesn't understand. I could have helped her understand. Kept her far away from these creatures. She would be safe.

"Don't let her see you. Knock her out if you have to." I nearly protested, but I knew what he would say. He would see how attached I'd become to her, he'd see right through me.

"Ok," was all I could say.

"Do not mess this up, Archer," he concluded before hanging up. No words of advice, or encouragement.

My goodbye hung dead on my tongue. Pocketing the phone, I slid my pack off my shoulders and reached inside for the materials I would need to feasibly complete this job. My truck was parked just off the street. The tarps were prepared to cover any cargo in the bed. My throat seemed to close with the reality of what I was about to do.

I could only hope Athena would understand why I had to do this, that she would forgive me for disappearing on her without an explanation. If she was even still alive after being subjected to whatever sick torture those vamps had planned for her. I wish I could be here to protect her. To help her in the aftermath.

With one last composing breath and a mindless trace of my fingers across the bite mark on my wrist, I headed toward the house.

ATHENA

FIFTEEN

I didn't know what to expect when Samara came over this morning. Heartbreak, pain, tears. That's what I had my money on. That's the fear that starred in my dreams last night. Never in my wildest imagination did I think we would share such a cathartic moment and release our inhibitions. Never did I think she would accept me as her mate.

But she did. My heart was almost too full, I was afraid it might burst. I felt my pulse in every inch of my body as Samara and I got dressed. It wasn't lost on me that Samara choosing to stay, also meant the obstacle that stood between Orpheus and me was now gone. A shiver wracked through me.

The bond.

I was about to complete a bond with four vampires.

My four vampire mates.

And I couldn't feel anything except excitement.

There was still the question of how long this bond would last. I didn't know if I was particularly interested in giving up my mortality to become a vampire. But all I know was my soul yearned for theirs and I deserved to indulge in the pleasure of them for as long as I could.

Samara led me through the streets of Shockgrove, a town I'd known my whole life. A town where I have lived, lost, cried, healed, and learned to trust again. The lighthouse stood as a beacon against the purple midday sky. The slightly chilled air caressed my cheek, and I couldn't help but think it was my mother's warm comforting embrace, telling me she was proud of me.

Samara's hand in mine felt like an anchor, holding me steady. I followed her down the sidewalk and came to the overwhelming realization that I would probably follow her anywhere she asked me to.

That thought should have terrified me, but no matter how hard the little voice in my head tried to pierce through the happiness I'd crafted for myself, there was nothing but bliss.

She twirled me, our melodic laughter mixing to create a sound so fucking pure I almost cried. Her lips grazed my throat, and I released a content sigh. There was something so right about her lips on my skin.

"Are you ready for this?" She asked, her breath dancing across my exposed throat. I let my hands trace a path along her back. "We don't have to do this if you're not sure." Her reassurance wasn't needed, but I enjoyed having it nonetheless.

I smiled brightly. "I'm sure."

Her dark eyes glistened with something that looked like pride, then she gripped my hand and pulled me onto the porch of a beautiful white beach house. Each step closer had my heart beating quicker until I almost wasn't sure it was beating at all.

Stepping through the threshold, I instantly felt enveloped by their presence. Their scents were so strong here, so saturated with their essence. It was intoxicating, sensual. I took a long languid breath, inhaling every ounce of them I could.

The living room looked positively touristy, and I stifled a laugh thinking about Orpheus willingly sitting next to a decorative bowl of seashells.

My eyes trailed along the walls, taking in the paintings, and tapestries when the hair on the back of my neck stood at attention. Goosebumps erupted across my exposed flesh, and I knew without a doubt they were there. My mates. I felt their eyes on me as if it were a physical touch. I bit my bottom lip, closing my eyes to revel in the sensation as their gaze caressed me.

When my eyes opened, I saw them.

Silas was leaning suggestively against the doorframe across the room, his arms folded in front of his chest offering me a clear view of the climbing serpents starkly contrasting against his cream skin. His honey eyes watched me with a hint of hunger, in every sense of the word. Laz had come to a stop on the staircase and sat down on one of the steps. Their hands were clasped in front of them as if they were holding themselves back. Their face was painted with a tortured expression. My eyes trailed up, landing on Orpheus, who was watching me from a perch on the second floor. He wore dark dress pants and a black button-down, but the top two buttons were undone and his tie hung loosely around his neck. Disheveled was a delicious look on him.

But just as I was admiring them, and the way their gazes trailed delicate passes across my skin, I heard a growl.

"Samara, she shouldn't be here right now." Orpheus. My eyes snapped to him. Looking closer now, I noticed his hands were gripping the railing in front of him, nearly digging into the wooden banister. Flicking my eyes to Laz, they weren't much better, their nails pressing into their skin as they forced their hands to remain clasped in front of them.

Looking over to Silas, I saw the tenseness of his shoulders more clearly now, the way his face was twisted.

I was wrong, they weren't just hungry.

They were starving.

"How bad is it?" I asked, my voice a timid whisper.

Samara put a gentle but firm hand on my shoulder and moved to stand between the others and me. Her body was rigid and poised. Fear clenched my heart. Not fear that I would be hurt, but that I was too late.

"The scent of you feels like barbed wire in my fucking throat," Silas whispered, his voice was animalistic, devoid of his typical cocky attitude.

"What were you thinking, Samara?" Laz lamented, grunting through held breath. "She's not safe right now."

"There was blood left this morning," Samara rasped, her body tensed.

"Half a flask," Silas growled, his body straightening. Samara put an arm out in front of me.

"Calm down, you need to get a handle on yourselves before you do something you might regret," Samara insisted, with an edge of worry. I felt my breath coming in ragged pants.

"Why did you bring her here?" Orpheus asked, his hunger slightly more restrained than the others, but there was an obvious hunger there.

"Because she is ready to accept the bond," Samara relented. I heard sharp gasps from Silas and Laz. Orpheus sighed deeply, his head falling forward.

"Fuck," Silas exclaimed, but it was not flirtatious, or even loving. He took a step forward like a predator. I stood my ground.

"Silas, back up." Samara had put her hand up, commanding him to cease his trek forward.

When I glanced back at the stairs, Laz was standing, their eyes full of guilt as they watched me. They were so close to losing every ounce of control they had.

"They need to drink," I whispered to Samara.

"They can't, not like this," she replied over her shoulder, without tearing her gaze from the others.

"Why not?" I asked.

"Because we're too hungry to control ourselves, Athena," Orpheus declared from his place above us all. "If we tried to feed on you-" I didn't miss the way his throat bobbed as he swallowed roughly at the thought. "In this condition, we wouldn't be able to stop."

A shadow of fear settled over me.

"You won't hurt me," I claimed, but it was met with a scoff.

"You have no idea what you're talking about," Orpheus spat as Silas and Laz continued to take stalking steps forward. Samara took a step back, herding me toward the door.

"You won't hurt me," I repeated with fervor. Deep down, despite their hungry gazes, and sharpening teeth, I knew it was true beyond a shadow of a doubt.

"We could kill you!" Orpheus screamed, his raspy timber echoing throughout the house. Laz and Silas were closer now, their closeness sent a shiver of anticipation where there should have been an air of caution.

"Samara, drink from me," I ordered. Her eyes darted over her shoulder to me in a brief display of confusion.

"If they smell your blood they won't be able to stop themselves." She turned back to face Laz and Silas. "We.. we won't be able to stop."

"You will. I trust you."

Samara groaned, and I saw her willpower waver. She wanted it, as much as they did.

"Samara, don't," Orpheus commanded, anger pouring off of him.

"Samara, do it," I reiterated, my eyes meeting Orpheus'. He pleaded back at me in silent gazes. Was I making a mistake? No, I don't think I was. I was listening to my heart, and trusting this bond thrumming between us.

"You won't hurt me." I said again, and as my eyes locked on Orpheus, I felt Samara turn to face me. Her eyes were ravenous, her careful composure slipping with every passing second. Laz and Silas stood flanking her.

Tearing my eyes from Orpheus, I stared at the stunning woman before me. Her chest heaved as she took me in, her eyes reddening.

"Do it."

The first strike of her fangs against the skin of my wrist was unlike anything I'd ever experienced. The mixture of pain and pleasure was so overwhelming I whimpered at the intrusion. Samara was locked on my arm, her mouth closed over the wound. Her eyes were closed as she drank, and as I watched her, my heart exploded with emotion. Every moment with Samara passed through my mind.

I put a hand on her cheek and silently begged for her eyes to meet mine. She opened them, and finally, the red orbs met mine, a moment later, she pulled her fangs from my skin. Her tongue darted out to lap up the traces of my blood that remained on her lips.

I leaned in, kissing her and loving the unfamiliar taste of copper.

When I opened my eyes, Silas and Laz were transformed, their ears tapered off to points, their nails elongated. I reached for them, the overwhelming desire to connect with them overpowering any hesitance. Silas reached me first. His hand snaked up to grab my throat, a gasp escaped my lips at the shock of his touch and his burning stare. His nails didn't puncture the skin, but their pressure offered a sort of delicious danger to his hold. He tilted my neck back, forcing my breasts to push forward toward him. His fingers tightened around my windpipe, as he released a feral growl. Silas' fangs connected with the skin above the swell of my breast just as the edges of my vision began to blur. My hands came up to his head, tangling in his long dark tresses. My heart was beating out of control, pumping blood directly into his willing mouth. Just when the pressure on my throat reached critical mass, it disappeared. I gulped down greedy gasps of air, as he continued his indulgence. My breathing returned to normal and I glanced down at this perfect man, this stunning creature. His mouth had not relented. I kissed Silas on the forehead and whispered.

"You won't hurt me."

His eyes flashed up to me, as I watched the internal battle he fought against his own insatiable hunger, but soon enough his honey irises emerged victorious, and he took a step back. His mouth was painted dark red, and I watched it with my own hunger, my chest heaving in time with his.

I turned my head and reached for Laz. Laz jolted forward at the beckoning and dropped to their knees in front of me. Their clawed hands tore at the hem of my shirt, raising it just enough to clasp onto the flesh at my hip. A cry of euphoria escaped my lips as the point of contact sent jolts through my entire body, this sensual action so close to my core had my walls tightening with ecstasy. I was so fucking close to a release from the deliciously torturous connections with my mates. My toes curled as I held them to me, beckoning them to drink. They sucked my blood down eagerly, grunts of passion pervading the air. I leaned my head back, enjoying the way Laz's hands gripped my thighs and pulled me into their hold. Their tongue brushed across the bite as they drank which had me nearly begging for the release that was just teetering on the edge of my senses. My hands came to a rest on their shoulders, digging my own fingertips into the hardened flesh there.

Once my hand brushed against their skin, they pulled back, a look of fear and disgust on their face at the thought they could have hurt me as they reverted to their human form. I smiled down at them, hoping they could see just how happy I was, how perfectly and utterly content I felt. My body ached from the explosion of emotions, I felt this connection to each of them solidify and crystallize. I was seeing their features more clearly, feeling their breath as if it were my own. I was wound so tight, my desire built so precariously, I feared a subtle gust of wind might be enough to topple me into oblivion.

I felt my warm blood sliding across my skin from the stinging wounds on my body, but I couldn't focus on that as my eyes tracked Orpheus stalking down the steps toward me. Silas, Laz, and Samara were watching me with rapt attention, I could feel them so intimately, as I waited for my final mate to claim me.

He somehow managed to keep his transformation restrained, only the darkened corners of his eyes and the elongated fangs gave away just how fragile his control truly was. He was beautiful, they all were, in this almost half form. Lethal, and powerful. A mixture of human and vampire. Beautifully monstrous humanity. When I saw them now, I saw creatures worthy of the second chance at life they've been given. I saw creatures who deserve love, acceptance, and passion. And I was going to give it to them.

When he reached me, his head lowered to the wound on my breast, where Silas had claimed me, and his tongue darted over the bite, a long languid lick. I moaned wildly, ravenous for him. He gripped my arm in his hand and lifted my bleeding wrist to his mouth, repeating the process. His control was slipping with each and every second, I saw the monster begin to take hold as he sank to his knees and tasted Laz's mark on my skin.

All four of my mates released a guttural groan of pleasure and pain all in one as I gasped.

Orpheus was on his feet again in an instant, the creature well and truly taken over, and before I could comprehend it, his fangs were buried in the skin of my neck, at the hollowed space where my shoulder met my throat. I screamed out as my orgasm wracked through me. I was lost in the blinding pleasure, feeling the bond snap into place as if it were some tangible thing. My legs quivered, from passion or blood loss, I wasn't sure. But it was a type of pleasure I couldn't even begin to describe. There was only his mouth on my skin. Only the bonds from my mates. There was only us.

As I slowly recovered from the release, I felt the painful draw of my blood into his mouth, and the blend of pleasure and pain began to lean towards pain.

"Orpheus," I whispered, putting my hand on his cheek. He didn't respond, didn't remove his fangs from my skin. "Orpheus, listen to me." I glanced over his shoulder to Samara, Laz, and Silas who were frozen in their place, watching the blood pour from beneath Orpheus' mouth. "It's me," I whispered, feeling suddenly lightheaded.

The others didn't see my concern, instead, they simply watched with hunger as my last mate drank from me. "Orpheus," I commanded, my voice raised, I felt my strength wane, as my consciousness started slipping away. "It's me, Athena. Your mate. Please." I gasped as the pain increased. "Please!" It was a whimper, a cry, but he heard me. The pain subsided as he withdrew his fangs from my veins. He darted away, leaving me standing up against the wall alone. His back was turned to me, but I could see his turmoil. The guilt, the shame.

I struggled to maintain my balance, using the wall behind me as a steadying force. Silas, Laz, and Samara watched me, their eyes full of worry, but the careful grasp they had on their monsters kept them at a distance. I stepped forward, strength returning to me with each stride across the floor. As I passed, I felt Silas, Laz, and Samara fall in line behind me. Flanking me. Following me.

My hand came to a rest on his shoulder and he spun to face me, inhumanly fast, but I didn't blink. I stood my ground in front of him, his dark hair was wild and his face was locked in the visage of his creature. Red eyes, long fangs, pointed ears, vicious claws.

Most would shy away from him, many probably have.

I did once.

But not anymore.

I lifted my arm, bringing my palm to press against his cheek. His skin was smooth and cold to the touch. He groaned, it was an angry sound but he leaned into the touch.

"I almost drank too much," he seethed, in that vicious-sounding voice. I shook my head.

"But you didn't." He closed his eyes taking shallow breaths.

"I could have killed you," he sobbed, his clawed hands in fists at his side. I gripped his tie in my free hand and pulled him closer.

"But you didn't."

His red eyes were darting around the room, looking everywhere but at me. No matter how hard he tried, he couldn't regain control.

"Orpheus. Name four things you can see." He exhaled incredulously, nearly scoffing, but his breathing didn't slow. "Now."

He struggled to focus on something, anything, and I watched him closely as he forced his eyes to focus on his surroundings. "Samara," he began. I nodded, a soft smile playing on my lips at the name of my mate. "Silas, Laz," he continued and I brushed my thumb against his sharp cheekbones. His eyes landed on mine. Settling for the first time. "You."

"Three things you can smell," I prompted. He struggled to sniff in one smooth breath, his chest still heaving, but the fists at his side had come unclenched.

"The ocean," he said. I glanced over his shoulder at the waves that lazily crept up the beach toward the house. "Blood," he relented, his eyes locking on the wound at my neck, but just as I worried he was reverting back into his panic, his eyes found mine again, the red irises slipping away to reveal his dark black eyes. "You."

I rewarded him with a soft brush of my thumb against his lips, finding my blood there. He moaned.

"Two things you can feel," I whispered, watching in awe as the tips of his ears slowly rounded in front of my eyes.

"The ground under my feet." He smirked and I felt my eyes sting with unshed tears. "You."

"One thing you can -"

His lips were on mine before I could finish, his kiss was possessive and full of unspoken promises. His tongue begged for entrance and I moaned into his kiss at the metallic tangy taste of my blood on his lips. My fingers tangled in his hair and I pressed my body against him, feeling warmth bloom in my core.

He pulled back, breathlessly resting his forehead against mine. "I almost lost you," he sighed. I held him tighter.

"But you didn't."

He pressed another quick kiss on my lips before leaning his head down to my throat, and the exposed wound there. His tongue darted out to taste it and I threw my head back to give him better access. He was in control, I felt it in every ounce of my body. This was Orpheus.

When he lifted his head, he smiled over my shoulder at my other mates who had been watching closely.

"Are you still hungry?" I asked aloud for them all.

"I'll always be hungry for you," Orpheus offered, sending a blush to my face. "But I am in control now."

I looked over my shoulder at the others, waiting for their response.

"I feel better than I ever have," Silas whispered, and Laz nodded in agreement.

"You were everything I needed." Samara brushed her hand against my arm, and I shivered.

I turned to face them fully, leaving one hand resting on Orpheus' chest.

"But we took too much," Samara lamented, her eyes full of worry as they scanned me,

"That was reckless," Laz interjected, guilt painted on their expression.

"I'm so sorry," Silas added at the same time.

I put a hand up to stop them. "I don't want your apologies or worries."

They watched me as I met each of their gazes. Seeing passion and power in Orpheus, care and love in Samara, adoration and trust in Laz, and desire and certainty in Silas. My mates. Standing here now, between them, I realized I never knew what belonging felt like. Like Laz, I'd been wearing this town and my past like an ill-fitting pair of shoes, but now with them at my side, with this bond burning so strongly in my soul, and suddenly I'd finally found my size. An unfamiliar feeling pulsed between us, something I can only really describe as magic.

"What do you want then, little nymph?" Orpheus asked in a dark, sinfully sensual tone.

"I want my mates to claim me as theirs, now and forever."

Silas was the first to move, his lips crashing against mine in a clash of tongue and teeth. I felt Laz pressing up behind me, their lips placing eager kisses against my shoulder. A hand gripped my jaw, drawing me away from Silas. Samara leaned in, replacing his lips with hers, her tongue danced along the seam on my mouth begging for entry. I moaned into her lips as Silas lifted my shirt enough to capture one of my hardened nipples in his mouth.

I opened my eyes to find Orpheus watching us with ravenous attention. A dangerous smirk on his red-tinted lips.

He leaned back against the kitchen island and studied us. Seemingly perfectly content to enjoy this from the sidelines. I'd let him, for now.

"Do you want your mates to play our little game with you, baby girl?" Silas teased against my breast, his cool breath on the moistened skin sending shockwaves through my body. I nodded. His teeth clenched around the peak, and I winced. "What do you say?"

Samara broke our kiss to look at Silas, her gaze curious. I smiled at her before turning my taunting gaze to Silas. "Yes, sir." I heard every single one of my mates groan as those words crossed my lips and I was struck with how much power I had over them. They may be nearly indestructible immortal beings, but they were falling at my feet.

"Why don't you tell them what our safeword is," he commanded, darkly.

"Blood," I whispered. Orpheus ran a hand down his face to stifle a moan, the evidence of his arousal straining against his dress pants.

"Very good, baby girl. Now do us a favor and take off your clothes." Silas stood back, offering glances to Samara and Laz in a request for them to do the same. Laz obeyed quickly and eagerly, and despite the slight hesitation in Samara's movements, the heat in her gaze told me she wanted this moment with me, with all of us.

"Who knew you were such a bossy lover, Silas," Samara teased.

Silas winked at me. "Athena knew."

I felt my face flush as I reached for the hem of my shirt to pull it off over my head. I savored every hitch of breath and soft moan. As I stripped down, I was not ashamed or afraid of my nakedness, there was an empowering sort of magic to the way they watched me. Silas growled, a sort of darkness to his stare.

"Touch yourself, baby girl. Show us how ready you are for us," Silas commanded. I bit my bottom lip, humming with appreciation at how the words made me feel.

My hands trailed down the planes of my stomach, inching lower, torturously. I ached to be touched, but I wanted to savor each second of their attention.

My fingers reached the apex of my thighs and I dipped them into the warmth of my folds. I groaned at the sensitvity I found at my clit. Drawing my fingers through my slick wetness there a few times and relishing the feeling, I tossed my head back and let the sounds tumble from my lips. I withdrew my fingers just long enough to hold them out for Silas. He stepped forward, capturing them in his mouth. Both of us groaned.

"Enough playing around, Silas," Orpheus called from his spot near the island. He was collected, his ever-present composure firmly in place, but I could see just how much this was affecting him.

"What do you say, baby girl? Are you ready to be fucked by your mates?"

All I could do was nod. I was blind with desire, there was nothing but them and their bodies. I needed them like I needed oxygen.

Silas smiled and lifted me by my thighs, urging me to wrap my legs around him. He stalked over to the couch and slowly lowered me onto the cushions, my head rested on the arm and I watched him with bated breath. I felt Laz and Samara follow after, but Orpheus stayed put, his eyes trailing me. Watching.

"I'm going to give you my cock while Samara sits on your face and you're going to use those perfect fingers of yours to get Laz ready," Silas rattled off with a sinful eagerness. I was so wound up I felt like my body was a livewire just waiting to detonate.

Silas and Laz stripped down, revealing their toned bodies. Laz looked like the picture of Southern comfort. Soft toned arms and a hard planed stomach, their golden skin on full display. Silas' tattoos never ceased to stun me. The dark trails of ink covered most of his torso, dancing down his arms and traveling lower on his body to his perfect length. I didn't want to think about how painful that might have been, but the design made him look so dangerous, so forbidden. It was enough to have me whimpering for him.

He settled between my open legs and gripped his cock in his fingers, pressing it lightly against my opening. His other hand gripped my thigh, holding me open for him.

He pushed in, inch after delicious inch, and I cried out at the welcome intrusion. He cursed under his breath as he seated himself fully inside of me. My walls stretched to accommodate him.

Laz came to a stop near my torso, dipping their head to take a nipple into their mouth. They worshiped the hardened peak with their cold tongue and I felt the shiver rush through my entire body. My fingers wrapped around their hardened length and they hummed appreciatively as I gave them languid strokes. I arched off the couch just as Silas withdrew nearly to the tip only to slam back into me again. Before I could cry out, Samara situated herself above me on the arm of the couch and lowered herself to my mouth. I drank up her arousal as eagerly as she drank my blood, and she rocked back and forth, riding me for her pleasure.

Every inch of my body was electrified by pleasure. I'd never felt this aware, this adored. As Silas pounded into me, Samara slid her sweet pussy along my willing lips. I quickened my strokes on Laz's length and they continued to taste my nipples.

The connection that thrummed between us, so completely obvious and strong now, was pulsing with lust, intensifying the emotions. Samara's breathing quickened and her fingers tangled in my hair as she neared her release. I sucked her clit into my mouth, and she cried out, her orgasm bursting within her.

Silas picked up his pace, his cock hitting the deepest parts of my body with each thrust. "You take me so well, baby girl," he grunted as he slammed into me. Samara stood from my face and I took gulps of fresh air, ragged and panting as Silas continued his delicious torture. I flicked my eyes to Laz who understood what I wanted and moved closer so I could take their length into my mouth. I let my tongue swirl around the head, and Laz moaned, the muscles in their abdomen twitching, eager to thrust into my hot willing mouth, but they restrained. I reached for their hips and pulled them into me, taking as much of them as I could into my throat.

"Oh, Athena," they whispered, a sound of passion, of adoration. I loved it so much. Their fingers caressed my face and I worked their length.

"You look stunning with their cock in your mouth and Samara's cum on your lips," Silas growled, their control slipping as they pressed in again and again. Their pace was relentless and eager. I cried out, the sound muffled by Laz's cock. Silas' fingers dug into my hips as he drove into me chasing that high, I felt him tense and pulse as he found his release. A string of expletives tumbled from his lips as he emptied himself inside of me.

I picked up my pace on Laz's length, their hands brushing loving touches across my forehead.

"You are the most perfect creature I'd ever seen," Silas whispered before withdrawing from me. The absence of him made me whimper, the vibration jolting through Laz. They moaned.

"Samara," Silas ordered, breathlessly. I couldn't see what they were doing, but a moment later, Samara had situated herself between my legs, straddling me. Her core was inches from mine. I mewled in anticipation.

She pressed her core to mine and the first brush of her clit against mine sent me tumbling into an orgasm that she rode out, the friction was so delicious, so intense that a second release came slamming into me before I'd even recovered from the second. Laz had lost control of the gentle lover and was thrusting into my mouth forcefully, and I swallowed each inch happily. With Samara dragging her slick folds against mine, she cried out, reaching another release quickly and a salty taste erupted against my tongue as Laz followed suit, spilling themselves into my throat. I swallowed every precious drop. When Laz stepped back, and Samara stood, I felt utterly used and satisfied, but still, a deep ache burned in my stomach. My eyes flicked over to where Orpheus stood. Somewhere during all that, he had lost his dress pants and unbuttoned his black shirt, it hung open to reveal his trim physique. Hard planes of muscle and a soft dusting of hair. My eyes trailed down to his erect and exposed cock as his hand trailed careful strokes down its length.

His eyes were locked on mine as he stalked forward. When he reached me, he knelt down, stealing a kiss from my lips. "That was the most beautiful thing I've ever seen," he whispered against my kiss-swollen lips. "Now it's my turn."

My thighs clenched at the promise.

"I will love watching you with them, little nymph. I could do that for the rest of my life. Seeing you take your pleasure from them. Cry out as they work your body." I smiled, and I heard the others release a soft sigh. "But when you are with me, I will not share." He moved to position himself behind me on the couch, spooning me. He lifted my leg and carefully adjusted our position. I could feel the press of his length against my slick opening and I gasped. "I will wait my turn, I will watch you ride all three of them for hours if that's what you want. But when it is my turn, you're mine and mine alone." Silas chuckled, lightly.

"Do you understand?" Orpheus asked, pressing slowly into me, the feel of him drove me wild.

"I do," I whispered.

"Leave it to him to be possessive." I heard Silas offer in a teasing tone.

I almost retorted, but then Orpheus was sliding home. This position made it so I could feel him so deep inside of me. His arm wrapped around my waist as he controlled our pace. A slow, torturous tempo. I tried to speed up, but his hands remained steadfast, forcing us to revel in this.

"God damn, baby girl," Silas vocalized, his eyes watching the place where Orpheus and I were joined with a look of wonder and lust.

Orpheus slid his fingers down to brush against my clit and I felt my release cresting again. He worked me slowly, savoring the feel of my walls tightening around him. His lips pressed against my throat, where his fangs had just claimed me. I released a heady sigh as his fingers continued their worship of my clit.

Each careful thrust of his cock into me was a promise. A reminder of who I belonged to.

My orgasm exploded claiming my body, and I was vaguely aware of him following me over the cliff of passionate oblivion.

When my breathing slowed and my heart rate returned to normal, I felt the weight of exhaustion for the first time as well as the light ache of exertion in my muscles. But above all of that, I felt the bond. This love, this connection. It gave me strength. I wondered how I'd ever gone without it. Orpheus stood from the couch, and I rolled back, resting my tired limbs.

Laz's hands were first to touch me, a gentle caress against my cheek. The four of them helped me dress and gave me a glass of water. I promised them I was fine, but they fawned over me nonetheless, and I felt like my heart might burst from the rush of love.

The others took seats near me around the living room, their hair perfectly mused, their chests rising and falling with content breaths. I looked around the room, studying them. My mates. How lucky was I to find people that not only knew my body as if it were their own, but made me feel so safe, and so protected?

"Your bites aren't bleeding anymore," I stated.

"Our saliva counteracts the bite," Samara said, a soft smile on her lips. "When we take the time to lick the wound it will disappear entirely, as if nothing happened. We always do. It's like an unspoken vampire rule to close the wounds before leaving." I felt my heart clench with fear and disappointment that my bites might not have left a permanent mark on anything other than my soul, but my eyes flicked down to my wrist, where Samara had made her claim. To my satisfaction, there was still a mark there, evidence of our connection, but it wasn't a bite mark as I anticipated. Instead, raised white lines formed an outline of hanging wisteria circled my wrist climbing up toward the elbow in a gorgeous fine-line design. Like a white ink tattoo on my skin, the floral pattern was stunning, and so perfectly Samara. She watched me as I brushed a finger across it. As I did. I felt her. Intimately, as if by touching this mark I could focus on the bond I had with her and her alone.

I lifted the hem of my shirt to see Laz's mark on my hip. Climbing up my upper thigh and just above my hip bone was a white design of the phases of the moon. Changes and exploration. Something new. Laz beamed at me with pride and honor as I stroked the design and felt that connection burn brighter.

I stood from the couch and moved to the mirror which was fastened on the wall between the two front windows. Immediately my eye flashed to the lightning strike that spanned the right side of my throat. Starting from the base of my ear to the top of my shoulder, white disjointed lines decorating the surface stared back at me. My fingertips brushed it and Orpheus pushed to the forefront of my mind.

Finally, I pulled at the neck of my shirt, revealing the loosely coiled serpent design that sat just below my left clavicle. Its detailed scales were so intricate. I ran a touch along the snake's body and suddenly my senses focused on Silas.

"They're gorgeous," I uttered, holding in sobs of pure happiness.

"How do you feel?" Laz asked carefully.

"Like I have a family again." They looked back at me with matching gazes of love. My heart was beating for them, and theirs for me. I could feel them through the bonds that decorated my body as if they were merely extensions of myself.

The sound of breaking glass echoed through the house as both windows shattered. I bent forward, covering my eyes as shards flew around me. My mates were with me in an instant, their bodies covered mine from the assault. I tried not to panic, letting the comfort of their presence soothe me, but then I noticed the smoke spilling from a small metallic device that had landed amongst the glass on the floor.

"Fuck," Silas cursed, weakly.

"They found us," Laz cried, falling to their knees, clutching their chest in pain.

'No, no, no, no," Samara cried, but each repeat of the words was weaker and weaker as she stumbled back against the wall, losing her balance.

I glanced around at my mates, their faces twisted in worry and fear as the smoke enveloped us. I waited for it to affect me, but I felt perfectly fine.

"What's happening?" I pleaded as Samara slipped to the ground. Silas crashed against the wall as he attempted to hold himself up.

"Athena…run…" Orpheus forced out before collapsing onto the floor.

I dropped to my knees, tears pooling in my eyes and obscuring my vision. "Wake up!" I cried, pressing my palms against their limp forms. "Oh my god, wake up!" They didn't budge, the smoke blanketed the area, covering their forms. I tried to wave my arms around across the floor, eager to be in contact with each of them. "Please, please," I sobbed.

I was too distraught, too focused on the pain in my chest to hear the figure slip through the open window and come to a stop behind me. All I saw was a brief glimpse of a shadow amongst the smoke before something hard crashed against my temple and everything went dark.

SILAS

SIXTEEN

The world was finally in focus. Suddenly there was nothing but her. Her blood on my tongue felt like electricity, oxygen, sunlight. It was powerful, and alive. Nothing in this world could ever compare to the feeling of my body inside of hers, her walls constricting around me, holding me there as if she couldn't bear to be separated.

These last few days have been agonizing. Knowing that she was so close but that there was this cavern of distance between us. My family was on the verge of falling apart, and I was so close to forgetting why I cared enough to continue existing.

And then…Athena.

Her kind heart, her pure soul…her.

She was exactly what we needed. All of us. Orpheus needed someone he got to relax with, someone he trusted enough to take the metaphorical 'tie' off around. Laz needed someone who they could tend to, someone they could worship. Samara needed someone to help her heal, someone who could fill the void left by Alora without erasing the memories she left behind. And I needed someone to love me.

I've had a family. I got lucky with Alora and the other Wanderers, but I have never been in what I would consider love. Not in the way Alora and Samara were, or Laz with that asshole from his hometown, before he took the cowards way out. I'd never experienced that. I'd only ever indulged in sex and physical pleasure. But now, it's her. I have her. And I love her. Without a doubt in my mind. I love Athena Landry, and she loves me. She hasn't said the words but she doesn't have to. I know what love is. I've seen it. And I see it in her eyes when she looks at me. I hear it in her voice when she says my name, I feel it in her touch when she places her palm on my face.

She is everything I never knew I could have. And now that I have her, I would do everything in my power to keep her safe.

I would burn down this entire world for her.

As my body began to betray me and I heard her frightened screams, I had one thought. One singular, overwhelming thought. That I was going to make whoever did this to us regret every breath they've ever taken.

My consciousness began to slip from my grasp as she cried for us. For me.

The mixture of holy water and garlic isn't lethal to a vampire, not in any capacity, but what it does is vicious. It sinks into the pores and freezes its victims from the inside out. Suspending them in time. My lips stilled, and my eyes dried out from the inability to blink. They tried unsuccessfully to focus on the white smoke that circled me.

I wasn't able to move, to speak, to call out for her, but I could hear everything. Every sob, every desperate call from her lips. The way my name, all our names, sounded like a broken scream. Hearing the woman you love fall to pieces and knowing you can do nothing to stop it is a fate worse than death.

A fate that I can't wait to force onto my captor.

I heard the sound of footsteps, heavy and crunching against the broken glass, and I wanted to scream to her, to tell her to get out. To get free. But I couldn't speak. I couldn't scream. I couldn't help her.

The sound of something heavy connecting against flesh threatened to topple my sanity. Suddenly, a loud thump vibrated across the floor, my eyes focused through the dissipating wisps of smoke to see her, unconscious and lying in a heap on the floor. I lost every ounce of control I had. Anger surged through me, but with nowhere to go, and no way to release it, it felt stifling, and overwhelming. Like I might explode at any moment.

I watched in rapt horror as she was dragged from my view, her red hair trailing behind. My heart, newly revived, felt cracked and split right down the center.

The footsteps disappeared, along with my mate, and I knew it was only a matter of time before our captor returned for us. I needed to do something. I needed to save my family. To save my mate.

But still, I couldn't move.

I wished I had been knocked out. I Wish I couldn't hear a single thing. Wished I didn't know what had happened, because having the complete awareness of what was occurring, and none of the ability to act on it was a special kind of torture.

Focusing every ounce of energy I had left, I tried to move a finger, but it felt as if I knew there was an appendage there, but it did not belong to me anymore. So far removed from myself.

I screamed and trashed against the mental cages that have been forged around my consciousness to no avail.

Eventually, the footsteps returned. I could see more clearly now that the smoke had lifted, but my vision blurred from the dryness. Dark boots, dark wash jeans, dark clothes… and there. There it was.

A confirmation of what I already knew to be true. The mask that covered my captor's face. A Nameless mask. They found us. They caught us. Again.

I tried once more to move a finger, a hand, anything. There was a sort of tingling sensation radiating through my arm, and despite the pain, and all the anger bubbling beneath my surface, I felt it. My finger bent. Slightly, barely at all, but it was a movement. Unfortunately, it was not enough to save my family. Not enough to save my mate.

I wanted to cry. I couldn't.

Not when I saw the figure drag Samara out of the room. Not when they returned for Laz. Then Orpheus. Not when I felt their hands close around my shoulders and hoist me up, dragging me across the floor. Not when I felt the broken glass from the windows dig into my flesh as I was pulled through the living room and out onto the porch. Not as I was tossed into the bed of a truck in a heap with my family with their equally stiff bodies feeling like rocks beneath me. Not when a bright blue tarp was secured over the top of us. Not when our captor started driving away.

The driver stopped and I couldn't hear what he was doing, but there were voices. Someone was here. If only I could signal for them. If only I could let them know we were here.

I focused on my hand again. I had nothing left. I felt so weak, so helpless. But that wasn't good enough. Athena deserved better. She deserved my everything. I let thoughts of the people I love fuel me.

Orpheus and his quiet strength. His determination and ferocity in protecting those he loves.

Laz and their soft devotion. The way they love with every ounce of their heart, unreserved and unrestrained.

Samara and her will. Her control, the way she acts only when she must and only as she should.

Athena and her heart, her soul, and her mind. The way she trusts, the way she heals. People who've gone through half the trauma she has would turn it all off, and hide themselves from the world. But not her. She opened her wounded heart. She continues to do so, despite the pain, and the past. Her courage. I could do this for her.

With those thoughts and the images of my family flashing in front of my face, I channeled it all into my hand. It moved, slowly, inch by inch, but it moved. I felt the cool rush of air brush against my skin and suddenly, my hand was poking out from beneath the tarp. The voices continued. I just needed whoever it was to see me, then maybe they could help. My mind and body felt exhausted like I might pass out at any moment. It wasn't much, but maybe, just maybe, it was enough.

With that thought, and that sense of accomplishment rushing through me, I let the exhaustion take me away.

ATHENA

SEVENTEEN

My head hurt.

That was the first thing I noticed as I came to. My body ached from blood loss, exhaustion, and exertion. My throat was dry, and each breath caused a sort of white-hot pain to radiate. My eyes blinked, struggling to focus on my surroundings. I groaned as I tried to sit up, my body felt heavy and worn out. As my eyes adjusted, I saw a familiar view. A normally comforting setting that at this moment was offering nothing except confusion and worry. The Maine Plotline was quiet and only soft rays from the evening sun were poking through the door. The rest of the light was blocked by the board that covered the front window. I glanced around trying to make sense of what had happened, to no avail. Pieces of the last few hours came back to me in flashes. Breakfast.The beach house. The bond. The smoke.

My head snapped around.

My mates.

I tried to call out for them, but my throat was searing. I glanced down at my wrist to see the floral wrapping design signifying one of my bonds and touched it quickly. Samara was there, I felt her, but she was weak. I repeated the motion on the other three bonds receiving the same alarming sense. One thing was abundantly clear. They were in trouble.

I grabbed my phone from my pocket and dialed their numbers. The line was dead. Each unavailable beep sent me closer and closer to spiraling. I slammed the phone down on the counter and paced, dragging my hands through my ratted hair.

My mind was spinning as I tried to piece together the muddled facts. The sound of the bell above the door had hope blooming in my chest. I turned eagerly, mentally begging to see my mates return to me, safely. But I was not so lucky.

A figure stood silhouetted in the door frame by the waning evening light. As he took a step inside I gasped with recognition.

His eyes burned with anger and hatred. I saw them so clearly. Felt his ire so intimately.

Greg.

He took a few menacing steps forward, and I stepped back.

"Greg, what are you doing here?" I asked nervously, my eyes glancing over at my phone on the counter. So far away.

"I came to give you one last chance to tell the truth," he replied, he sounded so unhinged. I couldn't get a hold of the shaky breath that came out in spurts.

"Please, just leave me alone," I begged, backing up against a bookshelf, the wood slammed into my shoulder blades and I winced at the soreness there.

He continued his slow deliberate steps forward. "See, I know for a fact something happened that night that you're not telling the police." His eyes scanned me with disgust. "So fucking fess up."

He was only a few feet from me now, and fear gripped me. I tried to make a break for it, heading for the phone, but his hands darted out, grabbing my biceps forcefully and holding me in place with a painful hold. I tried to scream, but he pushed me back into the bookcase, sending a jolt of pain down my spine as a few titles fell off the shelf to the ground below.

"Stop, please!" I cried.

"Tell me the truth," he demanded, his bloodshot eyes staring into mine.

"He tried to rape me," I shouted, trying unsuccessfully to pull from his grasp again.

"You're lying," he screamed before pushing me into the bookcase again, his fingers dug into my arms to the point of pain. I cried out at the pain. His breath reeked of alcohol and the scent stung my nostrils.

"I'm not! I'm not," I whimpered, tears flowing from my eyes. "He tried to rape me and those strangers saved me. They pulled him off of me and took me home. I swear." Now that I knew what my mates were capable of, I wasn't all that afraid of telling this one asshole about their interference. But my heart broke a little as the concern for my mates and their current situation returned in full force.

He watched me for a moment in silence, before a soft smile played on his lips. "He didn't try to rape you. You probably begged for it."

I shook off the sting of his accusation, not an unfamiliar phrase.

"I didn't," I yelled, but he dug his fingers into my arms harder, I felt the warm, sticky blood begin to trickle across my skin bubbling from beneath his fingernails.

"Don't fucking lie," he screamed into my face, and I turned my head from him, shutting my eyes. "You're a goddamn slut! You think I haven't seen you around town with your 'strangers'?" He spat the word. "I bet you're fucking them all too, aren't you?"

I sobbed, unable to manage words.

"Where is Louis?" He barked again.

"I don't know!" I cried out, I didn't even recognize my own voice. It was a broken, weak sound.

He pulled back, slamming me into the bookcase again with more force. My back exploded in pain at the impact and books flew off the shelf raining down on top of us. By some stroke of luck, a heavy tomb clipped Greg on the side of his face. He cursed and dropped his hands from my skin, cradling his head in his hands. I didn't dare wait another second. I sprinted past him, pushing through the door and out onto the pier. I called out for help. A familiar sense of deja vu hit me. There was no soul in sight.

I pressed against the bonds again as I ran, begging for them to feel me. To find me, but the connections laid dormant. Nobody was coming to save me.

I had to save myself.

Greg was behind me, I felt him begin to catch up. His presence was eerily similar to that ominous smoke back at the beach house. But this time, I was ready. I veered toward the railing of the pier, and his footfalls sounded behind me. I reached the railing and allowed myself only a moment to breathe, before turning to face my assailant. I stood my ground, gritted my teeth, and pushed every ounce of pain away from my mind. He barreled forward, a crazed obsessive look in his eyes.

I waited, watching his strides as he made his way to me, drawing strength from the connections that thrummed within my soul. My mates weren't there physically, but their influence was so visceral. I felt them in every step, in every breath. Their strength was mine. And I needed every ounce I could muster. Just as his arms rose to grab at me, I ducked. With his momentum he was hurled into the railing, but not quite over. The wind was knocked out of him and I knew I had to take advantage of the opportunity. I let loose a punch against his face and he groaned in pain. He tried to turn back to me, blood spilling from his mouth, but I landed another punch before he could react. I ignored the stabbing sting in my hand and let loose years of aggression on him. Punch after punch, I saw my step-father, I saw Louis, I saw the cops who never believed me, the townsfolk who judged me. I saw them all and I hated them. He whimpered under my assault, but I wasn't done. When he was weakened and his arms came up to protect his face, I gripped his arm and used every little bit of my remaining strength to push him over the railing. I heard his scream get cut off as he hit the water below and only then did the weight of his assault lift off of me.

Glancing down at myself I saw the bruises and blood decorating my arms like a gore-tainted work of art. I was so dangerously close to passing out. I had to get to somewhere safe. Soon.

I stumbled away from the railing, not even bothering to look for Greg in the crashing waves below the pier. He could disappear into nothingness and I wouldn't bat an eye. I limped toward the main street at the end of the pier feeling every injury throb violently, it was nearly enough to take my breath away, but I pressed on. My painful grunts echoed through the night air as I stepped onto the street. The sound of tires squealing startled me, but I wasn't strong enough to move out of the way. A pair of headlights illuminated me in the early evening light. The truck had stopped just short of me.

I vaguely heard the car door swing open.

"Holy shit, Athena. What the hell happened to you?" Archer's voice was strained, and worried. I forced myself to focus on him. The sight of him blanketed me in relief. I released a sob and fell into him. He held me up and I embraced him as best I could and cried. "Athena, talk to me. What happened?" He inquired angrily.

"Greg," I whispered and Archer cursed under his breath, his hands pressing gently against my back. My legs gave out slightly but Archer managed to catch me, righting me.

"Whoa, ok, ok. Here." He helped me over to his truck, leaning me against the passenger door. I pressed my body against the truck's frame and felt the extent of the injuries and exertion from the last twenty-four hours so vividly. I was lightheaded.

"I'm dizzy," I offered, meekly. Archer steadied me and looked over my shoulder into the bed of his truck.

"I have some water in my truck. I'll get it." He made sure I had a solid grasp on the side of the truck before he leaned into the cab. I gripped the metal and struggled to stop the world from spinning. I tried to focus on one thing, staring at the blue tarp inside the bed.

I calmed myself by studying it. Listing off what I could see as a way to focus on staying upright and conscious.

The bright blue color reminded me of a pool on a hot summer's day.

The silver rings had rope looped through them to tie it down.

The bumpy shape from whatever was beneath it.

The hand that poked out from beneath it.

Shock flooded my brain, I shook my head trying to make sense of what I was seeing. I stumbled a little but leaned onto the truck to ground myself and stared at the hand. Was it even real?

But as I continued to stare, I knew it was.

A gasp caught in my throat when I saw the swirling black ink painting the back of the hand and inching up the arm.

I knew those tattoos. I knew those fingers.

Silas.

Panic invaded my senses, and all I could feel was unrelenting, devastating fear.

"Here, drink this," Archer said, offering me a bottle of water. I was too weak to hide my fear. "What's wro-" his eyes followed mine and he saw it too. Silas' hand. Clear as day. He groaned with frustration. Something like guilt playing on his face.

"I can explain, I swear," he started anxiously, but I was done listening. I inhaled, readying a scream, but before it could escape my lips, Archer's hand clamps down over my mouth and nose, bringing a strip of wet fabric to brush against my skin. The scent of whatever he had doused the cloth with invaded my every sense, and the dark vignette around my vision blurred. I lost my balance, but Archer caught me, holding me tight to his chest as the world began to slip away into nothingness.

He looked down at me with traitorous green eyes, but they too were disappearing into the darkness of my own mind. Before I was lost to the void of my consciousness, I heard his whispered words.

"I'm sorry."